Brad Bateman

and the

Burgundy Bay

Brad Bateman

and the

Burgundy Bay

Colleen Pace

ISBN: 0-9711374-0-4

The American Association of Riding Schools, Inc.
8375 E. Coldwater Road
Davison, MI 48423-8966
810-653-1440
colleenpace@onemain.com
www.ucanride.com

About the Cover

Our cover horse is "Dark Horse Foxy Bay," an American Morgan Horse gelding owned by Amy Wertenberger.

Cover credits go to the DeGrandis family of Britton, Michigan—Mary, Amy, and Adrian. These members of the Michigan Justin Morgan Horse Association volunteered to develop this set of photographs especially for this book.

A very special thank you to Jackie Rodosalewicz and her son, Craig, who own Little Bit 'O Farm in Tecumseh, Michigan, for their assistance with the photography.

With Appreciation

I would like to include a very special note of appreciation to my husband, Gary, for his encouragement as I completed this manuscript; and a sincere thank you to my good friends, Cathy Larner and Judy Karns, who assisted with editing the text for publication.

BOOK ONE

1

"I got sixty-five, sixty-five, three-sixty-five," bellowed the man behind the loudspeaker. "Who's gonna give me seventy, seventy, I want three-seventy for this filly." Chuck Wheaten's voice crackled through the shoddy P.A. system. The filly was the twenty-second horse to pass through the auction ring. As each animal was ridden in, sold, and ridden out, they began to look more and more alike—four legs and a tail. Wheaten wiped his chapped lips across his dirty sleeve and returned to the microphone. "I got sixty-five, sixty-five, three- sixty-five," he repeated. "Who's gonna give me three-seventy?" Sweat beaded on and trickled off his weather-worn forehead.

It was mid-winter in Linden, Michigan, and freezing outside, but the lone spotlight shining across the forty-foot sale pen hung just a few feet from Wheaten's tired brow. His back was sore, too. He shifted his weight on the wooden stool. His aching spine gave a painful little snap and the tension eased momentarily. Cigarette smoke hung in the poorly ventilated room, burning his eyes as he surveyed the too-quiet and too-small gathering. Could he push for a few extra dollars on this filly? His mind wandered again to his aching back. Surely, it would not aggravate him so badly if he dropped forty pounds off his bulging, middle-aged belly. "Sixty-five, sixty-five, I got three-sixty-five," he called through the crackling speaker. "Who's gonna give me three-seventy?"

The little red mare ran frantically back and forth in the small confine of the auction pen. Dust rose from under her feet. The teenager on her back pushed his heels into her sides hard, trying to wake her up a little for the bystanders. She was wild-eyed, scared, and wanted out of the pen, away from the people, the cigarette smoke, and the terrifying sound of the crackling speaker.

She was fully surrounded by walls and rails with no easy way out, and she was not mean enough to fight.

Glancing down from his position in the worn western saddle, sixteen-year-old Brad Bateman could see the little mare's shoulder muscles quivering as he urged her on. Most likely, he thought, this little mare had been standing idle behind someone's barn for the last year, a forgotten and out-of-shape pet. Even this bit of excitement was too much for her.

"Aw, c'mon folks; this here's a nice little filly," bartered Wheaten into his mike. "I won't let her go for less than three-seventy. Who'll give me three-seventy?" He was really pulling teeth for an extra buck on the little red mare.

A tattered glove rose above someone's faded winter cap and the auctioneer jumped at the new opportunity. "Seventy, seventy, I got three-seventy. Who's gonna give me three-seventy-five. She's worth every penny folks, look at her run, ain't bucked yet."

The filly scurried back and forth. Brad's leg pressed, first right along with a pull of the right rein, then left. Someone in the crowd tossed a firecracker into the mare's path and she shied away with a shrill whinny as it popped in front of her. Wheaten bellowed a stern reprimand toward a group of rambunctious boys, as the teen rider pulled his right rein quickly, laying the heel of his boot firmly into the little red mare's side. Her mind was diverted from the firecracker as she spun around on her hocks. Brad's left hand, calloused and grimed with dust and sweat, grabbed the horn of the old saddle for support.

"Seventy-five, seventy-five, I want three-seventy-five for this mare," Wheaten bellowed over the loudspeaker. There was no response from the crowd and some of the spectators began to move off toward the concession stand. "Crummy night," he muttered to himself. "Ain't no one here with a decent dollar in his pocket." He decided to sell while he could to the man with the tattered glove. "Going once, going twice, SOLD," his voice boomed, "to the man in the gray parka for three-hundred-and-seventy dollars. A steal, mister, that's what you got. Your buddies here gave you a steal."

Turning away from the mike and casting a quick glance down the ladder behind him, Wheaten chided his teenage rider. "Git 'er outta here. I ain't got all night." He ran his sleeve across his forehead to wipe away the sweat. A few red-gray hairs were all that remained on the fifty-year-old head. His chest felt heavy and the night was passing too slowly. *At this rate, we'll be here past mid-*

night, he thought to himself. "Git 'er outta here, boys," he repeated brusquely. He reached under his counter for a warm can of beer and guzzled the remaining brew. It burned his parched throat.

The door at the far end of the pen slid open and Brad hurried the little red mare out of the crowd and into the quiet stall area in the rear of the barn. She had built up a nervous sweat between her front legs and was still quivering. The teen slid to the ground and dropped the reins over the filly's head. With one flip of his hand, he loosened the cinch and swept the saddle off her back and over his shoulder.

"Here, Tyler," he said quietly, passing the reins to a younger boy. He ran his fingers through his soft, dark hair, then pressed his hand against his shirt to soak up the sweat on his chest. "Put her in number three. She's a goner."

Tyler, redheaded and freckle-faced, led the mare away. His hand listlessly scrubbed her neck as they walked. It was warm under her mane, as warm as the inside of a mitten. "You're a good girl," he murmured quietly to his momentary friend. Tyler was well aware that all the horses in pen number three had been purchased by Mr. Croswell of Double R Farm. He also knew that Double R Farm was a broker for the meat packers. Before the night was through, this timid little mare would be crammed into an open semi-trailer and hauled north to the slaughterhouses in Canada. She most likely would not be fed again before she met her death two, possibly three, days away. The little mare pressed her head against Tyler's shoulder and rubbed hard. The sweat under her bridle had caused her to itch. He led her into pen number three and dropped the gate latch.

Why do I come here, anyway? he thought.

By the time Tyler returned to the edge of the auction pen, Brad had already mounted another horse. The age-worn saddle was firmly secured on the back of a black-brown gelding. Three riders were working the auction and they had about sixty horses to run through. Not even sixty spectators stood around the sale pen. That meant that more than the usual number of animals would be sold to meat packers or taken back home as no-sales. Not all of them could be ridden anyway—some too old, some too skinny, some too mean.

Tyler was only thirteen, but he hung around the barns every Saturday night and helped for free. "Brad," he said slowly. "Do they have to go to the slaughterhouse if Mr. Croswell buys them? I mean, can't Croswell sell them to someone else, or can't Mr. Wheaten buy them back?"

"Mr. Wheaten doesn't have a reason to buy 'em, Tyler." The response was matter of fact. "They're not his horses. He just sells them for other people. You know that. And, Mr. Croswell isn't a horseman," Brad added. "He's just a truck driver doin' his job."

Tyler persisted. "But Mr. Wheaten could buy 'em back and use 'em over at the riding stable."

"He already does that," reminded Brad. "But just how many horses do you think Mr. Wheaten needs at the stable? Besides, he's only going to keep the ones he thinks are fairly healthy and absolutely safe."

The door at the far end slid open and a lanky, rough-and-tumble sort of fellow named Willy ambled out of the auction area. A spotted pony followed quietly on a lead. Brad and Tyler had heard the sale price, a hundred ninety-five dollars. Wheaten sure wasn't doing very good for himself tonight. As Willy led the pony into a quiet corner, a really young girl, maybe eight years old, bustled through the bystanders to catch up. The girl's parents brought up the rear. The spotted pony pushed its muzzle from one coat to another looking for a possible carrot. The girl squealed with delight and threw her arms around its shaggy neck.

The third sale rider, Carter, spurred a big Appaloosa into the auction pen and Brad moved the horse beneath him up in line.

"You see, Tyler," Brad commented as he nodded toward the newly purchased pony, "we're not all bad. I bet that pony came from a good home. See how she's tolerating that girl hanging all over her?" The pony let out a huge snort and shook her neck vigorously. The family gasped and jumped away as spray flew from the pony's huge nostrils. The spotted pony shook her shaggy head again and resumed her search for carrots.

Brad and Tyler watched the family with their new purchase. The parents stood by as if they weren't sure what to do next. Willy stood listlessly with the pony's lead rope in his hands, waiting uncomfortably for the new owners to take the pony and disappear.

"Hey, Tyler," coaxed Brad. "Willy there won't help 'em any. Why don't you find a carrot in my backpack and wander on over. I bet they could use a crash course in horse care." Tyler took the cue and sauntered up to the new pony's owners, happy to bestow his wealth of thirteen-year-old equine knowledge upon the little audience.

The door at the far end of the sale pen slid open again and the Appaloosa reappeared. He was probably the biggest horse to come through, a light cream color with spatters of red freckles covering his entire body. His big eyes gazed the back area calmly.

Carter swung his far leg over the Appaloosa's neck and hopped forward to the ground. He turned and gave the horse a hearty slap on the neck. Brad could tell that Carter liked the animal and guessed that he had probably gotten a pretty good ride out of him. The horse's owners stood by grumbling that the auctioneer hadn't tried hard enough. They were taking their horse back home. The best price pulled from the waning crowd was not as high as they had hoped.

The fact was, no matter how solid the horse, tonight, just two nights before Christmas, there were only so many spectators with money in their pockets and the need for a horse. Most of them were there just to be there. It's where they were every Saturday night, for lack of anything better to do—an addictive solution to sitting home.

Brad was still sitting on the dark bay gelding when Wheaten turned and waved him in. He gave his horse the cue and it responded with a relaxed walk into the auction pen. *Not much pep here,* he thought, *but not any bad habits or noticeable obstinacies.* He would be a hard one to sell, but a likely prospect for the riding stable.

Brad pressed the calves of both legs into the horse's ribs a second time, asking for a trot. Its black mane shook a little in response, but no trot followed. Brad's original guess was confirmed. Wheaten slowed his pattern of speech over the speaker.

"Three-hundred-twenty-five dollars? Is that all I can pull on this 'ole boy? Three-hundred-twenty-five dollars? Come on, folks; he's a nice ole boy." Wheaten stopped to take a draw from a new can of beer. He rolled his auctioneer's gavel slowly back and forth on the countertop. "Three-hundred-twenty-five dollars?" he repeated. "Well, heck then, going once, going twice, sold to the fellow in the green cap for three-hundred-twenty-five dollars."

The lanky man in the green cap grinned and turned away for a cup of too-strong coffee. He was Wheaten's yardman, hired to handle the backhoe to clear the manure from the horse pens. However, on auction night he was posted in the crowd in case Wheaten wanted to buy a horse for himself. It might be considered unethical for an auctioneer to purchase a horse at his own sale because he could purposely keep a price down for his own benefit, so Wheaten posted "Green" in the crowd and the sellers didn't know the difference. For three-hundred-twenty-five bucks, the bay was a good addition to the riding stable lot, and the sellers wouldn't know whether the auctioneer could have pulled a few extra dollars out of the crowd or not.

It was nine-thirty when Brad came out of the auction pen and let the black-brown gelding loose into the stable pasture. His thoughts matched those of Mr. Wheaten. The night was going too slowly. By eleven, Wheaten's voice was sounding worse than the crackly P.A. into which he was calling, and the sing-song rhythm of his auction calls was slowing down.

By eleven-thirty, nearly everyone was gone. The floors were littered with Styrofoam cups and empty cigarette packages. Mr. Wheaten had already headed up to the house in search of something to calm his throbbing head and aching back. A couple of drunks were haggling out in the parking lot about which one had their truck keys. An elderly man emerged from an over-used outhouse and headed for his car. Dorie Wheaten, Chuck's dependable wife, cleaned up spilled coffee and cocoa from the condiment table before retreating to the office area behind the concession window.

Dropping into a chair at her cluttered desk, Dorie studied the night's take: ten percent of the sale price for each horse sold, a flat twenty dollars from each seller who pulled his horse from the sale and took it back home, twenty percent of any tack and equipment sold. Still, it didn't look like it was going to add up to much tonight. She pressed her slender fingers hard against her tired eyelids and rubbed. Her pixy figure, perky brown hair, and neat attire belied how tired she really felt.

Back in the stall area, Brad stretched his coupled hands over his head and pushed them high into the air, stretching as far as possible. His tired back ached as it arched backward into the bend. Slowly, he brought his hands back over his head and stretched until they touched the ground in front of him. His back ached again as it arched forward and down. He glanced to see if Tyler was still around, but found him nowhere in sight.

Brad stood looking over the empty sale pens. All the horses that were there four hours ago were on their way to new homes, either good or bad. He let his back fall against the wall and then slid down until his weight plopped onto a pile of old straw, his tired legs sprawling across the dirt floor.

This odd world of the auction barn was so different than his other world—the real world in the year 2000—the new millennium. Here, in the old and musty barn, it could have been 1965, or 1945, or even 1845, or even 1745. The dim lighting, the smell of rotted wood, and the ammonia of animal urine in pens with too-sparse bedding could make it difficult for one to understand how someone could love horses, when this was their only exposure. But Brad loved horses, and this was his only exposure. He looked forward to the summer when he could fill his hours as one of the riding stable guides. He and Jackson, the old white gelding he had grown so fond of, would lead blissful greenhorns on their hourly trail rides.

Passing his hands through his smooth, dark hair, Brad felt the grit that had been stirred up by the dozens of horses that had been under him tonight. He was tired, yes, but not bruised. Not one animal had bucked him, not one sly one had spun too fast or reared too quickly to unseat him. Mostly, the lot had been a quiet one, almost a sad one. No wild beauties, no fierce rebels, no elegant movers.

Brad pulled himself to his feet. He noticed the sleeve of his blue denim shirt was ripped and the tear in the knee of his jeans had grown to a bonafide gaping hole. He walked to the door of the tack room and, shaking his foot hard, kicked a boot through the door into a dark corner. The second boot followed as a rake or pitchfork clanged to the floor in response. Reaching just inside the door, Brad groped for his high-tops and slipped them over his blackened, smelly socks. He glanced at his watch as he headed for his mother's minivan. It was twelve forty-five. With his first driver's license just one month old, his folks would be waiting up.

2

Christmas for Mr. and Mrs. Bateman was quieter than usual this year. Brad's older brother, Robbie, did not come home from college for the holidays. The Michigan State University Ski Club's Christmas Getaway took him to the slopes of northern Michigan. To miss Christmas with the family was a big deal. Their mother, Susan Bateman, saw it as a sign that her Robbie had grown up and away from her. With Brad having his license now, she knew that he, too, would gradually be less tied to her. His job at the auction barn gave him control over his own money, so he no longer depended on her allowances. Instead of asking her about things he wanted to do or places he wanted to go, she now found him telling her about decisions he had made and then waiting for her response. Maybe it wasn't all that different because she still had veto power over those decisions with which she did not agree. But the approach was different, and she saw it as a clear sign that Brad, too, was growing up and away.

Mrs. Bateman still set out Christmas stockings for the entire family, including Buffy, their cocker spaniel. Mr. Bateman reached deep into his stocking and retrieved a banana and a tangerine to have with his Christmas morning coffee. Brad pulled a chew bone from Buffy's stocking and pretended to eat it while Buffy barked insistently, demanding her Santa's treat.

Later, when they were opening their Christmas gifts, Mrs. Bateman pulled a soft package from under the tree.

"Oh, leave those there, Mom. They're snowmobile socks for Matt," said Brad. "Leave that one, too. It's for Mrs. Wheaten."

"Oh?" replied his mom as she set the packages back under the tree. A gift for Brad's best friend was understandable, but she wondered at the gift for his boss.

Brad responded casually, "It's a business diary that has room for her to jot in what she spends each day and a pocket for her notes. I found it at the office supply store when she sent me up for receipt books for the auction barn. She's always complaining about having petty cash slips fall to the bottom of her purse, so I think she'll like it. Besides," he added, "it's got a horse head stitched on the cover."

Mrs. Bateman raised her eyebrows. "Do the other boys buy Christmas presents for the Wheatens?" she asked.

Brad chuckled. "I doubt that they buy gifts for anyone, but I like Mrs. Wheaten. She talks with me about the horses, and she tells me about the business. You know, like what it costs to run the concession counter and things like that."

As Brad talked, he opened a soft package and pulled out a light gray sweater. Flecks of dark gray and black formed a dappled stripe across the chest.

"I bet you picked this out, Dad." Mr. Bateman grinned and nodded. Brad knew the colors were his dad's—conservative. No one would go ape over it at school, but it was nice. Brad opened a large hardbound book from his mother. It was a photographic book by Robert Vavra, *All Those Girls With Horses*.

"I wasn't sure whether you'd like it for the horses or the girls," winked Mrs. Bateman, "but the photos are just beautiful." Brad browsed the pages. Vavra's camera had captured some of the most beautiful horses from around the world—all with female trainers or riders.

3

The day after Christmas a blue and silver truck and trailer rolled into Wheatens' auction lot. It was a double-axle Chevy, absolutely spotless. On the side of its door, the truck boasted a farm name, scrolled in shiny black letters:

McMichaels' Training Center

*Breeding * Training * Sales*

Northville, Michigan

The horse trailer that lumbered behind it was an elaborate four-horse gooseneck. It had a tack room at the front, and a sleeping compartment extended over the bed of the truck. It, too, boasted its owners in elegant black lettering:

McMichaels' Training Center

Home of 'Moriah's Black Magic'

World Champion Stallion

Not many horses came into Wheatens' during midweek. It was Friday night and Saturday morning that saw dozens of trailers stream in, dropping off horses for the Saturday night sale. Some rigs were new, but mostly they were rusty and noisy, and rarely did one boast a bonafide farm name. The sound of squishing driveway gravel caught Brad's attention. He laid the saddle he was cleaning over a stall wall and wandered up to the front of the building. Wheatens' barn man had wandered onto the front porch.

"Hey, Green, what's going on?" queried Brad. Green was a stupid name to give a guy, but that's what everyone called him. He was never seen without his green farm cap. A flying ear of corn was embroidered above its bill, and *Dekalb Seed* was printed below. Brad was sure that Green's cap had two-hundred-and-four years of grimy sweat embedded in the rim. Once, Tyler suggested throwing the hat, with Green still attached, into the biggest automatic washer in town. It was probably a good idea.

"Why, it looks like a fancy farm has come to buy up a string of our stable horses," Green grinned as he said it. "Gonna make 'em into show babies and sell 'em for a million dollars."

Brad curiously eyed the truck as a handsome man in his late twenties dropped from the cab. "You're kidding," Brad said slowly with quiet surprise. Green laughed loudly enough that the driver heard his voice.

"You gotta be the dumbest kid I ever met," chuckled Green. "I bet that guy's ashamed to drive into a place like this. Those fancy show barn trainers don't care much to socialize with auction barns."

Green was right. The man did not appear to be hurrying anywhere. He looked toward the office door and then looked hesitantly at Brad and Green. Brad stepped toward the truck, noting that the driver was clean shaven. He wore a crisp, light green shirt and sported a pair of clean black riding boots under a pair of gray slacks. Brad heard an impatient horse inside the trailer, kicking against the back door. He passed his cleaning rag to his left hand and extended a slightly oily right hand to the driver.

"Hello. I'm Evan McMichael. Mr. Wheaten is expecting this horse." The driver's voice was smooth and friendly. "Do you work here?"

"Yes," hesitated Brad. "Well, on Saturday nights, anyway. I'll find Mrs. Wheaten for you. She's probably in the office."

"Looks like you're cleaning tack," the visitor offered as they walked. Brad cast a quick glance at his own grimy hands.

"A saddle broke loose under me a couple months ago," he replied. "Dry rot on leather sort of scares me now."

Evan chuckled quietly. "It's not fun to see those hooves flash by your face as you hit the ground."

The comment let Brad know that Mr. McMichael had shared that experience at least once. He opened the screen door and Evan passed in front of him. Dorie Wheaten immediately stood and extended a friendly hand to greet the visitor. Brad wondered how she could be married to a guy like Wheaten who was probably up at the house sleeping off a drunk.

Dorie Wheaten's eyes landed warmly on Evan. "My, you're the spittin' image of your dad," she smiled. Evan responded with a slight nod, obviously not understanding what she meant. He had never seen nor heard of this woman before.

"I'm Dorie Wheaten. We'll take good care of your mare until Saturday, and I promise you," she added, "We'll do what we can to bring you the best price possible."

"She's not our horse and a bad debt is a bad debt," responded Evan matter of factly. "Whatever we can recoup from the deal we'll take and be done with it." Dorie Wheaten sighed but offered no further response. She knew that the highest bid ever cast in her barn was probably less than what the mare, waiting impatiently out front, was worth.

Dorie suddenly felt uncomfortable. She glanced quickly at the dust on the corners of her desk and on the chairs that had not been wiped clean by the backside of a customer since last Saturday night. It was the barn, with its infinite cracks and crevices, that made it impossible to keep anything clean. Still, she felt suddenly responsible for things over which she had little control.

"Well, young man, let's see what you have out there. Brad," she added, "would you please make sure the box stall in the back corner has clean bedding. We'll put her there." Brad left through the rear office door, passed through the tack room, and into the open stall area beyond. There were four rows of box pens, each about fourteen feet square. Aisles between the rows extended from the auction pen at the front toward the rear of the cavernous old barn.

There were thirty-two weathered pens all total, stabling as many as eight ponies or three crammed horses on any given Saturday night. The ceiling over the auction sale pen up front, plus the concession and office area, and tack room served as the floor for the hayloft above.

Brad dropped three bales of fresh straw down from the loft. Wheaten would shoot him, for sure, if he walked in right now. The barn rule was one bale per pen and that was expected to absorb the urine of up to three horses. But Brad stacked the three bales into the wheelbarrow anyway, teetering them as he rolled the barrow toward the back. He was quite sure Mrs. Wheaten would want him to use three. The pen was still soiled from last Saturday's sales. Green always left them dirty from Saturday night through to the following Thursday, just in time for the next sale.

Brad guessed that Mrs. Wheaten did not approve, but he never heard her address Green to the contrary. The employees were her husband's responsibility and she did a fair job of staying out of his part of the business. Handling the money, keeping the books, and making sure the concession stand was well stocked were her responsibilities. She also took it upon herself to serve as a sort of hostess to the customers as they came in for the sales.

Brad slipped his hands around the twines of the top bale and lifted it from the wheelbarrow. With a swift kick in the center, a huge poof of bright yellow straw filled the air. He repeated the motion with the remaining two bales and then pushed the mounds of yellow around the pen with his sneakers. Tucking the wheelbarrow back into the corner, he headed toward the front.

When he rounded the corner of the barn, he came to a dead stop. There stood the most beautiful horse Brad had ever seen! Evan McMichael gently stroked the mare's muzzle as he visited with Dorie Wheaten. Each time he stopped, the mare would push her face forward into the palm of his hand nuzzling for more attention. Brad walked quietly toward the couple, not wanting to interrupt their conversation.

The sun bounced off the horse's back as Brad's gaze streamed over her body. She had a fine, deep red-brown coat without a loose hair in sight. Her mane, the blackest black, was thick and coarse. Brad noted that it was shaved extremely short from the poll between her ears, down her neck a good six inches. The absence of mane at her upper neck made her throat latch appear sharp and well-defined. The tips of her ears were trimmed so crisply in black that one would have thought an artist had been hired to do the job. There was not a single long hair extending from the inside or the edges of her ears. They had been shaved to perfection.

The mare's inky black muzzle wrinkled and wriggled under the soothing scratches of McMichael's hand. She extended her upper lip, like an elephant's trunk, attempting to pull his fingers into her mouth.

Brad took a step back to look at her legs. They were black, too, typical of a bay horse, but this mare's black stockings were especially long. They were as inky black as her nose and extended beyond her kneecaps before blending in with the rich maroon of her forearms.

Brad cast a funny glance at her tail, or at least what should have been her tail. In its place was a neat wrap, thick and brown. A sturdy string, like kite string, was stitched neatly up the wrap, holding it firmly in place. The tail must have been braided and rolled inside because the entire affair did not hang much below the dock of the tailbone. McMichael smiled at Brad's questioning face.

"It drags the ground a good six inches," he boasted.

"Why?" asked Brad, still bewildered.

"Because she's an American Morgan Horse and Morgan owners are crazy," he chuckled. "This breed is known for having the thickest manes and tails of all the pleasure horse breeds," he explained.

Dorie enjoyed the men's conversation, a change from the usual auction barn horse talk. Brad was still studying the mare's tail wrap.

"How can you ride a horse with its tail dragging on the ground?" he asked. "Won't she step on it when she backs up?"

"Sure will," laughed McMichael. "Funnier yet," he added, "When we drive them in buggies, we have to tie the tail up to the front of the cart so it doesn't get caught in the spokes of the wheels!" Brad could not help but grin.

"So, why do they do it?" he again queried.

"Answer me this question," posed McMichael. "Why do girls wear high heels?" The grin on McMichael's face spread as he watched Brad struggle for a reasonable answer.

"I don't know!" Brad laughed an almost embarrassing giggle. "'Cuz they want to, I guess."

McMichael leaned forward and slapped his hand on Brad's shoulder. "That's absolutely right, boy. You're absolutely right. They do it because they want to." The filly nudged McMichael's shoulder and he returned his hand to her nose.

"Well, I've got to be getting back," he said, ending the small talk. "Dad's expecting us to work another fifteen head today and it's already noon."

Dorie re-entered the conversation. "Is the stall ready for her, Brad?"

"Yes," responded Brad. "And I put in a flake of hay and fresh water."

"Why don't you sneak in some oats, too," she suggested.

"I already did," Brad grinned sheepishly. They both knew that sale horses were not provided with oats and that this would have to be a secret between them.

Evan McMichael seemed to appreciate their special effort. He had worried, as he drove the mare over, about what would happen to her once he dropped her off. He found a sense of relief in the attention Dorie Wheaten was offering. He pondered Dorie's comment made in the office, about his looking like his dad. He made a mental note to ask his father how she knew him.

Evan handed the lead shank to Brad and the mare immediately began to dance anxiously. "Easy, girl, easy girl," Evan soothed. The filly relaxed.

"That's right," said Dorie. "We don't even know this woman's name."

Evan smiled sadly and shook his head. "This, Mrs. Wheaten, is Burgundy Delight, and it's a crying shame that she'll never have the opportunity to show what she can do. Both her sire and her dam are world champions," he explained. "Her daddy won the World Park Harness Championship in Oklahoma City a decade ago. My father trained him," he added with pride.

Evan realized that he was slipping back into conversation and time was escaping him. He had detested getting stuck with the job of bringing the mare here in the first place, and was surprised to find he was not particularly eager to leave.

"Talk to her, Brad," he coached. "She knows the word *'easy'.*" He stroked her smooth neck firmly and methodically.

"You've got to remember," Evan added, "She's not used to being handled by a lot of people. She's always been worked by just Dad and me." His voice dropped as he corrected himself. "By me. She's been my project. Sure wish I could show her this coming year." He blocked his dreaded thoughts of where she might go after this Saturday. The worst part was that he would never know. His throat tightened as he thought it might be a blessing not to know.

"Come on, girl," Brad coaxed the edgy horse. "At least for this week, you'll find a friend in me." Brad's brain was already beginning to fabricate fairy tales of how he might be able to keep this mare for himself. Goosebumps popped up on his arms and sent chills down his back. He wondered if Mrs. Wheaten had noticed. Of course not, what a silly thought.

"Evan, I know it's none of our—my—business," Dorie hesitated, "but . . . "

She was spared finishing the question as Evan McMichael followed them toward the stall, answering her unspoken question.

"Burgundy Delight was born at our place four years ago. She was assigned to me for halter training, so I've always sort of seen her as mine. Anyway," he continued as they led the mare to the rear of the barn, "the guy who owned her got caught in a nasty divorce and got way behind on his training fees. He kept saying he'd make it right as soon as his divorce was final." Evan shook his head. "Then, all of a sudden, the guy's wife decides she wants the mare. Don't ask me why, she was rarely around the place and I never saw her so much as pet the horse." Brad reached for the door of the pen and swung it open for the mare to pass through.

Evan reached behind the horse and dropped the latch on the gate. "I think she just wanted one more reason to hassle her husband, and she knew that he really loved this horse. Anyway," he concluded, "the divorce proceedings have been going on for over a year and the guy keeps getting further and further behind on his bills to Dad. We really wanted to be fair about things, but it wasn't just training fees we were losing. Any vet and blacksmith fees for horses in training are billed to our farm. Then we re-bill our customers. So you see, we were paying out money on her that we weren't getting back. Finally, Dad foreclosed on the horse. It's in our training contracts, so we have the legal right to move the horse quickly to recoup whatever money we can. I wouldn't mind keeping this one for myself, but Dad reminds me we're not in the business of owning horses. We're in the business of training and selling horses. We prospected our current clients, but no one's in the market for another horse right now, so here she is."

Dorie spoke up. "That's an important point, Evan. Do you have a minimum price we're supposed to accept next Saturday?" Brad could see Evan's throat tighten.

"Dad said she's not to come back to us. Just get him what you can and we won't complain."

4

Brad arrived early at Wheatens' the next morning. Dorie was not surprised when she heard his squeaky sneakers come through the door.

"Let me make one guess why you're here today," she teased. "And so early," she added. Brad dropped his parka across a chair and emptied a packet of hot cocoa mix into a Styrofoam cup. Dorie lifted a steaming kettle from the hot plate on the concession counter and filled the cup.

"You really like her, don't you?" Dorie already knew the answer to her question. Brad nodded an affirmative. She set the kettle back on the hot plate and sat quietly at her desk. "I agree with you; she's one pretty animal. It'll be sad to see her go through the sale on Saturday."

"Do you mind if I work with her between now and then?" Brad attempted to sound nonchalant with his question.

"Go right ahead," answered Dorie. "I'll enjoy watching. But didn't you say you were going up north with a friend this week?"

The hot cocoa burned Brad's tongue. "Well, we planned on it. Matt's dad said we could take both snowmobiles, but I thought maybe I'd stay and work the horse instead."

"Brad," Dorie cautioned, "you can't be falling in love with this horse." Brad ignored her comment.

"What do you think she's worth?" he asked. Dorie stared at her coffee for a moment before venturing a reply.

"It's hard to say. Horse prices are very subjective at the professional barns." Dorie set her chin in her hand and watched Brad's expression. "I'd guess maybe sixty-five hundred dollars."

"Wow," Brad responded. Then he continued, "Do you keep up with that stuff, Mrs. Wheaten? I mean, I've never heard you talk

19

about show horses. Do you read the magazines and know who's winning?"

"Oh, I used to," Dorie's eyes gazed out the window. "I kept my subscription to *Saddle Horse World* up to date until a few years ago. And last fall, when I went to Indiana for my niece's wedding, there was a show at the state fairgrounds. I stopped in for a couple hours to watch. Nothing's changed much."

"Nothing's changed?" Brad didn't hide his surprise. "Changed from what? Did you show horses?"

"Oh, a little," Dorie smiled softly and shook her head slowly. Then she added, "Most of my memories are very good ones. Anyway, you can work that mare all you want until Saturday. She hasn't really settled down since last night. It probably wouldn't hurt for you to ride her in and out of the sale pen a few times. I'd hate to see her spook and hurt herself on Saturday."

Brad pitched his cocoa cup quickly into the basket and pulled his parka around him. "I'll lunge her a little first, to get the ants out of her pants. Then maybe I'll saddle her up. Thanks for the chocolate." With that, he made a beeline straight for the bay mare's stall.

Burgundy Delight was playing in her pen. Her water bucket had been spilled and a lead rope, left hanging over the top rail, now lay in the straw between her legs. She nickered with interest as soon as she spotted Brad.

"Hey, girl, how are you on such a cold morning?" Brad noticed fresh hay in the corner and guessed that Mrs. Wheaten had beaten him to the feed room. Burgundy Delight wasted no time leaning over the rail to sniff at her new friend. She nibbled his collar and pushed against him with her nose.

"Oh, ho, what have we here? A spoiled horse?" Brad pushed the mare back so that he could open the pen gate. He pulled a carrot from his hip pocket. "I know you're looking for a treat and . . . I just happen to have one for you." Eager teeth reached forward to consume the orange stick, but Brad held firmly to the end of the carrot.

"Nah, nah, nah, you've got to bite. That's right, chew your food." She grabbed the second half of the carrot as he ran his other hand down her gently crested neck. Her thick and luxurious mane lay on the opposite side, exposing, on his side, the prettiest and smoothest arch of silky fur.

Brad studied her face. There were no traces of whisker stubble on her muzzle. Evan McMichael must have trimmed yesterday morning, before delivering her. Brad wondered why he would bother, knowing she was going to sit until Saturday and then be sold to someone who probably wouldn't notice the effort anyway.

After studying the tail wrap, neatly sewn in place, Brad thought it best to leave it as it was. He lifted the lead from between the mare's feet and snapped it to her halter. "Okay, Burgundy Delight—Burgie Girl—let's go for a walk." Taking her from the pen, Brad was careful to stay at her side. Burgie had no interest in behaving herself and danced back and forth across the aisle. The last thing he wanted was a shod hoof prancing on his toe. As they passed the tack room, he reached in and grabbed a fifteen-foot lunge line.

Outside the barn, there were patches of ice on the ground. Between the barn and the back pasture, there was an open area and, from there, by riding off to the left, one could enter an open field. Brad searched for a thirty-foot area that was safe enough to work the horse. He switched her lead rope for the lunge line. Holding the line in his left hand, he stepped back, giving the beautiful mare ten feet of slack. Lifting the free end of the rope in his right hand, he swished it gently in her direction to encourage her to move forward in a circle to his left.

Burgie responded with an immediate trot, smooth and even. "Evan McMichael called this green broke?" thought Brad as Burgie continued in an obedient circle around him. He continued her circle to the left for five minutes and then repeated the process to the right. Burgie never fussed but, rather, trotted along, perfectly happy.

Dorie had been leaning against the barn door quietly observing. "She's trying to sell herself to you," she said.

"Well, I'll tell you, Mrs. Wheaten," Brad chuckled. "She sure doesn't have to try hard. I think I'll saddle her up." He lowered his voice and commanded "Whoa." Burgie came to an immediate stop. *Impressive,* he thought.

"I'll get the tack for you," offered Dorie as the three of them re-entered the barn. She returned with her English hunt seat saddle, and Brad responded with an "Oh no, I'm not riding in that slip of leather. Get me the old black saddle."

"On her?" quipped Dorie. "She's probably never had a western saddle on her back in her life. Evan said they were training her for English pleasure. That's a flat saddle. The closest we have here is my hunt. You won't have any problems." She laid a well-used white-turned-gray pad and the saddle on the mare's back, and slipped a simple snaffle bit into her mouth. Burgie lifted a hind foot with a threat to kick toward Brad as he buckled the girth snug around her barrel. He made a mental note to saddle her more slowly next time. The little entourage returned to the rear of the barn, where Dorie stood at Burgie's head as Brad swung into the saddle. The mare immediately began to dance.

Dorie stepped to the horse's head. "Easy, easy, girl. Get your legs away from her sides," she commanded quickly.

"I'll take her from here," assured Brad as he collected his reins. But the moment he laid the calves of his legs against Burgie's sides, the horse spun completely around and began backing frantically. Dorie rushed to the rescue, calling again, "Get your legs away from her." She grabbed for the reins and pulled some of their tension from Brad's hands.

Brad corrected himself. "Maybe I won't take her outside after all. What am I doing wrong?" He sat quietly, rubbing his fingers firmly into the nape of Burgie's neck to sooth and gentle her.

Dorie encouraged him with a confident voice. "Your legs are too heavy. You're used to pushing auction and stable horses around—and they're used to being pushed around. However, this horse's sides are as light as a feather. Now, pick up your reins slowly, and as you do, watch for her reaction. As soon as she feels the slightest tension on the bit and gives you a response, hold it there. Don't ask for more until you understand her better. Do the same with your legs. Gently lay them against her until you get the slightest response from her. Give her a chance to tell you just how much direction she needs."

What Dorie said made sense enough to Brad. He began again, this time with a much lighter touch. But as soon as his legs came in contact with Burgie's sides, she bolted into choppy, unpredictable crow hops, stopping and starting and tossing her head. The more she fussed, the harder it was for Brad to not grip with his legs for support. Brad pulled his feet from the stirrups and flipped quickly to the ground. Burgie settled right down and stood quietly for the two of them.

"Either she's barely green broke, or she just doesn't like me." Brad stroked Burgie's neck and shook his own head in disappointment. Dorie wasn't listening. She was busy shortening the stirrup leather on the far side of the horse. She came around the near side and proceeded to shorten the second leather. Gathering the reins slowly in her left hand and securing her grasp with a lock of mane for support, she placed her left foot in the near stirrup and lifted herself nimbly onto the light-weight saddle. Burgie didn't move. Dorie leaned forward quietly and stroked the horse's neck.

"All right, woman," Dorie whispered. "Let's see what you can do. Walk, girl." Burgie moved forward in a slow walk. Brad never saw Dorie's legs press the horse. When she reached the end of the small fenced area behind the barn, she turned Burgie into the open field and pressed a second time, ever so softly. Burgie responded with a nervous trot.

Suddenly, the mare jumped four feet sideways and spun a full circle. Before Dorie could completely regain her balance, Burgie broke into a canter, attempting to pick up speed in the open field. Dorie lifted her seat out of the saddle to maintain her balance. With her weight in the stirrups, she passed both reins into her left hand and reached her right forward to the horse's head. She grabbed the right rein very near to the bit and, with a quick, firm, and deliberate tug, she pulled Burgie's head so unexpectedly toward the right that the horse had no choice but to break her gait and slow her speed. Dorie drove her into a tight circle until she came to a stop. By the time Burgie gave up fighting the woman, Brad had reached them in the field.

"Do you want off, Mrs. Wheaten?" Brad reached toward Burgie's mouth and took the reins in his hands.

"No, but you can walk us back to the barn. It's been a while since I've been on a horse at all, much less a sassy one." She added, "I doubt if she's ever been worked in an open field. Most likely, she's had ring work where there were walls or rails to give her confidence. We don't have anything like that here other than the auction pen. And that's too small to really do a workout."

Once back in the barn, Burgie got a good brushing before being returned to her pen. Brad put away the lunge line and tack thinking that maybe he would head up north with Matt after all.

5

The ringing of the telephone woke Susan Bateman from her sleep. The clock on her nightstand told her it was six-thirty in the morning. Scurrying down the stairs and across the cold kitchen floor, she lifted the receiver from its hook.

"Hello? Mrs. Bateman? Is Brad there?" It was Matt Foxworthy's familiar voice.

"For heaven's sake, where else would he be at this time of the morning?" As she spoke, Susan noticed a scrawled note that lay on the counter:

> Mom,
>
> > Please let Matt know I won't be going up north.
> >
> > I'm working at Wheatens' today.
> >
> > > > Thanks, B.

Susan read the note aloud over the phone. Matt grumbled a "Thanks, Mrs. Bateman," before hanging up.

"A horse," she mused aloud as she scuffled her sleepy feet back to bed. "A horse got him up at five-thirty in the morning." She slipped into bed and pulled the covers over her shoulders. Her oblivious husband snored softly at her side. Maybe she should stop in at the barn later. This must be some animal if her son could spend all evening complaining about it, and then get up at five-thirty the next morning to work with it.

☆   ☆   ☆

The auction barn was dark. The winter sun would not rise for another two hours. Still, a sleepy Burgie eagerly greeted Brad. The flicking of the barn lights caught her by surprise and her eyes squinted tightly as she chortled quietly from her pen.

The creaking of the feed room door wakened the bay mare completely. Off in a corner, Willy's caged chickens began to move around. Burgie nickered persistently as Brad scooped her oats from the bin. A few bales of hay had been thrown down from the loft the night before. He grabbed a flake and tossed the impatient mare her breakfast. Brad noticed that the water in the corner bucket was frozen solid. He returned to the front of the barn, collected a box of brushes from the tack room, and drew a fresh bucket of water from the spigot.

Burgie's head was lost in the pail of oats as Brad began grooming. He was determined that she would look as good on Saturday night as she had when she came in two days ago. He had reviewed his, *The Complete Pony Care Book* last night, after spending twenty minutes looking for it. He was not sure whether he had even kept it, seeing as it was a birthday present when he was in the fourth grade. But, for now, it was his only resource manual.

"Burgie, I'm supposed to start brushing at the top of your neck. Now, how can I do that when your head is stuck in a bucket?" The mare ignored him and continued hogging her oats. Brad began rubbing the top of her shoulder in a hard circular motion with an oval, rubber-toothed curry brush. As he worked the circle, he whistled her a quiet song. The harder he pushed, the more she leaned back against him. He was sure she was enjoying his effort. When his right arm grew tired, he switched the rubber curry to his left. Eventually, that arm became tired, aching in the shoulder, so he switched back to the right. Long before he was finished, his biceps and elbow joints ached from the constant action. It was a thorough curry job.

Burgie finished her oats and immediately went to work on the flake of hay. After giving her entire body a deep down rub, Brad dropped the rubber curry back into the box and picked up two bristle brushes. The green brush was thick and stiff while the blue one was soft. His hands simultaneously retraced the entire curry path on Burgie's body, rubbing straight down hard with the green brush followed by the soft blue. Even in the dim light of the auction barn, he could see her bay coat shine.

Brad used only the soft brush on the lower part of her legs, and then lifted each foot to clean the inner hoof with a metal pick. He was surprised to find a leather pad covering the entire surface of the bottom of the hoof. The pad had been inserted between the hoof and the metal shoe. Brad had never seen such a shoeing job and, with some measure of curiosity, dropped his pick back into the box. He again decided to leave the tail neatly in its wrap. He was eager to see how long her tail really was, but it seemed best not to mess with the meticulous job until Saturday. His pony manual suggested washing the inner ears, nostrils, and eyes with warm water, but the auction barn did not have hot running water so he skipped grooming her face. He noticed with dismay that new whiskers were beginning to sprout on her muzzle.

With the grooming done, Brad was suddenly aware that Burgie had had her breakfast but there was a growling in his own stomach. He collected the brush box, gave Burgie a hardy slap on the hip, and left her pen. He didn't get thirty feet away before the mare lifted her head from her hay and nickered what seemed to be a note of appreciation for the good grooming, delicious breakfast, and kind fellowship. "Ha," thought Brad as he walked away. "You're probably telling me I forgot the carrots!"

Brad set the grooming box on the ground and returned to the bay mare's stall. He quietly opened the gate and slipped alongside her. With a long, slow reach, he swept his arms around the huge base of Burgie's neck and gave her a warm, tight squeeze. She lifted her head and stepped away. "Yeah, well I don't love you neither," he smiled. And with that, he jogged quickly out of the chilly barn, hopped in his van, and headed for the Supreme Donuts shop.

When Brad returned to the barn with his small treasures from the donut shop, the sun was just beginning to peek across the fields behind the barns. Brad slapped his palms against the steering wheel in time to an upbeat tune on the radio. He turned the van into the barn lot and pulled to a stop in front of Dorie's office window. As he stepped from the van, he could see lights over at the next barn. The stable crew was already out and feeding the riding horses. He could see Jackson's dirty white head protruding from an open door. Whoever would want to go riding in twenty-degree weather? Still, it was Christmas vacation and, if the sun shown brightly enough, it might warm into the thirties. Besides, even though Wheatens kept fewer stable horses during the winter than in summer, whether the riding stable had business today or not, the horses still needed to be fed.

Brad glanced at the office window. It was dark inside. Dorie was not yet up and about. He ambled to the side of the building and pushed hard against the sliding door. It creaked open slowly and he headed for the concession area.

Hot cocoa and three cream-filled doughnuts soon warmed his stomach. A fourth was on its way down the chute. Now, Brad needed to decide what he was going to do with Burgie. After all, he gave up the chance to go snowmobiling with Matt just to be with her. When he reached her pen, the pretty mare stole the last bite of his cream stick and began to snoop for more.

"Sorry, girl, all you get today is a saddle." At the tack room, Brad flicked on the light and stared at the saddles on the racks. He still was not sure what he wanted to do. Cobwebs hung from the ceiling rafters and a thin layer of dust covered most everything. His gut feeling was to reach for the dependable western saddle; then, he remembered what Dorie had said about Burgie most likely not being used to such a heavy piece of equipment. Removing the protective towel, he lifted her saddle from the rack. He then decided against it and set it back in place.

The thought of not riding at all was what actually came to mind. Brad could just lunge Burgie to keep her exercised until Saturday. Then, during the auction, he could simply walk her into the sale ring. Of course, everyone would think she was still truly untrained because the auction boys always rode anything they could mount. If Brad chose not to ride her, one of the other guys would probably take her in. Maybe, he thought, he just would not work the auction at all this coming Saturday.

With each passing thought, Brad realized that he was afraid of not one, but two, possibilities. First, he was afraid to ride Burgie because he did not want a second disappointing experience, a repeat of yesterday. And second, he did not want to see her sold on Saturday. *That's pretty stupid,* he thought to himself. *If I'm afraid to ride her, then why do I care if she gets sold?*

With that, Brad made a resolute turn and headed up front to the office. Although the outside door to the office, leading from the concession area, was locked, the inside door, leading from the tack room was not. Brad found pencil and paper on Dorie's desk and scrawled a quick note:

8:00 a.m.

Mrs. W,

> I'm taking Burgie for a walk. Don't worry about us.
>
> (We don't have a saddle with us so we can't hurt each other!)
>
> Ha. Ha.

Brad

With Burgie snapped securely on her lead, Brad and the mare headed out the back door of the barn, around the back pen, and across the forty-acre field that had been the scene of her fussing the day before.

There was no wind and no clouds. The early sun was exposing a crisp, blue sky. Maybe it would warm past freezing before the day was through.

The boy and horse spent the next three hours exploring. Every time something spooked Burgie, Brad would turn her to face the source of fear and wait patiently until he was sure her curiosity was satisfied. A rabbit running from under a small pin cherry tree was the biggest ghost of the day. The cawing of a band of too-close crows rising from a grove of pines and the barking of two dogs that suddenly came romping upon them made her stop, but her response was not too skittish. A diesel truck passed along the expressway across the roadway beyond the auction barn, and bellowed its horn, but the sound seemed far off and Burgie did not even notice.

Brad and Burgie walked the entire length of the field, all thirteen-hundred-and-twenty feet. They walked along the dilapidated, paint-worn fence that made up the south side of the Wheatens' back paddock, and along the simple wire fencing that extended beyond. The two of them crossed into the open cornfield that led toward Tyler's house. The ground was frozen and they had to pick their way, stepping around clumps of dirt and corn stubble. A light breeze picked up and Brad could feel the late December chill on his ruddy cheeks. A nice beard would do him good right about now, but his folks had given him an adamant "No!" to his attempt to grow whiskers.

After a mile or so, they came out on the open road and continued their aimless wandering. A car came up behind them and

Brad waved his free hand downward emphatically, urging the driver to slow his speed. The driver ignored the request but Burgie offered no reaction to the passing car. Evan McMichael had said that she had been shown extensively in halter classes and was accustomed to being trailered. Obviously, she had had plenty of time to grow used to cars.

Brad walked the horse past Tyler's house and thought about stopping. His fingers and toes were frozen and his nose was runny. Tyler's mom would probably invite him in to get warm but he wasn't comfortable leaving Burgie tied outside. So, instead, he turned and began a silent walk back toward Wheatens'.

As Brad entered the back side of the barn, he glanced at his watch: eleven thirty. He was impressed to see how much he had accomplished and how much of the day was still ahead. It sure beat his usual roll out of bed on non-school days at eight-thirty or nine, especially when he often added two hours of Looney Tunes to the late rising. He wondered at how his Christmas vacation was turning out so differently than he had planned.

Green had the backhoe in action, cleaning out the thirty pens for Friday's arrivals. Chuck Wheaten was up front, under the auctioneer's stand, trying to fix the faulty P.A. system. Dorie was in the office, taking inventory of concession supplies.

With everyone busy, Brad suddenly felt like he had wasted the morning, but watching Burgie in her stall let him know he did a good thing. First of all, he did not usually work on Thursdays anyway, so there was nothing for him to do. And the walk had done Burgie good. She was relaxed and happy, and that was the way an animal should be—besides, it sure beat being in school. The sudden thought that school would start again on Monday made the Christmas holidays seem too short. The thought that immediately followed was even worse: Burgie would be sold in just two days. By the time he returned to school, everything would be just as it was before she had come into his life.

"My, my, aren't we the early one?" Dorie's voice surprised him. Brad turned to find her walking down the aisle. She stepped over small piles of loose manure that had fallen from Green's machine. Brad recounted his morning activities to her.

"Did she shiver at all while you were out?" Dorie questioned the boy. Burgie had been kept blanketed at McMichaels' so her winter fur had not grown thick, and the blanket had not accompanied her to Wheatens'.

"No, not at all," Brad replied. "The sun's bright. The only parts of me that are cold are my fingers and toes."

Dorie rubbed her hands on Burgie's neck. "Are you riding today?"

"Yep," Brad replied. "As soon as I grab a sandwich. I've already walked off four cream sticks."

"Are you sure you want to do that?" Dorie queried.

Brad looked at Dorie and contemplated his answer. "Yes, I am. I want to. I know she's not my horse, and I know I don't ride well enough to do her justice. But, by golly, I've never had the chance to ride a really nice horse and she's going to be gone in two days. Then I'll be sorry that I didn't ride her when I had the chance. So, I'm going to ride her now!"

"That's the spirit," Dorie responded. "I'll even make that sandwich. Will you run up town and pick up supplies for Saturday night? I don't want your new license to go to waste."

Brad took the list from Dorie, along with a hundred and a fifty dollar bill: four hundred Styrofoam cups, six boxes of sugar packets, six three-pound cans of coffee, two cases of cocoa packets, and a bottle of Jack Daniels. Brad looked up at Dorie.

"Forget the bottle," she mused. "I'll use you as an excuse. I can tell Chuck that I forgot you can't buy liquour. He doesn't need it anyway."

☆　☆　☆

By one that afternoon, Brad had Burgie saddled and ready for what he and Dorie had agreed was to be a short workout. She suggested that he ride inside first. The ceiling rafters were high enough and the aisles were twelve feet wide. He also listened to her advice about what tack to use. Burgie stood ready in the aisle, sporting the light hunt saddle. She was tacked in a simple snaffle bridle, its mild bit jointed in the middle. Any tension from the reins would be felt at the corners of her mouth and nowhere else.

Brad decided to pull no surprises today. Everything would go as smoothly and quietly as possible. He was intent on being sensitive to how Burgie responded to his smallest motions. When saddling, he eased the girth up to the desired tightness and slowly latched each buckle to the saddle billets. The mare stood quietly and tolerated his effort. He then gathered his reins in his left hand so that they barely formed a straight line from her mouth to his hand. A half-inch more tension would have caused her to back or fuss. Setting his fist against the lower crest of her neck, he collected a tuft of mane to steady himself, as he had seen Dorie do the day before. With his right hand on the pommel of the saddle, he quietly set his left foot in the stirrup and raised his body off the ground. As he settled gently into the saddle, he kept the calves of his legs absolutely away from the mare's sides. She stood, quietly mouthing at her bit.

Brad lifted the reins and Burgie immediately took one step back. "Well, now I know how easily you back," he said aloud.

Burgie had not been trained to rein western style. It was therefore necessary for Brad to hold a rein in each hand. Here at the barn, they called it plow reining but, in fact, it was the traditional English way to maneuver a horse. Only when it was necessary for the rider to use one of his hands for some other task, such as holding a rifle, lance, or lariat, was it necessary to train a horse to western, or neck, rein.

Brad thought about how he worked the auction horses in the small sale pen. In order to turn a horse in the tight confine, it was necessary to press into the animal's side at the same time that he drew on the rein. A rein pull alone would throw the animal off balance because there was not enough room to make a big and sloppy turn. By pressing his heel behind the girth, however, Brad could encourage the horse to draw his back legs up under himself and maneuver a neat, tight circle. He figured the same should work with Burgie; he just needed to be much more gentle with the requests.

Brad squeezed his right fist around the rein just enough that the bay mare could feel the movement, but not a tug, at the right corner of her mouth. At the same time, while keeping his left leg away from her side, he gently laid his right calf just behind her girth. She spun quickly around and came to a stop facing the opposite direction. Brad breathed a sigh of relief. Now, he knew his mission. It was he, not Burgie, who needed work.

Brad evened the tension between the reins, still just barely feeling Burgie's mouth in his hands and touched both her sides lightly and simultaneously. She broke into a trot, tossing her head incessantly. He quickly remembered the advice Dorie had offered while he was eating his sandwich.

"While you're riding, put an imaginary cup of hot cocoa in each of your hands. All the while you ride, be sure that you don't spill a drop." It was impossible. Dorie's hunt saddle was too small and, as Brad bounced to Burgie's choppy trot, his butt kept falling in an obnoxious double bounce against the back of the saddle.

Burgie continued this choppy trot around the circle formed by the two aisles running through the barn. It was true that the walled building gave her emotional security that she had not found in the open field yesterday. The teen was thankful for that.

Brad could tolerate the trot no longer. He squeezed the reins once and Burgie dropped to a still-choppy walk. After a few moments, in response to Brad's soothing words, "Easy girl, easy girl," she relaxed and walked quietly along. He pulled both his feet from the stirrup irons and let them hang loosely away from the horse. They circled the empty pens four times before he dismounted and returned the mare to her stall.

Brad left feeling good about the horse but really disgusted with his own riding. He had always thought he could ride with the best of them. Now, he realized that staying with a horse whose jaws and ribs had become hardened to the tugging and kicking of joy riders was not the definition of quality horsemanship.

That night he lay awake in bed, figuring how to make these few rides before Saturday's sale as enjoyable as possible. In a western saddle on a western trained horse, Brad could ask the animal to give a jog rather than a trot. A jog is easy to sit, albeit much slower than a normal trot. Really good western horses were called daisy-cutters because their hooves barely lifted from the ground as they ambled along. This caused the jog to be very smooth, and much easier to sit.

Brad figured it would be impossible to ask Burgie to jog. It simply was not in her personality. She had a natural style that was full of pizzazz; as if she was always turned on, always saying, "Look at me. I want to show off." Still, he knew he could not reap a rewarding ride if he could not steady his hands. And it would be impossible to steady his hands if he could not steady his body.

Dorie had sent Brad home with a stack of magazines. Lying in bed, he flipped through back issues of *Practical Horseman* and noticed that riders over fences lifted themselves out of their saddles before sailing over the rail. He figured that he could avoid the bounce of the trot if he would put himself in such a position. After all, he was using a hunt saddle intended specifically for jumpers, so, why not? Sleep came gently. Horses sailed over fences and clouds and stars. Brad fell off a golden steed, dropped through the billowing whiteness, and landed on a black stallion. The night was long and sweet.

6

Friday morning found Brad at the barn early again. Following the same schedule as the day before, he fed and groomed Burgie and then headed up to Supreme Donuts. Upon returning, however, he skipped the morning walk and saddled the mare. Like yesterday, she stood quietly as Brad eased himself into the saddle.

Brad asked Burgie to walk the inner aisles. But Burgie had just come off a full night's rest; she didn't want to walk. She fussed and pranced and begged to trot. Without dismounting, Brad guided the mare out the back door of the barn. The winter sun was just rising over the cornfield beyond the open meadow. He courageously encouraged Burgie left around the paddock and into the field.

As Burgie lifted herself into a springing trot, Brad shortened the reins and buried his fingers into her mane. He pressed the balls of his feet against his stirrup irons and let his heels drop low. Laying his knees into the saddle's padded knee rolls, he lifted his seat into the air. By lowering his back until it was parallel with Burgie's neck, much like a racing jockey, he could keep from losing his balance.

Burgie trotted eagerly along the entire tree-lined fencerow. The meadow disappeared behind them as a cornfield came into view. The crows that had scared her the day before meant nothing to her today. The crunch of the frost on the meadow weeds seemed to make her spry and happy. When the trot became unruly, Brad shortened the reins by scooting them between his thumbs and forefingers, making sure to keep them even. His knees and ankles buoyantly absorbed the motion of the horse, while he held his head and body steady.

Upon reaching the edge of the cornfield, Brad remembered the frozen ruts they encountered the day before. Instead of venturing onto them, he just squeezed his left fist and touched Burgie with his left calf. She automatically turned and continued along the perimeter of the meadow. Soon, they were at the next corner, a full forty acres away from the barn, and shadowed by the wood-lot. Brad asked for a *whoa* and Burgie obeyed. He ever so quietly set his butt into the seat of the saddle.

Not until this moment was he aware that his body ached all over. It was worse than being bucked. His inner thigh muscles, holding his body out of the saddle, had been taut for the entire distance. His buttocks were tight. His contracted biceps had kept his back steady as his hands had moved with the come and go of the mare's neck. His Achilles tendons and his knee joints had served as buoyant springboards but now ached from the effort.

The pair headed diagonally across the open field toward the barn. The return walk was relaxed. The sun cast a measure of warmth across Brad's back. He had conquered Burgundy De-light. No, he corrected himself. She had educated him.

Two hundred feet from the barn, Brad noticed a woman standing at the corner of the paddock. She was bundled in a long, tan coat and wearing no hat—definitely, not an outdoors-woman. The figure raised a hand and waved to him and the con-nection was immediately made. Brad raised his hips from the saddle, totally forgetting his aching muscles. His mother had never visited the barns in the two years he had worked for the Wheatens'. Even in past winters, he had peddled his ten-speed back and forth to his weekend employment. All she knew of Mr. and Mrs. Wheaten, Green and Tyler, and all the horses was what Brad had told her at home. Now, here she was, waving to him across the open field.

"Let's go, girl," he said aloud as he asked for a trot, while hold-ing the reins snug to discourage an unwanted canter. But Burgie had a natural surprise for Brad. Her trot toward home was im-mensely different than her trot away from the barns. Instead of a choppy trot, or even just a smooth and natural trot, the beauti-ful bay mare lifted her feet high and extended her legs well in front of her. As Brad felt the power rise beneath him, he thought she might break into a canter at any moment. He began giving her reins extra little squeezes with his fists. Still, her body swelled under him and swept the ground beneath her. It was a physical and emotional lift he had never before felt in a horse. Glancing over her shoulder as they glided along, he could see the tops of her knees as they rose up high with each stride.

Burgie came to a sure stop right in front of Susan Bateman, and Brad slid quickly to the ground, staring aghast at his mom.

"Your feet must be freezing, Mom! Where are your boots?"

Susan smiled at the thought of her son looking out for how she was dressed. It was a unique role reversal.

"I was just on my way to your father's office when I thought I'd stop in to see this latest girlfriend of yours." Brad silently noted that Wheatens' auction barn was in no way on her way to his father's office.

"She's pretty, isn't she?" Brad encouraged a positive reply from his mother. Actually, it was the first time his mom had been this near to a horse at all, so she was in no position to compare the mare's beauty to any other horse.

"Well, I have to admit, I thought I would be afraid of her, but this horse has such a gentle eye. I never realized horses had such big eyes." Her response was enough to please Brad.

"Where should I pet her?" asked Susan earnestly.

Brad answered with authority. "She can see better at her side, and don't move too quickly or you'll startle her."

"Me? Scare a horse? That's hard to believe!" Susan whistled ever so softly and Burgie's ears perked up in full attention to the hesitant woman. She laid her open palm against the mare's wide, flat cheek and scratched the circular jaw with her polished nails. Burgie stretched her head forward in response.

"Oh, you like that. You're such a good girl." Susan ran her hand softly over Burgie's eye bone and around the back of her ear. "Oh, I found another itchy spot." She giggled as Burgie pushed for more attention.

Dorie Wheaten watched from the door of the barn. She was thinking that Brad's mother looked just half her own age, yet they surely must be closer than that. Working out of doors wears so badly on a woman's face, leaving dry skin and crow's feet long before they are deserved.

Earlier, while waiting for Brad to return, Dorie had shared a cup of coffee with Susan Bateman. As they chatted, Dorie had worried that something terrible might have happened during Brad's ride and he might not return at all. Would this woman hold her responsible for letting the boy out on an unpredictable horse? Now, however, that worry was behind her and Susan Bateman was happy with Brad's horse. Dorie mentally corrected herself. Susan was happy with the horse that would be sold in tomorrow night's auction.

7

At nine o'clock Saturday morning, Brad had still not arrived at
the barns. Dorie wondered whether she would see him at all.
Maybe he would skip work tonight. Under the circumstances, she
felt it would be justified. If Brad decided not to be around when
Burgie went on the auction block, she would see to it that Chuck
did not reprimand him for it.

Just then, Dorie caught the sound of Brad's mother's minivan
pulling up to the office. The lot was busy with trucks and trailers
coming in with horses for tonight's sale. It was the night before
New Year's Eve but Dorie was right in her speculation that the
holiday would not lessen the number of sellers. She was just hoping it would also not lessen the number of buyers. On the one
hand, a lot of people were off work for the holidays and may be
looking for somewhere to spend some time. On the other hand,
everyone was broke after Christmas so, even if they showed up,
maybe they'd be lookers but not buyers.

Without stopping by with his usual "hello," Brad proceeded to
tack up Burgie and head out back. There was something specific
he wanted to test with Burgie, and today would be his last opportunity to work with her.

The pair started off along the meadow's northern fencerow as
usual. Burgie picked up a pleasant trot on request, and was much
more easygoing than the day before. Brad thought it amazing
how quickly they were adjusting to each other. Again, he lifted
his body from the saddle, though not as high as the day before, to
avoid her bounce. The mare's trot fell into a smooth and rhythmic motion and Brad began to gauge her length of stride.

After a few hundred feet, Brad felt ready for his test. He gave
the slightest restraining squeeze on the reins to let Burgie know

he wanted her to keep her neck arched and her nose tucked. His calves then touched her sides, asking for more energy from her hips. The mare brought her rear legs up under herself with greater emphasis, and there was noticeably more spring in her hocks. The restraining reins discouraged her from turning this extra energy into forward speed. So, the energy went upwards instead. She lifted her front legs higher and extended them in a greater arch. That was it! It happened just like yesterday. Her motion swelled under him. The meadow passed under them as they bounded forward in high, round, gracefully sweeping strides. She was gorgeous! Absolutely gorgeous! And he was in heaven. Absolute heaven. The bright winter sun glistened off the deep burgundy red of her body; the crisp chill of the wind bit his face and blew her mane. Brad could feel her full thousand pounds of massive, moving muscle pumping through his entire body. She was so unlike the stable horses. She was so . . . pizzazzy. No wonder she was named Burgundy Delight!

Before they reached the back corner of the cornfield, Brad brought Burgie down to a natural trot, then a walk. Her body was warm and she snorted three loud snorts to clear her lungs.

They rounded the corner and Brad loosened his reins and gave the mare a slight nudge with his right boot just behind her girth. She broke into an easy canter along the edge of the cornfield. Brad's face began to burn from the wind, cold and sharp, and the warming sun could do nothing to help. Burgie's body rocked methodically in her beautiful canter along the edge of the field, the meadow to their left, and the cornfield to their right. The cold whipped his face, tears streaking across his cheeks, flowing behind him, leaving his ears momentarily wet. The meadow became a blur as Brad squinted his eyes in the cold. He could barely see the woodlot, a huge dark mass, coming toward them. Today, however, he had confidence in Burgundy Delight. She made a long, wide left curve and cantered along the woodlot. Brad slowly pulled in on the reins but Burgie didn't feel his message. She didn't want to stop. Brad lightly wiggled the leather between his frozen fingers—left-right-left-right-left-right.

The bay girl listened now and bounced as she broke her gait. The teen slid forward on her neck and dug his fingers into her black mane to keep from sliding over and off her shoulder. Bounce. Bounce. Burgie came to a stiff, panting walk. Brad leaned down and to the side, stretching to stroke the front of her neck. She had no sweat. She, too, tingled with the brisk morning.

"I got eighty-five, eighty-five, one-eighty-five," bellowed Chuck Wheaten over the loudspeaker. It was just as crackly as last week. Obviously, he had not figured out his wiring problem.

Back in the pen area, Dorie laid her hand on the boy's shoulder. "You've got to get her out there, Brad. You and I both know that there's only so much money out there in those bleachers and the longer you wait, the harder she'll be to sell."

Brad couldn't look Dorie in the eye.

She continued, "We have an obligation to Mr. McMichael. It's the business we're in, Brad, and you're here to do a job."

Brad still didn't answer. He thought he'd be able to handle the situation better than this. He had spent all last evening dumping his bad feelings in his mother's lap. By the time he went to bed, he felt weary and defeated, resigned to losing Burgie. His mother had suggested that he ask for the night off but he had decided not to wimp out on the Wheatens.

Now, standing with the mare, his stomach was sick. Burgie paced nervously as dozens of horses passed by her stall. The constant bellowing of the static loud speaker put her on edge. She was not used to all the people milling about the barn, hanging over the rails of her pen, waving their arms and poking at her. And that blasted, crackling speaker. It just plain put her on edge.

Earlier, Brad had groomed Burgie to perfection. Her tail was combed smooth behind her. The glossy black hairs extended beyond floor length and were becoming caught up in her fresh straw. Without answering Dorie, Brad entered the stall and lifted Burgie's tail from her bedding. He wrapped the tail around his arm and pulled it through itself to form a soft slipknot up off the ground. He pretended to be intent about picking the remaining bits of straw from the tail.

"Saddle her up, Brad." Dorie became quietly snippy. "I'm not your mother and we don't have all night. I'm going back up front. I expect to hear her coming on the block within the next ten minutes." Without waiting for an answer, Dorie headed up front. It was her fault that it had come to this. She should have known better than to have taken the situation so lightly. She had given Brad more credit than his age called for and now she had to take part blame for his having a rough time with it.

No thoughts passed through Brad's mind as he blindly saddled the mare. She was skittish as he mounted her, but he was insensitive to what she was feeling. He was too busy blocking his own bad feelings. Carter teased Brad about the saddle he was using, but Brad didn't hear. Willy just stood back and watched in silence.

Tyler was nowhere in sight. Brad had barked at him so harshly an hour ago that the youngster wanted nothing to do with him tonight. But it was not Tyler's fault. The younger boy was so taken by Burgie's shining coat and impressively long black tail that all the wrong phrases rolled from his lips. "Boy, she'll sure sell for a mint. Someone's going to be a lucky buyer tonight. Wonder where she'll end up."

"GET LOST!" Brad had shouted, which sent Tyler scurrying on his way. He could always spend the evening playing with Willy's chickens.

Brad was so wrapped up in self-pity that he forgot to pull Burgie's tail out of its full and fluffy slip knot before maneuvering her into the sale ring. Still, it looked elegant compared to the sock that had protected it all week. That sock would have raised a real hoot from the crowd.

"Now look here, folks." Chuck Wheaten began over his P.A. "We've got a little something special for you all tonight." Burgie stared wide-eyed at the smoky crowd and nervously danced about the small arena. "One man's misery is another man's luck. Someone didn't pay their bills so their beautiful show horse ended up right in your hands." Burgie continued to pace her small confine with tiny, choppy steps—not the sweeping, high-arched strides Brad had come to know. There was, of course, no room in here for that even if she could relax and perform the way she had been trained. She chopped and stared, and hopped and stared, distrusting the crowd, the smell, the smoke, and the dizzying crackle of the loudspeaker.

"Twenty-five hundred dollars." Chuck suddenly bellowed. The booming of his voice caused Burgie to stop short, then restart her choppy pacing. There was nothing Brad could do to help her relax. "We're gonna start the bidding at twenty-five hundred dollars. She's a ten-thousand-dollar baby and you all know it. A once-in-your-lifetime opportunity to own a real show horse. Who'll start me out with twenty-five hundred dollars?" The quiet crowd just watched Burgie chop the little runway. A few laughs, grunts, and chuckles murmured through the gawkers.

"Twenty-five hundred dollars!" called out one spectator. "She ain't got four hundred dollars worth of meat on her bones. She won't hold up on the trail. Bet I can run her plum dead in an hour!" The man's friends all laughed and nodded in agreement. Brad tried to bring Burgie to an easy trot but she continued her spooky chop.

"Two thousand dollars," Wheaten corrected himself. Then he boomed over the speaker, "Two thousand dollars, two thousand dollars, who'll start the bidding off at two thousand dollars?" A man sitting further up in the dim bleachers called out, "Let 'er run a bit." Wheaten nodded for Brad to put the mare into the short to and fro spurts typical of the 4-H speed-and-action horses.

Brad's response was quiet and was meant only for Wheaten's ears. "She can't do that in here. And, she doesn't neck rein." But the fellow nearest the pen overheard and let out a hoot, "What, boy? She ain't neck-reined? You got a plow-reined hoss there?" He laughed hard and spit a wad of tobacco into the ring. If there were decent 4-H families in the crowd, they weren't coming forward with money for an English pleasure horse. "Kick her anyway. Let's see what she's worth," continued the old geezer.

Brad brought Burgie to a stop and turned to face the old coot straight on. His temper was flaring. "She's not a horse to be kicked. I've never rode a horse like this before. She's incredible!"

"Incredible my bum end," mumbled the tobacco chewer. "How do you ride a hoss you cain't kick?!" The every-Saturday hang-arounders were beginning to have such fun at Burgie's expense that even the fair-hearted 4-H families in attendance were becoming annoyed. Maybe, they weren't looking for a high-stepper, just a steady pet for their child, but most of them quietly contemplated that Burgie was, in fact, a pretty horse. Too high strung, but pretty.

A young girl on the far edge of the ring had been working her way forward. Finally, she was able to stretch her arm over the rail and reach Burgie's soft nose. A friendly muzzle leaned forward in its search for a friend.

"I like this horse," the girl said quietly. "Can I have this horse?" Wheaten's eyes scoured the crowd quickly to find the man

who had been standing with the little girl earlier. He was leaning against the wall near where the horses were being brought
in. Wheaten pointed his gavel at the man and asked, "Will you
give me two thousand dollars for this horse?"

The man shook his head in the negative but held up his in-
dex finger. Wheaten jumped at the response. "I've got a thousand
dollars," he bellowed. Dorie had come from behind the concession
counter to see what was happening. Brad's head was spinning.
Even he could afford a thousand dollars! What was happening?
How could these people not see the value in the mare that had
stolen his heart? What was going to happen in the next few moments? Could Dorie really satisfy Mr. McMichael with a mere
thousand dollars?

But Chuck Wheaten's attention was drawn to the far front of
the barn, to the door leading toward the concession area. Dorie
stood in the doorway, her lips pursed, shaking her head. Chuck
wiped the sweat from his face. "I ain't taking no thousand dollars
for this handsome mare. Listen here, folks. She may not look like
a lot to you in this here little box. But I been watching this flashy
little darlin' all week. This here boy's been workin' her out yon-
der in them fields, and I'll lay my name to her, she's a pretty sight
to behold. Who's here ever dreamed of winning one of them there
English classes at your shows? This here girl will do the job for
ya. Now, we ain't askin' no ten thousand dollars and you all know
that's what she's worth. Some poor fella's lost all he's got in a divorce and the prize sits right here. That is if the right person is
sittin' right out there." He paused for just a moment, waving his
auctioneer's gavel toward the bleachers, and then continued.
"Now, who'll give me eleven hundred dollars for this here mare?"

Three women sat halfway up the bleachers. Maybe they were
single. Maybe they left their husbands home. No matter, now
they whispered among themselves. Finally, the one on the left
raised her hand to start the bidding. With a silly grin and shake
of his sweaty face, Chuck drawled, "I got eleven hundred dollars,
who'll give me twelve?" This was like pulling teeth.

Chuck Wheaten glanced back up toward the open door and
there stood Dorie still shaking her head. He wiped the sweat
from the bottom side of his chin and around the back of his neck,
swearing in the process. He searched the crowd for Green, caught
his eye, and slowly rolled his gavel back and forth on the counter.
Green took the cue and slowly raised his hand.

"I've got twelve hundred dollars!" And, without a moment's hesitation, he added, "Sold to the man in the green hat for twelve hundred dollars!" His gavel slammed the counter and Burgie gave a little jump.

"Get 'er outta here," he snapped at Brad. "I ain't got all night and we got horses to sell!"

Late into the night, long after the crowd was gone and employees were home and fast asleep, Chuck Wheaten stomped the wooden floor of the old two-story farmhouse he called home. The smell of beer was heavy on his tired breath. "I didn't want that damnedable horse here in the first place!" He pitched his empty can in the corner basket and in the same swing, opened the frig for another. "You, Dorie Wheaten! You're going to call them blasted McMichaels in the morning, and I'll tell you what. I'm not gonna have some high strung mare causing an accident over at the riding stable. My liability insurance is high enough as it is. Either you come up with a way to pay for that blasted horse or I'll sell it to Double D Farm next Saturday. You hear me? I didn't want that blasted horse in my barn! And, I don't want to hear the name McMichael! Why'd you go and bring those blasted McMichaels back into our lives anyway? I did just fine without them all these years! Hope you're happy, Dorie." He guzzled half a can, belched, and pitched the remainder in the sink. "Blasted McMichaels," he muttered as he stumbled into the living room and crashed on the couch.

Dorie remained at the foot of the stairs, fingers gripping the door jam. She watched her husband roll off into a peaceful snore on the sofa, and then turned and quietly climbed the stairs alone.

8

Brad didn't return to see Burgie on Sunday. In fact, he didn't get out of bed all day. Dreams would come and go as he fell in and out of sleep; dreams that didn't make sense. Every so often, he would wake and roll to look at his clock—8:30; 10:15; 12:32. He thought about school starting on Tuesday. What a bizarre Christmas break. When he left school on December 22, Burgundy Delight didn't even exist for him. Now, on return, he could not let her exist either. He would make a point to stay away from the auction until after next weekend. Seeing his mare would just deepen his pain. It was supposed to be over last night. How could things turn out so unfairly? What Christmas witch was pulling so harshly on his heartstrings? Would Chuck Wheaten let Burgie suffer under the harsh hands and heels of ignorant riding stable customers? Would he turn her over to the meat packers for what little he could? Brad decided he just would not go near the barns.

It was early. Susan Bateman sipped her coffee in Wheatens' auction office while Dorie scurried to clean away the mess from last evening's sale. She shamed herself silently for not taking care of it last night, but her mind had been on other things. In particular, a necessary late night call.

Now, Susan Bateman was here with questions. What was going on with this horse, anyway? Is she for sale or isn't she? What's she really worth? What would it take to keep a horse? How much money? How much time? What about school? The questions came at Dorie faster than she could answer.

Susan blurted, "You know, Mrs. Wheaten, we never intended for Brad to own a horse. His father and I don't know the first thing about horses."

"You'd be surprised at how many parents don't know anything about the horses their kids own." Dorie gave up on cleaning the concession window and poured herself a cup of coffee. "They think it's like going out and buying a family dog. Horses are big, and they're expensive. Not the purchase price, mind you, but the vet bills, the blacksmith, the feed, the barn repairs. And that's nothing compared to what it'll cost if you decide to start showing. Then you've got trucks, trailers, show equipment, riding clothes, entry fees. It can get to be a nightmare if you're not prepared."

"So, why did you even call?" Susan asked. "And even if we could come up with the money, we hear horror stories about people being injured and even killed with horses. Just how dangerous are they?" Susan pressed.

Dorie offered a friendly chuckle and took another sip of coffee. "Horses are only dangerous when you mix them with people. If you don't understand them, you're bound to get hurt. Isn't that true with motorcycles, playing football, or bicycling on public roads? Every activity has a set of rules and, if you don't follow them, you get hurt. The only difference with horses is that they make the rules. We call them laws of nature. And, when you stop to consider that humans and even dogs and cats are predators but horses are animals of prey, believe me, our rules don't match. The old cliché, 'think like a horse,' is a good safety rule."

Susan finished her coffee. It was probably a little late to be asking about Brad's safety when he had been running auction horses for two years, but as another cliché' goes, "ignorance is bliss." Dorie poured Susan a second cup of coffee and topped off her own as she said, "It's hard to try to pull together a dream for your son when you don't know the first thing about it. Is that what I'm hearing?" Susan nodded and felt a momentary sisterhood with Dorie Wheaten.

Dorie pulled a pad toward her and picked up a pencil. "All right. Let's go from the top." Susan was not aware that Dorie had already spent some time going over these figures.

"First of all, can you afford to buy the horse? Second, how many and what kind of places are there to keep a horse? Third, what's it going to cost, say, per month, to care for her? And fourth, a question you've probably missed, what's Brad going to end up wanting to do with her?" Susan agreed that Dorie had summed the matter up quite well.

"Dorie, am I crazy to be here? Does Brad really need a horse? This horse? I'm scared to death that the time spent with the horse will cause his grades to fall and totally steal his time from the family."

Having no children of her own, Dorie was jealous of Susan's concerns. She had come to see Brad as a pseudo-son. She chuckled at the thought that Brad, like all kids, was totally oblivious of these maternal yearnings. If only kids knew how a parent's pride in watching their child grow independent was so sadly shadowed by the heartbreak of watching them grow away.

"Susan, I think he needs the horse," Dorie said. "I don't know about his grades, because I've never asked. I guess I've just assumed he was a bright boy because he speaks so well. He's also my best worker. Your second question I can answer right now. He can keep Burgie here as long as we can figure a way to earn her keep. Chuck won't have it any other way and, on that point, I suppose he's right. I'm crazy about the horse. Admit it, so are you." Susan nodded. She was beginning to really like this woman.

For the past year and a half, Susan Bateman imagined that Dorie was an older, overweight, drab woman. The image must have been conjured up to match the condition of the auction barn itself. When she drove into the lot on Friday, she had not expected to meet a well-kept, physically fit woman near her own age. Dorie began to write on her pad.

"If we continue to feed Burgie grain along with her hay," she said, "which we will want to do, then her feed and bedding are going to run me around a hundred a month. Right now, Brad earns $30 every Saturday night. We have four boys employed as riders, but as best as anyone could guess, we might as well have just three. I know for a fact that Chuck is going to fire Brendan before January is out. We never know whether he's going to show up for work, and when he does he's got either a bottle or a girl with him. God knows how he finds some of his girls. They would really shock you.

"Anyway, if the other three boys are willing to pick up the slack, they can split Brendan's pay, and I think they can handle it. Plus, we got this little volunteer named Tyler." Dorie drew a quick line across the page.

"That will leave Brad with about $50 a month to work with after feed. That won't go far, Susan. Can you help?"

"Please remember that Brad's father and I have not had much time to discuss this," Susan replied. "We thought it best to gather the facts before we said anything to Brad. However, we figure that we can spare a couple hundred a month, if that would help."

"I'll tell you the truth, Susan." Dorie leaned forward in her chair. "A couple hundred dollars will be more than enough right now. Brad can use some of our tack and equipment. Can you make a point of putting half that money in a special account so that whatever Brad doesn't use can be saved for when he needs it?"

"Why, sure we can." Susan was becoming more optimistic by the minute and more comfortable with the idea of horse owner- ship. In fact, she was getting just a little excited.

"Wait, Dorie," she said. "We're forgetting a major point. What's this horse going to cost? I've heard ten thousand and I've heard one thousand. Horse people must be crazy." She got up and poured a third cup of coffee from Dorie's pot.

Dorie responded quickly. "There's two points to consider. I can pick up the phone and call Joe McMichael right now. In my heart, I believe that mare is worth about $6,500. She's got excellent bloodlines, she's a good age, and she's got all her ground training done. Under the right set of hands, I bet she could grow into a quite a show horse, but don't get your hopes up. Brad may love horses and he may be good with our stable horses, but he's no competition for these big show barn trainers. What she needs is a year of advanced training. I think between Brad and me, we can turn her out pretty nice for the open show circuit. That should be enough to thrill Brad during his last two years of high school. And, he'll get the chance to work with 4-H horse kids his own age. However, can he take her farther than that? I guess I wouldn't encourage it if I were you. Too much time and money. To compete on the class A circuit, he should have been out there years ago."

Switching back to the matter at hand, Dorie continued, "I won't be lying if I tell Joe that the best price we could pull was eleven hundred and that we topped off the sale at twelve hun- dred and kept her here." Susan Bateman could not comprehend how a horse, supposedly valued at better than six thousand dol- lars could not draw over eleven hundred at an auction. She shook her head in puzzlement and Dorie noticed.

"These people who come here, Susan, they want something they can pet and climb on and play with in the summer. They often sell them back in the fall or tuck them away behind a barn. They don't expect the horse to change during the time they have it, and they aren't interested in improving the way it works for them. They're just there and you ride them and you love them. Most of them are just good animals with good hearts. The top of the line coming through our barn become excellent 4-H horses and, if you ask me, that's probably the best kind of horse all 'round.

"But, there's all sorts of people in the horse industry," she continued, "many of whom see their horses as more than just a pet. Parents enroll their children in private riding lessons like you would dance lessons or gymnastics. It's not the tutu or balance beam they are interested in. It's the reward of seeing their child grow. They expect the child to improve and they hope to one day see a peak performance. Trainers are the same way with their horses. They see them very much like dancers or athletes; living bodies that improve with time and effort. And with the improvement in the animals, they can measure the improvement in themselves.

"Burgie has good bloodlines, and you can compare the horse industry to the dog industry. You know there are purebred dogs and there are mutts, and that some people prefer the purebreds while others prefer the mutts. If you're going to simply keep your dog in your backyard, then maybe a mutt will do just fine. However, if you're going to spend a lot of time working with your dog, then you might as well invest in a purebred; one that has a club and shows where you can enjoy being with other people who enjoy the same breed. The horse industry works the same way.

"The other fact about Burgie is that she has been handled by professional horse trainers who really know what they're doing. That is part of what makes Burgie so special. I suspect that Mr. McMichael, and certainly his son, Evan, had hoped to bring this horse along over the next couple years. It's been a long time since I've been around the show circuit, but I think she would have been World Championship material had she stayed with them. However, the general rule among horsemen is to move bad-debt animals as quickly as possible.

"Burgie can take your son a long way, Susan, if he has the heart for that, and the time, and the money. And I bet you'd enjoy the result. Also," Dorie smiled warmly at Susan, "I know you'll be proud of Brad. It's a long gruelling road to turn out a horse for show, whether it's on the class A circuit or the open 4-H circuit. Those 4-H kids work darn hard for the rewards they earn." Finished with her lecture, Dorie returned to the facts.

"We know that Joe needs to move the horse. He'll hate hearing twelve hundred dollars, but he apparently has no other choice. If he had a possible customer waiting for a good horse, then I know Burgie would never have been shipped over here in the first place. If I tell him we sold her out at twelve hundred, do you have the money?"

"I think we can count on Brad for most of that," Susan responded. "He has some in savings toward a car. If he'd be willing to ride his bike in good weather, then I'd be willing to continue scheduling my van with him at least through the rest of this winter. And, if he doesn't want to use his car money, then he certainly doesn't need the horse."

"Good, then. Let's put this show in motion." Dorie flipped through her stack of business cards until she came to the one Evan had left on Tuesday. She picked up the telephone and placed the call. Silently, she shuddered at the thought of suggesting the twelve hundred dollars and, as the phone rang, she wondered who might answer. If it was Joe, would she recognize his voice? Twenty-five years is a long time.

A husky female voice answered, "McMichaels' Training Stable."

"Hello, this is Dorie Wheaten at Wheatens' Auction Barn. May I please speak with Evan?"

"He's down at the barn until dinner," returned the curt voice. "This is Mrs. McMichael. Did you sell the mare?" Dorie's mind raced. Was it Evan's wife or Joe's? Dorie was put off by the woman's abrupt telephone protocol. "We were offered twelve hundred . . ."

Before she could finish, Mrs. McMichael cut in. "That's ridiculous. What kind of business are you running down there?! I'll have Joe get back with you." She hung up the phone before Dorie could respond.

Susan was surprised when Dorie raised her eyebrows, shook her head, and dropped the phone onto its receiver. "Did they say no?"

"I don't know what's going on over there. Let's just wait until they call me back before we say anything to Brad."

Susan gathered her coat. She was going home with more information than she had hoped for. As she left Dorie Wheaten's office, she wondered where horse shows were held, and she felt baby butterflies in her stomach.

An hour later Dorie received a telephone call from Evan McMichael. She was relieved it wasn't Joe. Ten minutes later, Susan Bateman knocked on Brad's bedroom door.

"Honey?" Brad pulled the covers down from over his head.

"You've got yourself a horse!"

9

Returning to school was the last thing Brad wanted to do. Usually January was a good time to be in school. The days were short and cold and it was easy to keep one's mind on American History and Keyboard Skills II. But now Burgie was competing for Brad's time and attention. Mr. Wheaten had worked out a schedule for Brad to spend some afternoons doing handyman chores around the auction barn to earn extra money and Mrs. Wheaten set four o'clock in the afternoon on Thursdays as her time to work with Brad and his horse.

Sunday night had found Brad up late talking with his mom. She was excited about helping Brad with his new venture, yet knowing that it could not come at the expense of his schoolwork. It had been a number of years since Susan needed to watch over Brad to make sure his homework was done correctly and in on time. Brad understood that it was now totally up to him to be responsible about keeping up with his classes.

Brad sat listening to Mr. Cleveland explain how the students were to go about dissecting their frogs. Brad's mind wandered, leaving the biology dissection notes to his lab partner, Matt Foxworthy. During this junior year, he had signed up for six classes instead of five plus a study hall. Now, however, the extra class was one more bother keeping him from Burgie.

After school on Tuesday, Brad stopped off at the lumberyard to pick up a square of roofing shingles for Mr. Wheaten. They were going to replace a section of roof on the loafing shed behind the barn where time and the elements had taken their toll. Brad hoisted the ninety-pound block of shingles over his shoulder and struggled up the sturdy ladder. He was thankful this was a low building as the effort was nearly beyond his strength. Mr. Wheaten followed behind, remaining on the ladder to supervise Brad as he pulled and replaced old nails and shingles. Burgie was in the back paddock with Jackson, rolling in the muddied snow and making a general mess of herself.

Brad's Thursday lesson appointment with Dorie offered the first opportunity to saddle the mare since she passed ownership the Sunday before. If Burgie could have been kept at his house, then Brad would have at least given her a good grooming before leaving for school. He considered driving to the barn each morning, but it wasn't practical. First, he needed to share the minivan with his mom, which left him riding the bus. Second, a really good grooming warrants a really good shower afterward and there just wasn't enough time. As it was, he was up every morning by five-thirty. He did not think caring for the horse warranted getting up at four.

Now, Brad saddled Burgie in the same steady matter-of-fact way that worked well for her last week. He mounted and worked her down in the area between the barn and the back paddock. Dorie chuckled when she came out to find him trotting his mare back and forth, his seat in the air and his hands steadying himself on her neck.

"Enough two-pointing, sir. Today we're going to teach you to post a rising trot!"

Brad wheeled Burgie around to face Dorie. "We're ready when you are. I'm sick of this!"

Dorie stepped up to the duo and gave Burgie a few friendly slaps on the neck. "I suspect it won't take you long to catch on. You already know the feel of a horse and that's half the battle. Beginners need to catch on to that one-two motion before they can learn to post." Dorie stepped back and gave her first command.

"Take her away from me and work as large an oval as you can in what space we have here. As you trot, let your mind concentrate on the motion of her legs. Call out loud to me, *one-two-one-two-one-two*. Make sure you're saying it in time with the movement of her legs."

Brad began his two-point trotting: feet touching the stirrups, knees touching the saddle, shoulders low, butt not touching at all. As Burgie trotted her oval, Brad called out first one, then two as the horse's alternating front feet hit the ground; "One-two-one-two-one-two."

Dorie's voice trailed behind Brad as he rode away from her and then became louder as he rounded the oval and trotted back toward her.

"Now," she shouted, "instead of saying *one-two* say *up-down*." The request was easy enough as Brad kept his up-downs in time with the feel of Burgie's front hooves striking the ground.

Finally, Dorie instructed Brad to put the words and the motion together. "When you say *up,* be in the air. When you say *down,* let your seat touch the saddle. But the moment—the absolute moment—you do, let it return to the air. Don't resist the momentum of the horse. If you tighten up, you'll double bounce. When you're relaxed and in time with Burgie's one-two motion, the natural movement of her hips will actually help to put you back in the air."

Brad let himself come down on cue, but when his hips touched the saddle, they bou-bounced, bou-bounced not at all in time with Burgie.

"Relax, Brad. Let the motion of the horse help you. When you come down, let yourself pop right back up again. Keep working at it. Keep going. Again. There! I saw one! Did you feel it?"

"Yeah, I did," shouted Brad.

"Again. Hey, that's not bad," said Dorie. Every six drops or so, Brad would feel a one-two post without the double bounce, but this exercise had consumed a good ten minutes of nonstop trotting and his legs were aching. He reined Burgie to a halt and caught his breath.

"That's fine for today. Beginners would take three or four lessons to reach that point. That's all I want you to do this week. Work your posting trot until your motion is absolutely smooth and one with your horse. Next week, we'll work on her head set."

Brad slid to the ground and the three returned to the barn. Even though it was just four-thirty, dusk was already setting in.

"You know, you're really lucky." Dorie opened the gate as Brad led Burgie into her stall. "Someone else paid a lot of money to have Burgie's training come along so nicely. You just happened to be in the right place at the right time. We'll have fun with her on the open circuit this summer. I wonder if the McMichaels ever put any of their new riders out on the open circuit to warm them up for the class A."

During the next two months, Brad had little time for anything other than Burgie. He spent all of January smoothing out the trot and working on a slow, smooth canter. Dorie would shout, "Get those hands up! Get those shoulders back! Get that chin up! Look where you're headed, not where you are! Smile! Relax!" Her womanly voice barked like a miniature military sergeant and her commands seemed totally contradictory. She promised it would all fall into place as time went by.

January turned to February and, with every week that passed, Brad could feel himself becoming closer to Burgie. His hips rocked the canter in time with the flow of her back. His heels stayed down. His thighs remained smooth against the saddle. No more air space between his knees and the smooth leather of the saddle flap. Brad was sure that he really could ride while holding two cups of hot chocolate without spilling a drop. His posture was good and his stiffness had all but disappeared.

Brad's February report card showed a drop in two of his classes, which raised both eyebrows and comments on the home front. He promised to get up an hour earlier each day to study so that he would not be so pressed for time in the evenings. His parents were skeptical that he would keep this promise for long, but Brad made the morning schoolwork sessions a habit not to be broken. In fact, he was surprised to find that hour, when his parents were still asleep to be a special kind of solitary time that he grew to enjoy. It gave him a sense of ownership of the house he had never felt before.

The auction barn became busier by the week. The least little hint of an early thaw brought people in to see what kinds of horses were coming through the sale pen.

February turned to March. Brad's grades showed marked improvement. As a midterm paper topic for his history class, Brad chose "Horses in the Revolutionary War." The library research had been interesting and the paper fun to present to his classmates. Each spring day fought to stay light a few minutes longer than the day before. Friends Matt Foxworthy and Mike Donaldson complained because they never saw much of Brad.

Every weekday, at three-thirty sharp, Brad had Burgie saddled and out the back of the barn. She would spring across the thawing meadow and slop through the cornfield, mud smacking against her belly as she headed toward the open road. Once out on the road, Brad would put his mare through her paces up and down the mile-long stretch: two minutes in a pleasurable trot, then thirty seconds of a bounding road trot, followed by a relaxed walk. He would then repeat the routine, insisting that the walk not be uppity. He wanted to feel a nice four-beat walk beneath him—not lazy, but not fussy. He would finish each workout with a slow and rolling canter, his hands steady, his back comfortable, his hips moving with the animal. He would hear an imaginary Mrs. Wheaten snapping, "Raise yourself up. Look proud! Be proud!" Then he would hear the crowd clapping and cheering as he made his victory pass. Tri-colored streamers flowed from Burgie's brow band, just as he had seen in Mrs. Wheaten's *Saddle Horse Report* magazines. Finally, when the roar of the crowd died away, he would head for home—across the sloppy cornfield and meadow and up to the back of the barn. He would tack down; wash the mud from Burgie's belly, from her legs, from his legs, and from the saddle. He would then go home, exhausted and happy, and ready for dinner, and, yes, homework. Every weekday.

10

"Hey, Craig, what'd you get on your bio quiz?" Mike Donaldson dropped the question as he joined the group of boys, lunch tray in hand.

"Don't remember. Eighty-seven, I think." Craig Watts popped another chicken nugget in his mouth and chased it down with a slug of milk from a half-pint carton. Cafeteria trays clattered on the stainless steel counter tops in the school kitchen. The room was filled with the squeaking of bench seats being pushed in and out from the long rows of lunch tables and the hum of teenagers.

"How about you, Brad? And, hey, why didn't you go out for track this spring?"

"I got a 92 on my quiz and I don't have time for track." Brad wadded his potato chip bag into a ball and tossed it over two students to hit Samantha Seager on the back of the head.

Mike stole a chicken nugget from Craig's tray and chided Brad. "You don't have time for track, you don't have time to shoot hoops after school, and you don't have time to do anything on weekends. You might as well drop off the face of the earth! What's with you anyway?"

"It's his horse," said Matt Foxworthy. "He's with that horse all the time. We have girlfriends, he has a horse."

"Yeah? Well, my horse needs work," Brad drawled back through his french fries. "You run track, I run the horse, so what?"

Mike joined back in. "What do you mean, the horse needs work? So what do you do other than ride it?"

"Tell him, Matt. You've seen my Burgie. Mike, the horse is a quality piece of equipment. I'm going to start showing her this summer."

"So are you going to sell her for a bunch of money, or what?" Mike couldn't see Brad's attraction to such an unorthodox pet, so Brad made an effort to explain.

"You know that '72 Rally Nova you've got in your back yard? Well, you've been working on that car for a year now, haven't you?"

Mike and Craig both nodded in agreement. "Yup, her body is completely buffed out now. You wouldn't believe it's the same car. As soon as Dad has time to help me with the engine, she'll be ready for the city parade this summer."

"So, are you going to sell her for a bunch of money, or what?" Brad mirrored Mike's earlier question.

"Heck, no. I've put too much work into her. Besides, I want to show her off."

"Well," remarked Brad, "You just answered your own question. I want to put Burgie in shows, where people who have been working horses a lot longer than me can let me know how she stacks up. And, maybe I'll put her in the city parade, too. I'm putting just as much work into her as you are that car."

"How do you show off a horse, Bateman? A horse is a horse. It's got four legs and a tail."

"Yeh? Well, I bet I can find you a hundred kids right here in this cafeteria that think a car is just a car. Even your Rally Nova."

"He's right, Mike." Matt Foxworthy joined in Brad's defense. "Brad's horse is real pretty. Don't know how to say it, rounder, bouncier, I dunno."

"Pretty's not the word," Brad corrected. "She's dynamite. She's full of vinegar and spunky as heck. No matter how much I ride her, she still has energy left when I'm done. I might not know what it takes to make a great show horse, but I think I've got one. The lady I work for is helping me, so I figure I got a good chance of bringing home some blue ribbons this summer. You guys are gonna have to come watch me win."

"Yeah, well, if you decide to put your horsey in the city parade, you better just make sure she doesn't kick my Rally Nova, or drop anything squooshy that will mess my tires!" Mike howled at his own joke and Craig chimed in.

Craig closed the lunch conversation on a sour note. "That lady you work for. Doesn't she own the auction barn? How can she know anything about show horses? Her place looks pretty grungy to me. I don't see how you can work there."

Brad didn't offer a reply as the boys cleared their trays and headed off for class. Mrs. Wheaten seemed to know what she was talking about. Besides, he didn't know anyone else who knew anything more than she, and if it weren't for Mrs. Wheaten, he wouldn't have a horse at all. As Brad gathered his books and headed down the hall he wondered to himself where Dorie Wheaten might have learned what she knew about training and showing horses.

11

Brad and Dorie agreed that it was time to purchase a more suitable saddle and bridle for Burgie. She would need a Lane Fox show saddle, sometimes called a cut-back or flat saddle. It would be as lightweight as Dorie's hunt saddle but without the supportive knee rolls. In place of the simple snaffle bridle she had been using since Christmas, Burgie would need a double, or Weymouth, bridle.[1] Even if they stayed at the low end of what was available, the investment in the tack would still run near a thousand dollars. Brad could not afford a separate set for workouts and a set to keep for shows. He would have to use the equipment carefully and keep it clean and oiled if it were to look good when the first shows rolled around in May.

Dorie made arrangements to have a blacksmith stop by to fit Burgie with a new set of shoes. By the end of January, the mare had outgrown the shoes she came with and had since been left barefoot. Now, the edges of her hooves were chipped from her workouts on the gravel road. Dorie had set the worn pair of shoes aside in the tackroom and brought them out when the smith arrived. He didn't recognize the style of shoe, said he had never seen anything like them before, wider up at the toe with a clip that extended up the front of the hoof. Instead, he set Burgie up with a standard set of trail shoes.

Working with the Lane Fox saddle was like starting all over again. The knee supports were gone and Brad dearly missed them. He was now required to refine his balance with a very different feel under him. Dorie encouraged him to not slow down at

---

[1]For a visual description of various saddle and bride designs, see Appendix A.

the trot while trying to gain his balance. On the contrary, she assured him that a little speed would help him to smooth out and flow in time with the animal.

"When you're on your horse," she said, "you have to know that you're not just riding her, you're actually driving her. Don't be a passenger, letting her get ahead or behind you in the motion. Drive her forward with your thighs against that saddle, your chin up, tummy tucked, back straight, and look where you're going, not down at her ears."

The double bridle was a royal pain in the neck. The reins were much thinner than either the western or hunt reins Brad had been using. In addition, he had to figure out how to make minor adjustments in the lengths of each to get the desired headset on his horse. What seemed correct when Burgie was standing still, needed adjusting when she moved out. This whole process was particularly difficult because Brad didn't know what the "desired headset" was even supposed to be. Dorie and he sat in the office one day going through old *Saddle Horse* magazines, examining and evaluating all of the pictures. They discussed every photo, researching the rider's relation to his horse as it moved before the photographer. Brad commented that it was so unfair for them to be sitting in this dusty old barn office criticizing all those people who at least had the guts to get out there and try. Dorie quickly pointed out that they were not criticizing the riders or the horses, they were critiqueing the pictures in an effort to learn. She assured him that no horse or rider should ever be judged with a single click of a camera. Even after scouring the magazine photos, once Brad was up on Burgie's back, it was too difficult to tell from above what she looked like from the ground. However, Dorie continued to coach and encourage him.

"Tighten up on the snaffle. A little more curb. Raise those hands." Brad found it difficult to follow her directions quickly enough because he was still having trouble figuring out which rein was which. All of March was consumed with catching up with the new equipment to the point where he had left off with the old.

With each passing practice session, Burgie would toss her head less, a sign that Brad was smoothing out and settling into the feel of the new bridle. By the end of the month, he was back to his usual routine up and down the road.

March was a beautiful month, much warmer than most other years. Soon, Brad found himself sharing the road with an occasional bicyclist or jogger, or a parked car with its owner stealing young daylily roots from the country ditch for spring transfer to a private garden. One jogger in particular passed him as often as two or three times each week. He found himself looking forward to her blonde ponytail bouncing toward him with a friendly "Hi there!" as she passed and disappeared behind him. Brad would turn to watch her trot away and it would throw Burgie's trot off balance. The horse would break cadence and miss a step or come down to a walk, reminding Brad to get his mind back on business.

By the end of March that yellow ponytail was bouncing past Brad at exactly the same time every day. It just didn't make sense to let that daily "Hi there" fall on deaf ears forever. So on the last Monday of the month, he purposely headed out twenty minutes early. By doing so, he would be at the end of his route and turned and coming back by the time she rounded the corner. The plan seemed easy enough, but somehow, he had to be heading home when she came around the corner without looking like he had been stopped at the corner waiting on her. *Why do we play these silly games?* he thought. *Why can't I just stand here with my horse and wait. When she comes jogging along, I can trot along beside her and say, "Hi. I thought it was about time I got to know you. My name is Brad Bateman. May I trot along with you?"* Brad waited nervously as the swinging ponytail rounded the corner. He attempted to time his posting in such a way to make it possible for her to jog up alongside him.

"Hi, there," she said and kept on jogging. "Pretty horse."

"Thanks." Brad didn't know what to say next so he said nothing.

"Do you call that jogging?" the blond queried.

"What?" Brad wasn't sure whether she was referring to him, the horse, or both of them.

"What your horse is doing. It's two-beat like a human. So, do you call it a jog?"

"Oh," surmised Brad. "If you're a western rider, you call it a jog. If you're riding English, you call it a trot." The blond kept jogging.

"So, why two names? Does the horse know the diff'?" the blond kept jogging.

"Well, yes and no." Brad ventured. "The western jog is slower than the English trot."

The blond thought for a moment. "Wouldn't speed be determined by the size of the horse?"

"How can you talk and jog at the same time?" Brad asked in honest surprise. "I'm having trouble keeping my breath while I talk and I'm on the horse."

"If you don't want to talk, then why did you wait for me?" she asked in a friendly, but forthright tone. Brad was caught off guard and embarrassed.

"I do want to talk. I'm just impressed. That's all."

"I'm Pat Spielman. Who are you?"

"Brad Bateman."

"Where do you ride from? I don't see a farm around."

"I keep her stabled at the old auction barn. We cut across a meadow and along the edge of that cornfield to reach this straightaway. How far do you run anyway?"

"Six miles a day, five days a week. Eight on Saturdays. Off on Sundays."

"Do you compete?"

"Yeah," Pat was beginning to pant and had long been sweating, even in the fifty-degree March temperature. "I want to run the Bobby Crim up in Flint again this August. I ran it last year but didn't place well. At least I finished."

"Isn't that a ten-miler?"

"Yep."

Brad shook his head. "That's a lot of hard work!"

"That depends," Pat responded. Brad had reached the edge of his cornfield and, if he didn't turn in, it would be too obvious. After all, he had already told her that was his turn off. So, as much as he wanted to extend the conversation, it was just not the place for a first date. He turned Burgie off to the right and through the ever so slight ditch. "Gotta go," he said. "Maybe I'll see you tomorrow."

"Sure," and the blond ponytail trotted off down the road. Brad gave Burgie a sharp nudge with his right calf and the mare picked up an easy canter most of the way back to the barn.

12

Brad and Pat became a good workout team. Pat's incredibly regimented running schedule made Brad more consistent in his own. Brad's presence on the road gave Pat someone to talk to, which helped her regulate and monitor her breathing as she ran. Burgie's steady trot helped Pat to pace herself better. It didn't matter that Brad never had an interest in running nor that Pat never admired horses. There was still a common ground between them.

Burgie loved the open road. She picked her way quickly across the meadow and along the cornfield each afternoon to get out on the road where she could put away the miles on a straightaway. At Dorie's suggestion, Brad spent most of each workout putting those miles on in a steady easy trot. At this point, they were looking for aerobic strength and consistently growing muscles. They were up to six miles a day, which, coincidentally, was exactly Pat's route. Toward the end of each workout Brad would have Burgie pick up that bounding road trot and Pat would sprint to keep up. The young runner loved the challenge of competing with Burgie's inky black legs, which were, actually, not any longer than hers and a whole lot thinner. When Brad would cue for her big trot, Burgie's whole body would swell and reach out to the road ahead. Pat would immediately dig in and one-two-one-two-one-two, trying to eat up the road, elbows pumping as hard as her knees. Sometimes, she would imagine that she was a horse, larger and more powerful than "the Burg" in an attempt to pull additional energy from her own imagination. She never mentioned these thoughts to Brad. How silly.

Somewhere during April, the two young athletes made a pact to attend every horse show or run meet that did not interfere with their own event. In and amongst their growing friendship, they were beginning to share a bond of commitment to persistence and consistency that would be needed to carry them through the summer. Pat was already blessed with a personality that seemed to incorporate the concept of consistency. She admitted in conversation that her days were fairly regimented in terms of study, eating habits, personal care, and the like. Brad thought about how undisciplined his own had been. Having Burgie come into his life gave him something to work toward. He told Pat that he daydreamed about her winning beautiful ribbons for dynamic performances, but to actually believe that it would happen sometimes seemed more like a wish than a sure thing.

"But you can do whatever you want," claimed Pat.

"Right," responded Brad. "I can get the Burg into the ribbons, if I have the time, and if I have the money, and if I can find the know-how, and . . . "

"Hey, don't blow my mind with that crap," retorted Pat. "Do you think I come from a family of runners? Heck, my mom rarely rolls out of bed in the morning and my brother's favorite hobby is watching the boob tube. I started running because I didn't know what else I could do, and running is free. I'm constantly criticized for the time I 'selfishly take for myself,' according to my mom. So, I sure didn't look to anyone in my real world for running support or any belief that I could ever run the Bobby Crim."

"Geez, Pat, get off my case," Brad jumped to his own defense.

"No, I won't! I get enough negative crap dumped on me and the last person I need it from is you!"

Brad was bewildered. "I was only talking about myself. Not you."

"It doesn't matter. Don't you see? If you talk about not having faith in yourself, those doubts will bleed toward me whether they're intended to or not. Then I'll have to stop running with you." Brad definitely did not want to lose his jogging companion.

"Pat, I never realized you were so wrapped up in all this I-gotta-win stuff. I like riding with you."

Pat dropped down to a fast walk, and refrained from talking for another two hundred feet. Then she stopped, dropped her waistline over, and touched her fingers to her toes. She just hung there, panting.

Brad wondered if she was sick, then realized that Pat was crying. He nudged Burgie a little closer.

"Hey, Pat, I'm sorry. What's with you?"

The blond ponytail regained her stand and turned toward Brad, stroking Burgie's neck, the sweat from her hand mixing into the mare's still dry coat.

"Every morning I stare at running magazines. I don't look at the advertisements for shoes. I stare at the people, deep in their faces. I tell myself they're just people—not the sons and daughters of famous runners—just people who run. And, all the time everywhere, I never think of myself as a student, a daughter, a girl, a whatever. I am a runner. Even when I'm not running, I'm still a runner. Maybe I'm a runner doing the dishes or a runner finishing my algebra, but I'm a runner." Brad pondered her reasoning and felt the determination in her voice. He stared at Burgie's ears because he felt uncomfortable meeting Pat's eyes when she was being so personal. If he had glanced her way, he would have realized she was staring at his boot, not his face, as she talked.

"Last year was terrible, Brad." Pat started walking again but talked as she went. Burgie walked along on a loose rein. "Mom never waited to see that my grades were okay. She just harped constantly, 'You better not let your grades drop from all that running.' What made her think the grades would drop? Where's the correlation? Besides, I've never had a 'D' in my life and not that many 'Cs.' She has no right to harp. My brother even laughs at me from behind his four hundred bags of Doritos. My only goal last year was to run the Bobby Crim. Ten miles seemed like running around the world. They weren't even there to watch. Dad dropped me off at six but had to work at the office that Saturday, so he says. Mom wouldn't come to pick me up until most of the crowd was gone. Keeping away from all those 'crazy people' was more important to her than seeing me cross the finish line." She stopped dead and turned to look Brad in the eyes.

"You know, she never even asked if I finished. Her entire conversation on the way home was about everything and anything except the fact that I had just ran ten miles."

Brad pulled Burgie to a halt and swung his boot over her rump, dropping off her left side.

"Come on. Let's walk the long way round to the barns. You can help me put Burgie up, then I'll drive you back to your car. Tell me what it felt like while you were running the Crim. Not the whole race. Start at the sixth mile. I want to hear the gruesome parts."

☆   ☆   ☆

March turned into April and April into May. The Saturday night auctions were becoming busier by the week as 4-H and open show families, plus all the happy trail riders, were sizing up horses for their summer adventures.

Based on her past professional training, Burgie was probably overqualified for the open show circuit.[2] However, with Brad's lack of experience, the open circuit would prove tough competition even with an excellent horse. Dorie Wheaten had committed herself to coaching Brad during this first year of showing, and Susan Bateman appreciated the effort. Two women, who had lived reasonably close to each other for nearly twenty years, with completely different lifestyles, were coming together as friends over a boy and his horse.

And now, a third woman was on the scene. A muscular little blond ponytail, who knew little about horses and didn't particularly care for the smell of the barn. Still, she would sit on a hay bale and visit while Brad rubbed down his horse and put his tack away.

"Sure wish I had someone to rub me down like that," quipped Pat.

Brad came at her with his deep brown, grungy, sweaty horse towel and Pat screamed, "I take that back, I take that back!" Dorie just watched from afar and quietly giggled.

By the end of May, Pat had run two small 10-K races. Ten kilometers is just over six miles, which is no more than the three of them had been doing each day. Her timings were good and Brad was waiting at the end of both finish lines. Pat requested size XL race T-shirts and gave them to Brad.

The end of May also brought Brad close to his first show. The Rambling Ropers 4-H Club was sponsoring the first show of the summer at the county fairground, and Brad and Burgie were signed up for English Performance and English Equitation. In the performance class, Burgie would be judged on how well she performed. Brad's role would be to help her bring out her best. In the equitation class, Brad would be judged on how well he rode. Burgie's role would be to help him bring out his best. Brad had

[2]For a better understanding of the various levels of show-ring competition, see Appendix B.

really only wanted to enter the first of the two, but Dorie insisted that he sign into every class he could. So, by the time the entry form was completed and submitted, the pair was entered in five classes. In addition, to performance and equitation, Dorie had suggested three fun classes: Musical Stalls, Command, and Egg-and-Spoon. Brad had absolutely no idea what he was in for, but signed his name and attached his check for four dollars per class.

"What's this?" Pat asked as she studied the registration copy. "Egg-and-Spoon? Do you have to jump over the moon?! Musical Stalls? What's Command? 'HEY, YOU! WIN THIS CLASS!'" They both laughed.

"I guess we'll just have to wait to see whether I survive the day. Thank heaven no one out there knows me."

"Aren't you inviting Matt and Mike?" Pat had met both the fellows during biology study sessions and just assumed they'd be on hand for Brad's first performance.

"What makes you think my friends and family are any different than yours? If there are no cars there, you won't find Matt and Mike anywhere in sight. Besides," Brad added honestly, "I really don't want them there. Mom's coming though so you'll have someone to sit with. And speaking of Mom, I need your help."

"How's that?" queried Pat.

"Please, please, please, don't let my mom cheer too loudly. She can be a total embarrassment, if you know what I mean."

Pat didn't know what he meant. She would have given anything to have her mom embarrass her at a race.

It was a week away from show time. The late spring days warmed to the seventies and the trees were in full bloom. Yellow Lady Slippers were wilted in the ditch beds and daylilies were filling in with long rushes of deep green leaves. Brad continued to work extra hours at the auction barn to keep Mr. Wheaten from complaining about Burgie's room and board. He found himself staying up later yet getting up easier and, ironically, his schoolwork seemed to be finding a place in all of this.

Maybe, it's the natural maturation that comes during the junior year of high school but more likely, not. At some subconscious level, Brad was getting to know himself. Less and less, he felt like an extension of his family. Interestingly enough, the more he felt he was growing away from them, the more he seemed to enjoy being with them. Without realizing it, his conversations with Pat about her relationship with her family were affecting his relationships with his own. When Robbie came home from college for Easter and mentioned a devastating experience he had in his physics lab, Brad asked him to explain. Robbie just stared across the dinner table. Since when was his little brother interested in what went on in his life? But long after Mr. and Mrs. Bateman had cleared away their own plates, Robbie and Brad talked about life on campus. It was one of the best times the two boys had spent together in years and they weren't even doing anything.

As Robbie headed out for the night, he stopped at the kitchen door and said, "Hey, Brad. Think you could find time to show me that big dog of yours while I'm home on break?"

Across town, Pat laid her *Runner's World* magazine on her nightstand and turned off the light. The blurred conversation of her mother's television program seeped through her bedroom floor as she floated into solitary sleep.

13

"You're gonna flood the whole gah-dam barn, boy! Get that hoss outta here!" Chuck Wheaten was sick and tired of that Bateman boy and his high-falutin' horse changing the nature of *his* barn. "Ya hear me, boy? I wun't na keep ya around here if it weren't for yer always showin' up to work on time! Now, move her outta here!"

Mr. Wheaten was right. Brad was flooding the whole darn barn. He pulled his mare farther out onto the drive, where they had started this fiasco in the first place, and returned to preparing Burgie for the suds that were to follow.

Dorie heard the commotion and came trotting out of the office. "No, no, Brad. Let's do this right." She reached to the spigot and turned the water off. "Do you want her afraid of baths all her life? If you don't make that hose her friend, you'll replay this mess before every show." Dorie took the hose from Brad, returned to the spigot and turned the water on ever so slightly. Just a slow stream came forth and when she pointed the hose toward the sky, the water bubbled over just enough that one could easily drink from it. She approached Burgie and let her do just that.

Burgie watched the water suspiciously. Then she reached forward and nudged the bubbles. Her upper lip wiggled like the end of an elephant's trunk as she investigated this new toy.

"There you go, girl. That's not so bad, is it?" Dorie slowly moved the water flow to the ground in front of one front hoof, then up the hoof wall and onto Burgie's pastern. Burgie stomped once but let the foot rest back in place, water running slowing downward. In an ever-so-relaxed way, Dorie talked to the bay mare as she moved the hose up the leg and, eventually, over the shoulder. If Burgie thought of prancing, Dorie backed the horse to an earlier position. Mrs. Wheaten handed the hose back to Brad.

"I don't care if it takes all day. You shampoo her slowly and rinse her thoroughly. Do one side at a time so the soap doesn't dry. I'll be back in an hour to see how you're doing."

By the time Dorie returned, Brad had done him and his horse proud. She was shampooed, rinsed, and grazing at the end of a lead on the side lawn. Mr. Wheaten had warned him to "git 'er out on the grass before she drops and rolls on ya." Brad had no idea that for every rider who dreamed of a gleaming horse, there was an equal number of horses that dreamed of rubbing the dirt back into their coat as quickly as possible. Some say dust is a natural sunscreen; others say possibly a natural fly repellent. Either way, horses think it's just natural to be dusty. But now Burgie's shine was shimmering radiantly through her drying coat.

Dorie ran her fingers through the horse's bridle path, testing to see if it was dry enough to clip. They would start between the ears and shave the mane about six inches back. It was easy to see where Evan McMichael had clipped, so they would do the same. Dorie handed Brad the clippers and instructed him to not use the outside outlet. The puddles of water would surely send a shock through all six legs.

"Where'd you get these?" Brad asked.

"Oh, I've had them," was all Dorie replied.

Brad studied the clippers. It was obvious they were brand new. He walked Burgie to the cross-tie chains Dorie had installed in the door leading to the auction pen. Burgie could stand in the barn area with her head facing into the sale pen. If an audience had been present, they would be staring right back at her, but today the barn was relatively quiet. It was a Friday afternoon but, being nearly June, most horse sales had been made for the summer; only a few were showing up for tomorrow night's sale. While business was slow in the auction barn, this was the time of year when it was in high gear over at the riding stable. A steady stream of greenhorns rode quiet horses back into the meadow and on across to the woodlot and, an hour later returned, sore but happy. It was easy to spot Jackson's white rump carrying children to and from the field.

Brad flipped the switch on the clippers and Burgie stood perfectly still.

"Thank you, Evan McMichael," whispered Brad. This mare handled well in the cross-ties, while being shampooed (when Brad did it correctly!), and during her clipping. Brad shaved her bridle path, the short hairs overhanging the top of her hooves at her coronet, and the whiskers on her muzzle. Most of his time, however, was spent on the inside of her ears. By the looks of the finished product, it probably wouldn't have mattered if Burgie had been hopping around. There were little choppy spots on the bridle path, and the whiskers, well, they were still mostly there.

"I'll never again complain about the shape of my face," Brad told his horse. "At least I don't have a big lob on the bottom of my chin, hair inside my nose, and I sure don't need to shave the inside of my ears!" Brad was most disappointed with the ears and said so when Dorie came back around. She took the clippers from him and deftly swiped quickly up toward each eye from beneath and across the top of the lid. Burgie's long eye-hairs were gone, perfectly, leaving nothing but her natural lashes. "Want to fix up the rest of my mess?" Brad queried.

"No, you did just fine for your first show." Dorie unplugged the clippers and glanced toward Burgie's stall. "I see you've got plenty of clean straw. Put her away now and get yourself home for dinner. Tomorrow's going to be a long day. You'll need to be here by five."

That night, Brad lay in bed wondering what to expect tomorrow. He had never seen a horse show and now he was going to be in one.

☆ ☆ ☆

The next morning, Brad brushed and brushed and brushed Burgie's glistening coat. He still wasn't particularly happy with his clip job. Dorie showed up with a dozen-box of Supreme Donuts.

"I didn't know you were up and around yet," Brad reached for an appreciated maple nut roll.

"These are from Chuck. He said to tell you they're your good luck fat." Dorie set the box on a straw bale and disappeared into the tack room. Brad wondered at the gift from Mr. Wheaten. He had already said he wasn't going to any "gah-dam hoss show." Dorie returned with a dark plastic jar labeled "Hoof Black."

"Whatcha got?" Brad watched as Dorie opened an obviously brand-new jar.

"Oh, just something I've had around the barn." Dorie swirled the dauber inside the jar. "Take her out front on the pavement. We'll put the first coat on here at home where there's less commotion. That way we can get a nice line around her coronet. Then, when we're ready for her classes, we can add a second coat, but won't need to go all the way to the top."

This made sense to Brad and, moving Burgie out onto the paved part of the parking lot, he watched as Dorie painted three perfect hooves. Burgie stood stone still.

"Here you go," Dorie handed the jar to Brad.

"You missed one!"

"No, you've got to do at least one," laughed Dorie. "It's your show, not mine."

Brad crouched and steadied his hand as he held out the inky black dauber toward Burgie's leg. Immediately, a small amount of Hoof Black accidentally spread into the hair.

"How'd you do that so easily?" he demanded.

"Just be glad she's bay and not chestnut. That black would show much more on a red leg."

Brad thought about it and agreed. "I'm glad she doesn't have a white sock," he added.

☆   ☆   ☆

Later that morning, Brad was surprised to discover horses with striped hooves—black where color met the coronet and natural where there was white hair above the hoof. Their owners had painstakingly painted the black parts black and used a high-gloss clear on the natural. And, every one of them seemed to have done a better job than he. Burgie was tied with a quick release to the side of Mrs. Wheaten's two-horse trailer. Brad grumbled out loud as he tightened down her saddle girth.

"Well, Burg, I can see now that neatness, or rather the lack of it, is going to cost us on the show circuit."

"Quit being so hard on yourself." Brad turned to find the friendly face that matched that voice. Pat stood admiring his gray suit and Sunday hat. She grinned because he looked like some guy from an old '50s movie. But, when he asked if he looked silly, she just said, "I've never seen you out of your jeans. It's quite a change."

"Did you come with my mom?"

"Yea, she's looking for a cup of coffee. When's your first class?"

"'Bout a half hour, I think. They're finishing up the show-manship classes now and I'm the second class after that." Pat glanced toward the ring to see a number of "naked" horses lined up with their handlers standing at their heads. As the judged proceeded past each animal, its handler would move smoothly from one side of the animal to the other, so as to not block the judge's keen inspection.

"What's she judging on?" asked the blond ponytail.

"How well they're prepared for show," responded Brad, as if he had known this information forever when, actually, Dorie had told him just a few minutes earlier. "I guess it doesn't matter how fancy the horse is. They're being judged on how well they're cared for. They'll be marked down for being flabby or dull because that means they've not been exercised, fed, or groomed well enough. And, they're judged on how well they're shampooed and clipped." Brad glanced back at Burgie's ears. "No wonder Mrs. Wheaten didn't suggest that class for me."

"Now, now," Pat petted Brad's shoulder like he was a horse.

"I know, I know, practice makes perfect," quipped Brad.

"That's not what I was going to say," grinned Pat.

"Oh, no? Well, then, just what were you going to say?"

Pat giggled. "I was going to say you have to suffer doing something poorly before you can enjoy doing it well."

"So, isn't that what I just said? Practice makes perfect?"

"Yep." Pat plopped her seat on the trailer's wheel fender.

The two absolute novices watched and listened as the judge called the winners in the showmanship class. Brad noticed that girls dominated the class. In fact, by the end of the day he was wondering if girls dominated all horse shows. He pondered why he was here while Matt and Mike were working on their cars. His subconscious mind registered the first place winner as she received her blue ribbon and exited the ring. A huge, chocolate brown bun, bustled in netting, sported a silver barrette under a deep rose-pink western hat. Her lipstick matched her hat absolutely perfectly. Brad shook his head nonchalantly wondering, *How'd she manage that?* He dropped the reins over Burgie's neck, unsnapped the lead rope, dropped the halter from her head, and raised the bit to his horse's muzzle. Burgie accepted it equally nonchalantly and, a moment later the buckles were latched and Brad was in the saddle, walking off toward the warm-up ring. He purposely didn't look back at Pat, for fear that nervousness was showing on his face.

As Brad moved Burgie in and amongst the other teens, he was glad that Mrs. Wheaten had encouraged him to ride out a few times with the stable customers. Riding with a group certainly had a different feel than riding alone, constantly watching who was coming up on his flank and being careful not to cut off a fellow rider's right of way.

Brad's first class was English Equitation. He was the last to enter the ring, simply because he was busy watching everyone else. The fifteen-minute class seemed to come and go in an instant. One moment, they were trotting one way of the ring, the next they were cantering the opposite direction and, before he knew it, the judge was calling for them to line up. Somewhere in the blur he had noticed that chocolate brown bun under a velvet black hunt cap and, when numbers were called, she was the first to step forward to accept the blue. Six places were awarded and out of nine riders, Brad found he was left in the line up when the announcer asked to have the ring cleared for the next class.

Back at the trailer, everyone was talking all at once. Mrs. Bateman swooned over her son, her hero of the class, even though he had totally lost. Dorie said he looked really good, and Pat said he looked nervous.

"Well, I wasn't," Brad retorted, and then admitted, "I was too busy trying to pay attention to what the judge was saying. Once you're in there, it's hard to pay attention to what your horse is doing. There are so many other horses pounding around you."

"That's okay, Brad, you did just fine," reassured Dorie. "Performance is the third class coming up so keep her saddled and just walk her out." They ambled toward a nearby field while Mrs. Bateman opted to regain her seat in the bleachers. Pat walked along Mrs. Wheaten's side and listened as she coached Brad.

"This second time in, you'll have your head about you better. Ask her to make smooth transitions from trot to walk and walk to canter. Try to space yourself so you're not being crowded by other horses. They were judging your riding in the equitation class, but they're not judging you now. They're judging Burgie, so put your attention on her."

This second class did seem easier already. Brad looked around to find open spaces and moved Burgie into them. On one occasion he cut the ring short on one end to do so and hoped that was okay. By the time the fifteen-minute class was over, Brad was beginning to feel sort of like when he was driving his mom's van. He and the van were one but, out on the road, they were also part of a bigger one—the flow of traffic. Here, he encouraged Burgie to time herself amongst the other horses so she could take advantage of what open space was available. Unlike the equitation class, the judge requested an extended trot. Brad held Burgie's head in as his calves quietly asked her to move into her bounding road trot. It was more difficult to bound here because there was a ring full of horses instead of a long straightaway road. Still, Brad could feel his mare was making the best of it.

In the line-up, Burgie would not stand perfectly still. Brad noticed the horse closest to him, a bright chestnut with a wide white blaze, was practically a statue. Only his ears pivoted as the judge walked by to inspect. When asked to back, the red took three perfectly spaced and perfectly straight steps to the rear, then quietly returned to his original position. The blue went to this well-deserving horse. Brad suddenly wished he had asked Pat to videotape the class. He would like to have watched that horse perform.

The red second-place ribbon went to the big, chocolate bun except, this time, it was demurely tucked beneath a navy-blue saddle-seat derby. Red button earrings matched a red scarf over a bright white blouse. Yep. The red lipstick was a perfect match. Brad watched the white, yellow, and pink ribbons leave the ring.

"Number 138. . . . Number 138." Brad snapped back to the announcer's voice. "Young man, you are Number 138. Please walk forward to accept the sixth-place ribbon."

Brad had forgotten his back number. The thought of bringing home a ribbon had never really settled in his mind in any real sense. Just getting ready to be in the show had clogged his brain well enough during these past weeks. Now, a sixth place out of seven entries was not bad. His mom was in a tizzy and Pat grinned from ear to ear. Brad didn't admit in words how pleased he was. He slid to the ground and gave Burgie a hardy slap on the neck. After all, this had been the performance class. It was Burgie's ribbon. He clipped it to the side of the trailer window and stripped and toweled his horse. He imagined showing it to his dad and Robbie that night.

After a lunch of hot dogs, Mountain Dew, and a Snickers bar, Brad resaddled Burgie for the afternoon "fun" classes. His gray saddle suit was sweaty and dust-filled. He made a mental note to bring an extra white shirt next time.

The Musical Stalls class was a mess. On the inside of the show ring, at the near end, ten-foot poles had been leaned against the railing every twelve feet making, well, sort of little standing stalls. All the horses gathered at the far end of the ring and the amplifiers played lively music. The horses rode in a small circle. On cue, the music would stop and all the horses would rush for the stalls—only one horse allowed in each space. With each round of music, one rail was removed so there was always one stall too few. Brad was not aggressive enough to get to a space quickly and Burgie was completely confused. In no time at all, the less than dynamic duo was eliminated and left to stand outside the ring watching the remaining spectacle.

"Next time." Brad chided Pat. "Next time. You watch me. Now I know how this thing works."

They did no better in the Egg & Spoon class. A ring attendant handed each rider a tablespoon and a clean white egg. Brad asked whether the egg was raw or boiled. The attendant chuckled and said, "If you don't drop it, it won't matter!"

The announcer instructed the riders to command their horses according to his requests while balancing the egg on the spoon. Not even a fingertip was to help keep the egg from falling. Brad's egg lay neatly in the bowl of the spoon throughout the walk, and he impressed himself by keeping the egg in its place during the trot, even while two other riders lost theirs. Brad's earlier question was answered as one of his opponents' eggs smacked on the front of an elevating front hoof, creaming it with slimy yolk.

Brad was determined to keep his egg throughout the announcer's call for a canter but, with Burgie's first sweeping stride forward, Brad's egg went flying in the air. The teen instinctively whipped his outstretched arm and caught the egg as it fell toward the ground showing, if not balance, at least a great recoup. "Nice work, young man!" proclaimed the announcer as a small group of bystanders clapped good-naturedly at the small feat. The announcer continued, "but not nice enough; the egg left your spoon and you're disqualified."

The Command class was Brad's favorite of the day. There were fourteen horses in the ring at the start of the class, carrying both teen and preteen riders. In the two morning classes, the judge had simply asked for the trot and extended trot, walk, and canter each way of the ring. In the Command class, the judge mixed the calls and included a "stop" or "reverse" here and there.

On each call, the last horse to respond was called to the center of the ring until only the blue ribbon winner was left on the rail. Burgie didn't place in the ribbons but Brad got a really good feel for the class and decided to enter this one at the next show.

As Brad was packing his gear, he noted that he never saw the chocolate brown bun after lunch. She must have only stayed for the morning classes. As quickly as the thought came, it went, and the tired, dusty, Wheaten barn crew packed it in for the day.

14

During the next two weeks, both Brad and Pat were settling well into their summer missions. Pat ran another 10-K race and placed well. She kept her practices during the week to six miles but did ten-mile runs on Saturdays. This way, the 10-K races were just like practice and she felt the once per week ten milers were preparing her well enough for the Bobby Crim up in Flint in August.

Brad's workouts after the first show became much more focused. He had a better feel for what the judge was looking for and how the other riders performed. When practicing for the equitation class, he really concentrated on feeling "one with the horse." Smooth unity was his goal. For the performance class practice, he encouraged Burgie to be bolder. He was looking for a full-bodied, self-confident horse that was extremely steady at the trot, with a clear distinction between her pleasure trot and her extended trot. They practiced standing still and backing straight, even though it was boring. Patience was not Brad's strong suit, but Pat was always there to support him with just the right cliché at the right time. One of her favorites was "A spectacular performance is always preceded by a great deal of less than spectacular preparation."

Brad and Burgie put a lot of practice in for the command class. He had been impressed with how responsive some of those horses had been during the June show. He would canter Burgie slowly down the road, and then bring up a sudden halt. With each attempt, his cues became subtler and she became more responsive. Dorie explained that Burgie was actually learning to feel hints coming from Brad's body before he gave his actual cue to halt. A shift of his hips or a tensing of his arms that was too subtle for him to be aware of was not too subtle for Burgie to feel.

"What these big animals can sense would amaze you," she had said.

☆ ☆ ☆

The third week in June found the Wheaten crew at the Happy Trails 4-H Show in Howell. The class line-up was almost identical to the June show. There were no musical stalls or egg-and-spoon classes but there was command, so Brad signed in for the three. Again, equitation was first, performance second, and command last. All three classes were after lunch so, even though it was a little farther away, Brad had plenty of time to prepare and still enjoy observing most of the morning halter and western classes.

During the halter classes, he noticed the girl with the large, dark brown bun at the nape of her neck. He wondered how many of the other riders here today had also been at the first June show. Studying the crowd, he recognized a few, including the red horse with the big white blaze that had won his performance class last time. Gary Shortner, the owner of a flashy silver-white Arabian, was also there. Gary had spent a moment small talking with Brad in the warm-up ring at the first show. As the red and its owner came out of the ring and past Dorie's trailer, ribbon in hand, she cast a friendly smile in Brad's direction. He nodded a return and she went on her way.

By the time the lunch hour was over and people were wrapping up their bags of trash, Brad was saddled and working in the warm-up ring. Pat had spent yesterday afternoon with him, coaching him on his clipping job.

"What are you telling me?" Brad had quipped. "You've never clipped a horse."

"Yeah? Well, maybe not," Pat responded, "but I do know how to slow down and do a job right. You're concentrating on the wrong thing."

"What do you mean?" demanded Brad with a chuckle. "I'm concentrating on my horse and on my clippers!"

"That's what I mean," responded the blond ponytail. "Your brain is holding an image of *your* horse and *your* clippers. Get rid of that picture. Replace it with a picture of the most perfect horse you saw at that show."

Brad thought of the red and also of the bay ridden by the brown-bun girl. "So? Okay. Now what?"

"Now trim like what you see. That's how artists draw. They always see the finished product and work toward it." Pat took a sip from her can of Mountain Dew.

What she said didn't make much sense to Brad, but it did make him think about the horses he would be with the next day. He found himself slowing down and working just a little more meticulously.

Now, as he worked in the warm-up ring, he glanced down at Burgie's bridle path and thought, yes, he was happier with this clip job.

This was a larger show. His equitation class had seventeen entries and, again, Brad did not place in the ribbons. He thought maybe he just wouldn't bother with equitation at the next show, but Dorie reminded him that the more times in the ring, the better for both of them.

There was only one class separating his equitation from his performance so, upon exiting the ring, he rode right on around and back into the warm-up ring. As he watched the class in progress, a western pleasure class, the brown bun rode up beside him.

"What's your horse's name?" she asked, deep red lipstick flashing over bright, white teeth.

"Burgie," he responded, taken quite by surprise at the girl's approach.

"Morgan?" she asked.

"How'd ya know?" Brad responded.

"She's good looking. What's her line?" The girl waited patiently but Brad didn't answer.

"Her bloodlines. What's her bloodlines?" the girl repeated.

Before Brad could respond, the announcer called them into the ring, which was a good thing because Brad didn't know Burgie's bloodlines. *What is one supposed to do,* he thought. *Keep his horse's family tree tucked in his back pocket just in case someone might ask?*

Brad was disappointed with Burgie's performance in this second class. She picked up the wrong lead the first time the announcer called for the canter and he had to pull her in and start again. When riding in the opposite direction later in the class, the brown bun cut him off as she came around a corner. He wondered if she had done it on purpose. She took the blue ribbon and second place went to the red gelding with the big white blaze. Brad was left in the line up which irritated the heck out of him. He would have to keep his anger to himself because Pat would just remind him that he had not shown enough to earn the right of passage into the winner's circle yet. She was so matter of fact. That part of her bugged Brad and impressed him at the same time.

There was a five-class break between performance and command. Brad had time to rinse his head and wash his face, brush Burgie and reblack her hooves. In the warm-up ring he small talked with a couple other riders and began to feel more at home. Brad and Burgie re-entered the ring refreshed and reasonably sure of themselves. Dorie had said more times than Brad could count that ninety percent of riding took place in the six inches between one's ears. Now, Brad took her words to heart. He entered this sixth class of his career with the intent to win. Burgie responded by taking heed of the clear requests coming through her rider's hands, legs, and voice. Brad counted. It took six steps for her to make the transition from her canter to her walk. He wanted to get that down to no more than four. There were twelve entries in the class. One by one, the judge would call a command and the slowest horse to respond would be called to the center of the ring. When the sixth horse was called in, Brad's heart jumped. He was in the ribbons. A seventh was called in after the judge asked for a canter depart—a canter from a halt. An eighth was called in on a halt-and-reverse from a trot. The riders were working counterclockwise in the ring. From the trot, the judge asked for a canter. Simple and routine, but Burgie picked up a right lead when she should have taken the left. Brad was called in and garnered a white fourth-place ribbon. He was well happy enough with that. It was a good day. As he collected his ribbon and walked Burgie through the exit gate, he caught the eye of the pretty girl with the dark hair walking toward him. He didn't even know her name. She stopped when she saw Dorie Wheaten reach his side, and when he looked a second time, she was gone.

15

It was early July. Four months of near daily riding was quickly turning Brad and Burgie into a fairly altogether duo. During workouts, they now veered off the road often. The fields and trails were dry and solid beneath Burgie's hooves, and a real sense of confidence had taken the boy. With school long behind them, early morning rides were quite possible and were much more cool and comfortable. Brad would investigate human footpaths or old snowmobile trails that led into the county park. Eventually, they would become nothing more than deer trails and, at some point, would become overgrown enough that the two would have to turn around or back out and catch another trail.

Today, they crossed a fair-sized bridge and watched the deep, dark water flow silently beneath them in stark contrast to the light gray boulders that supported its banks. They dropped left through a few pines and slipped into a meadow that once housed a baseball field. All that remained was the rusty wire of the home plate fence. Burgie broke into her bounding trot, consuming the field. Brad could feel the firmness of the ground beneath them surge through the horse's body and into his own. Why couldn't the show rings be a quarter-mile long field like this? This was Burgie's glory ground. They followed the north bank of the river until a small rise took them away, past abandoned tennis courts with cracked cement and, there, Brad and Burgie found another trail that returned them to the cool of the woods. They slowly picked their way along the path, catching deer tracks in the black edges of puddles and dodging frogs that hip-hopped up from the riverbed. The combination of beech and maple trees offered a welcome canopy to shade the boy and his horse.

The trail straightened toward an open field north of the river but still south of private properties fronting the next road. With the woods behind her, Burgie broke into a slow canter. Brad wondered if her shoes would slip in the slick black of the river path so he played with her reins—left, right, left, right—to let her know he wanted her to check her speed. At first she denied his request and he could feel her pulling away from him. The coolness of the woods and the promise of the open field tugged a little too strongly at her heart. Momentarily, Brad cussed his English saddle and wished for the security of the big western. He dropped his hips hard into Burgie's back and spoke harshly through the reins, calling "Hup, Hup, Hup," in a sharp, barking voice. Burgie, near the field's edge anyway, yielded to his command and came to a panting trot—boom, boom, boom, and finally a heavy, working walk. Burgie cleared her nostrils over and over again, indicating that she had finally warmed to the workout. Her body had broke sweat and so had Brad's. The slimy leather slid in the palm of his hands and he passed his reins from right to left as he wiped the sweat on his jean thighs.

The path dropped back into the woods and they walked along the riverbank until they stopped at the edge of a parking lot leading to a fishing dock. Ahead, cars traveled past on a paved road. A man and a woman were lowering a canoe into the river on his left. A doe and her fawn, unaware of his quiet approach, were drinking water from an inland pond on his right. How funny, he thought, that neither the humans nor the deer were aware of each other's presence, or of his for that matter. As Burgie stepped forward, the doe raised her head quickly and then stood stone still. A brief moment passed, and she disappeared into the woods in two simple bounds, the spotted fawn at her heels. Brad gave Burgie a pat on the neck and congratulated her for giving no more than a small hop at the movement of the deer.

They caught a break in the traffic and quickly crossed the paved bridge. They dropped through the ditch and headed back the way they came, only now along the south side of the river. They wrapped around behind a BMX bike track with a few kids peddling their maniacal little legs up and down the hills, and caught a path into a pine stand. A flock of crows rose raucously from the trees and Burgie shied to the left. Brad grabbed a big tuft of mane to help keep his balance. His mare regained her composure and he settled back into his rhythmic posting. At the far end of the pine stand another field opened and the two cantered across the open field toward the last woodlot that separated them from the road home.

"You got yerself one solid hoss there, boy." Chuck Wheaten slapped Burgie hard on the rump as he passed under her cross-tie and up toward the office.

"Thanks, Mr. Wheaten," Brad replied in earnest. It wasn't often that Chuck Wheaten had much good to say about anything, and Brad jumped at the compliment. Mr. Wheaten, however, continued. "I don't know if I'd get any crazy ideas about moving her up to the A circuit, boy. You ain't got the money nor the know-how for that stuff. And my Dorie here is stretching her run-around time and money a bit thin. You hear?"

"Yes, Mr. Wheaten, I've been thinking I need to help Mrs. Wheaten with things like gas and stuff, and . . . "

But Mr. Wheaten cut him off. "Your offer's a little late, boy. Between you working here and my wife covering your extras, seems to me that I'm the one supporting that there animal."

Brad now realized that Mr. Wheaten's friendly talk up front was just a conversation opener for what was really on his mind. Brad thought better than to respond at all so tossed his brushes back in the box and put Burgie up for the night. There were still four more summer shows before school started in September. As Brad drove home, he thought about picking up a second job. As it was, he was pretty much on call when Mr. Wheaten needed him to mend fence or nail down new roofing shingles. The cool of the evenings were spent painting the exterior of the main part of the auction barn. Mr. Wheaten had enough work available, but only so much money to pay.

The selfish part of Brad wanted to keep some of his time free for another reason. Pat had taken a job babysitting the children of a nurse who kept incredibly crazy hospital hours. Her running schedule had been disrupted to fit that of the nurse's. At best, she and Brad worked out together just two or three times a week and he missed her. He wanted to find a job where he could pick when he worked and that was pretty tough with most entry-level jobs.

And, yes, the thought of trying the class A circuit next year had already crossed his mind and maybe even settled in there quite snuggly. He intended to ask around at the next show to learn more about where and when they were held. Dorie probably knew, but he didn't want to ask. Like Mr. Wheaten said, she was already supporting his effort on the open circuit with too much of her own time and money.

16

The second week in July found Brad and Burgie well prepared for the Flying Hooves 4-H open show at the Shiawassee County Fairgrounds. Dorie's assistance was now rarely required. Brad's quiet observation of the competition, who was winning and why, gave him the insight he needed to better prepare for each show. When he was not in the ring, he was in the stands watching halter classes, western pleasure classes, English pleasure classes, and the mix of versatility classes chosen by each show committee. Some chose speed-and-action classes like barrel racing and pole bending. Others preferred jumper over fences or low-level dressage exhibitions. Brad found an interest in all the offerings while choosing to keep Burgie dedicated to the English pleasure classes. He wanted a blue ribbon, and if McMichaels' Training Center thought Burgie was an English pleasure horse, then Brad was not going to question their expertise.

As much as Brad was becoming more comfortable with his horse with each passing show, he still felt a bit of a stranger on the show grounds. All the teens who milled around him seemed to know each facility in every town as if it were their own back yard. Brad wondered how many shows each of them competed in to become so comfortable and at home. Unlike school, where everyone in a class is in the same grade, here, one could not tell how seasoned each competitor was. One might try to guess from the number of ribbons they were taking home, but that guess could be far from true. Some riders might be naturals, and with enough money for a quality horse, lessons, and equipment, they could come into the winner's circle fairly quickly. Others may not have natural talent for riding and may have been showing for years on their favorite pet, loved for attributes other than its ability to put out a great performance. They could have been on the circuit for three or four years, still be bringing home fourth-place ribbons, and still loving the hobby. Brad found himself studying the people as much as he did the horses.

The equitation class did nothing for Brad's ego. As much as he felt he was really becoming one with Burgie, it obviously did not show to the judge. In a class of eleven entries at this third show, Brad still took the gate. First place went to the young woman with the deep brown hair and second to the girl with the big red horse. Brad noted that these two girls were mildly pleasant with each other, but he never noticed them visiting outside the ring. They were obviously direct competition for each other, he decided, trading the first and second place position back and forth from show to show. It must have been frustrating for the other riders. As soon as they saw these two girls' trailers pull in, they must have assumed their chance for the blue was gone.

Not being one to start conversations with strangers, Brad found himself with his own Wheaten crew between classes. Today, however, Dorie was held back with work in her office, and Brad and Pat drove over on their own. Although Brad's mom continued to encourage his effort, she began to find the show grounds uncomfortable and preferred to hear the results from the comfort of her kitchen. Pat had misjudged when the lunch break would start and was off doing her six miles when Brad grabbed his cheese hot dogs and Mountain Dew from the concession stand. He swung both truck doors wide open so that a breeze could pass through, tuned in the radio, and sunk in behind the driver's wheel. Burgie stood tied patiently to the trailer's side.

Somewhere between the first and second cheese dog, Burgie gave a friendly nicker. When Brad took notice, he heard Burgie crunch down hard and begin chewing with her big equine molars. He swung his head around and out the door to find his mare enjoying the company and the carrots of the girl with the big, brown bun.

He collected as casually confident a voice as he could muster and said, "So, okay. I'm Brad Bateman." The girl held a carrot suspended in air. He continued, "And if you're going to keep beating me at all these shows, you might as well introduce yourself."

The brown bun continued the carrot's path toward Burgie's waiting and wiggling lips, then walked closer to Brad. "Well, I've tried to, like, a half-dozen times but you walk or ride away."

Why, thought Brad, had he not noticed these half-dozen efforts?

"I'm Cindy Ramsey. That, over there, is my trusty steed, Po-Diddly. You can call him Pogie." She pointed off to her bay standing quietly alongside a mammoth fifth-wheel trailer. Brad thought it looked large enough to haul eight horses and said so.

"Oh, no," Cindy chuckled. "It has a tack room in front of the stalls and living quarters extending over the truck bed. I had to bring it today because my dad took the two-horse to Ohio."

Silently, Brad was incredibly impressed that a sixteen-year-old girl could handle such a big rig out on the road, and that her folks would trust her with it. But out loud he just asked, "What's in Ohio?"

"We're taking two mares to Fairweather Farm for breeding. To Washington's Pride, you know."

Brad didn't know and his face showed it.

"Washington's Pride won the Regional last year. Are you new in Morgans? Or just new here in the Midwest?" Cindy reached, without asking, for Brad's Dew and took a sip.

"Yes. She's my first Morgan and, as you can probably guess, this is my first year showing. I've watched you take a lot of ribbons. You been doing this for years?"

Cindy returned the pop to Brad's waiting hand, reaching to brush wisps of hair back over her ears. "Forever. My folks own Riverside Stables. All we do is show. If there's not a breed show available, Pogie and I drop back to an open show."

Brad took a slug of Dew but didn't respond.

"Ever been to a Morgan show?" Cindy prompted.

Brad answered her question with a question. "How do I find where they are?"

That was just the prompt Cindy was looking for.

"You join the club. The state club," she concluded. "I'm this year's president; I'll get you an application form. Hey, why don't you come to a youth meeting? They're held at the high school in South Lyon."

Brad looked at her, and then quickly looked away. This was moving a little too fast.

"Here." Cindy reached over his arm and pulled the wrinkled show program off the dash, tore the corner off, and handed it to Brad. She pulled a pen from her jodhpur pocket and said, "Give me your number. I'll check the date when I get home and give you a call."

Without indicating whether he actually wanted to go to a youth meeting, Brad wrote his number on the scrap of paper and handed it back to Cindy. She sensed that he was uncomfortable and made a friendly excuse to be on her way.

"I better get Pogie ready for the performance class." With that, she was gone. It was just like his first class at that first show—in and out of the ring before he knew what had happened. He was eating his cheese dog, she was there, she was gone. He had her name but not her number or where she lived. The thought of her calling him gave him butterflies. He glanced back at Burgie, practically dozing on her lead rope, shook his head, and finished his Dew.

Brad was buckling the saddle onto Burgie's back when Pat returned from her run. She was surprised to learn that lunch had come and gone early and he was already tacking up for performance.

"Go ahead and shower," Brad assured her. "I won't go in for at least a half hour." Pat had learned early on that she could get her runs in on show days and use the show ground showers right along with the riders. She actually got to know a lot of the performers, at least the females, more quickly than Brad. She may not have known their names, but a lot of chatting went on in the showers.

During today's run she questioned whether she really wanted to be at all the shows. The first was fun because they only stayed while Brad was showing. Now, however, he wanted to spend the entire day studying the other classes. And, although she totally agreed that was necessary if he wanted to improve, she just wasn't horse crazy enough to want to spend the whole day. Now, she was toweled, dressed, and was back in the bleachers well in time to watch Brad boldly direct Burgie into his afternoon class. She didn't concentrate much on which horses won and why. But she did notice, at every show since the first, that Brad had an attraction to the girl with the dark brown hair. Was he impressed with her ribbons or her smile? Pat wondered whether she should feel slighted. Brad had never indicated a romantic interest in her, nor she in him. The fact that it had never crossed her mind must have meant it wasn't meant to be. Now, she watched Cindy Ramsey accept the second-place ribbon, as the blue was awarded to the white-blazed chestnut. That left four ribbons for the remaining nine riders. When Brad's number was called forward to accept sixth place, she let out a loud whistle from the bleachers and clapped alone for him. She watched Cindy glance briefly in her general direction and then hold her horse outside the ring, obviously waiting for Brad. Pat chose to stay seated while the two performers rode back toward the trailers. Bittersweet feelings flooded inside her because she still needed, or at least wanted, his support at her meets. She had some thinking to do.

When Brad had Burgie loaded in the trailer and all his tack and equipment was tucked in the bed of the truck, he found Pat, still up in the bleachers, reading a paperback. He waved his green ribbon between her and the book.

She quietly smiled down at him. "I got goose bumps when they called your number."

"I heard you whistle," his eyes squinted back up at her as the afternoon sun sneaked over her shoulder.

Pat bent the corner of her page to save her place, closed her book, hopped off the edge of the bleacher and down to the ground. She motioned an offer from her bottle of warm Gatorade, but Brad said, "You know I'm a Dew man," as they headed toward the truck.

17

The two weeks between the Flying Hooves 4-H Club Show and the late July Boots 'N Spurs 4-H Show flew by. Brad and Burgie did not miss a single day's workout and Pat often ran right at their side. She was pushing harder now, trying to better her time. The Bobby Crim was just a month away and she was up for it. It had been a good summer already. Having Burgie as a running mate was a challenging motivator, and Brad had become a very good friend. Their constant conversations comparing and contrasting physical fitness and competition in sport running and in the world of show horses drew them into deeper conversations about other things—the meaning of life in general, and meaning in their lives specifically.

Pat found a bit of family in Brad, and Brad learned to appreciate his own family just a little more. Before knowing Pat, Brad saw his dad, mom, and Robbie as just three people running here and there with very little in common. But there was an emotional distance between the people in Pat's family that made Brad realize there was an emotional closeness in his. Even if he wasn't always aware of what Robbie was up to while away at college, it didn't mean he wasn't with him in his heart.

Pat never mentioned her dad and, when asked, just commented that he wasn't around much, and it was pretty much like her mom wasn't there either. She was there physically, but mostly tuned out. Television talk shows idled away her afternoons, news programs interrupted dinners, and sit-coms filled her evenings. No matter how Mrs. Spielman filled her time, the television rattled on in the background. One evening, when Pat was about thirteen and in a sad state of frustration, she asked her mother why the television was always on. Her mother replied that it filled the void. Pat didn't know what she meant.

This coming Saturday, Pat would be running a 10-K fundraiser race for a burn unit at a Lansing hospital. In some small way, Brad was glad she would miss the Boots 'N Spurs Show. He had not heard from Cindy Ramsey and hoped to find an opportunity to strike up a second conversation. Somewhere inside he was feeling guilty. Pat had never struck him as a romantic possibility, and she had never indicated any such attraction in return, so it wasn't like he was being a traitor when he felt a curious tummy tingle at the thought of seeing Cindy again. Still, he felt like he was hiding something.

Pat slowed to a panting walk and pulled her sport bottle from her pant loop. Without stopping, she squirted her face and handed it up for Brad to spray a warm wash down his throat.

"I'm sorry I'll miss your run on Saturday," he said.

"No, you're not," Pat responded matter-of-factly.

"Yes, I am. Why do you say that?" he came back defensively.

"Because you're going to ask someone out on a date this Saturday and, if I were there, it would be uncomfortable." She looked up at him with the funniest grin on her face.

Brad was dumbfounded. Were they such good friends that they were thinking on the same wave length? He brought Burgie to a dead stop. "No, I'm not."

"Yes, you are."

"Am not. She steals all my blue ribbons."

"Oh, so we *are* talking about the same woman." Pat seized the opportunity to tease. Brad shifted uneasily in the saddle.

"Are you upset?" he ventured slowly. Pat stared intently at Brad. He was being very serious.

"Brad, you're my best friend. I've never had a boyfriend, don't really have any close girlfriends." Her left hand touched Burgie's rein and her right ever so slightly played with the crease at the knee of Brad's jeans. "You're the first person I have ever really been close to, but I can't imagine ever dating you. We're already doing more rewarding things together." The fact was, Pat couldn't imagine herself dating anyone, being that close, physically close, to any other person. There would be many years and a lot of silent pain before she would be able to grow away from the isolation she felt in her own family.

Brad shook his head in disbelief as she continued.

"Go ahead and ask her out, then tell me all the juicy details. But don't you dare tell her things I've told you or I'll hate you forever. I mean it."

Brad could not take his eyes off Pat. For the first time, he saw the glimmer of a woman staring back at him. He slid to the ground and slipped the reins over Burgie's head, letting his arm wrap itself around Pat's sweat-soaked shoulder. As he started toward home, pulling her after him, he gave her a sloppy kiss on the side of her sweat-slimy forehead.

"Will you be here when she breaks my heart?" he asked.

"What makes you think she'll break your heart?" Pat countered.

"I've watched her show." Their heads nodded in perfect agreement and they ambled down the road.

18

It was late July and Michigan was boasting one of its hottest summers in recent history. The Boots 'N Spurs 4-H Club Show at the Genesee County Fairgrounds would prove to be a real swelter. Cindy had not called as she promised and Brad began that terribly human habit of second guessing himself. Should he start a conversation with Cindy when he saw her and pretend the missing telephone call was no big deal? Or should he assume she was less than impressed with their first meeting and just decided not to pursue the friendship? Should he devote his day to showing Burgie as best he could and treat Cindy as a mere competitor? That thought frustrated him. He wanted control over his decision and his heart and brain were in a tug of war. He slid the electric clippers along Burgie's bridle path and concentrated on the task at hand. Burgie would show up for her part looking her best yet.

Pat was at her own meet and Dorie was held back at the riding stable. Brad was on his own, so whatever happened or didn't happen with Cindy, however humbling, could be kept to himself.

As Brad wheeled Dorie's rig into the grass field parking lot, he wondered if he had misread the show program. The field was practically empty. By this time at other shows, a great deal of bustling by a fair number of people would be underway. He backed Burgie out of the trailer and let her search for a few blades of grass as he sized up the gathering.

Gary Shortner was pulling the leg wraps off his flashy little Arab at the far corner of the warm-up ring. Tugging Burgie's head up from her munchies, Brad led her in Gary's direction.

"Hey there, Bateman, whassup? Didn't expect to see you here today."

"Why not? Where is everybody?" Brad asked in response.

"The All-Morgan," offered Gary as his brush set to work on his silver gelding. "Thought you'd be down in Detroit. Don't you show the breed circuit?"

"Right," Brad said with just a hint of sarcasm. "Like three mediocre ribbons justify the big time. Where in Detroit?"

"At the coliseum on Woodward and Eight Mile Road. It's only the largest and most prestigious Morgan show in the Midwest! You've never been there?" Gary continued without waiting for a response. "Ole Silver and me will be down there next week for the All-Arab. You should go down and check it out."

It suddenly dawned on Brad that he wouldn't see Cindy Ramsey today. Surely, she would be competing Pogie in Detroit. Now, Brad was sorry he was here. He'd rather be snooping the All-Morgan than competing here. After asking Gary about the possible time schedule of the Detroit show, Brad led Burgie back to their rig. If the All-Morgan ran the same as the All-Arab, then today, Saturday, was the last day of a four-day show! Championship classes would run all afternoon and into the evening.

Brad checked his own show program. Saddleseat Equitation and English Pleasure Performance were both before lunch. Command was the first class after lunch. With a crowd this small, lunch surely would come early and, it was feasible that Brad could get home in time to be in Detroit for at least some of the afternoon classes. He desperately wanted to see Cindy Ramsey in her other world.

There were only eight entries in each of Brad's three classes. In addition to Cindy's absence, the big red chestnut was nowhere to be seen. In fact, there were only three Morgans competing. The equitation class seemed to go slower and smoother, simply because there were fewer horses vying for good ring positions and the judge's attention. Brad surprised himself with a sixth place ribbon—his first equitation ribbon. As much as he publicly discounted the value of the equitation classes, he cherished a secret pride in this green ribbon; someone finally thought he looked good on his horse.

The performance class was a better story still. With the big guns out of the ring, new talent blossomed before the judge's eye. Was it because the intimidation factor was no longer there so these kids were really riding better? Or did the absence of that female dynamic duo simply leave room for others to move up into the ribbons?

In any case, Burgie came out with her first yellow ribbon—third out of eight. Brad accepted the award, leaned forward in his saddle, and tucked the ribbon clip into the side of Burgie's brow band, as he had seen others do. When they trotted back toward their trailer, the ribbon floated in the air and the hot sun glimmered off the satin. Brad imagined that Pat was there to greet him, and he made a mental note, a prayer, or a meditation, that she had done well with her running in Lansing that morning.

With the small turnout, lunch break came as early as ten-thirty. Brad shared his nachos with Gary as they bantered about the day's performance, peppered with various "my horse is better than your horse" jokes. Gary introduced Brad to another fellow Brad had only known by sight, and the day became a generally good and just plain fun time.

Burgie and Brad outdid themselves in the command class, earning, once again, a third in a field of eight.

"Let's see," mused Brad as he pulled his rig away from the show grounds. "That makes three sixths, no fifths, a fourth, and two thirds." That first show in early June seemed so long ago. As he swung out onto the highway, he checked his watch: 12:45. It would take an hour and a half to get Burgie home and the tack and trailer cleaned and put away, another hour to get home and cleaned up, then another hour to find the Michigan State Fairground at Woodward and Eight Mile. He would miss the afternoon classes but would be there well before the evening session started at seven.

Susan Bateman was thrilled to see Brad bound through their kitchen with additions to his ribbon collection. She didn't know the rankings yet, but knew these were the first yellows to grace her dining room curtain rods. Before heading for the shower, Brad grabbed the phone and rang through to Pat. As usual, she had run well and congratulated Brad on his successes, too.

"I thought we could do pizza tonight," she ventured, "but Mrs. Cronin called and needs me to sit the kids. I couldn't say no. She's in such a pinch."

That tinge of guilt poked Brad's belly as he said he understood. Off the phone, he bounded up the stairs two at a time.

It took a little work to convince his folks that he could handle driving into Detroit on his own. With a promise that he would call home when he got to the coliseum and again before he left for home, he gave them the assurance they were seeking. They had no clue he was going down to check out more than the horses.

19

As Brad pulled off I-75 and headed west on Eight Mile Road, it seemed hard to imagine there were any horses, much less four hundred of them, anywhere near. Eight lanes of traffic wove in and out and he was glad he was not pulling a trailer. Obviously, the state fairgrounds had been built decades ago and the city had grown up, and grown old, around it. Not until he passed under a viaduct and swerved left onto southbound Woodward, did he see the huge coliseum marquee. In large letters the sign read WELCOME MICHIGAN MORGAN HORSE SHOW. He paid a four-dollar parking fee to the gate attendant and wound his way around the monstrous curved-roof coliseum until he saw a sprawling expanse of horse trailers: many two- and four-horse rigs; dozens of fifth-wheel rigs with their hitches reaching up into the beds of pickup trucks, with tack room and sleeping quarters included; and huge semi- or near semi-trailers with elaborate farm names and logos emblazoned on their sides. He spotted the mammoth Ramsey Riverside Stables van but decided to tuck his mother's minivan further away, in and amongst a row of two-horse trailers.

As he walked the long, wide drive between the coliseum and the horse barns, the sounds of visiting people mingled with the smell of coffee and caramel corn. Traveling tack shops had their wares displayed around their vans: whips and spurs, gloves and jewelry. Nearby, a blacksmith smacked a shoe between his gavel and anvil to form-fit it on a waiting horse. The barns were not made of wood. They were huge steel structures and, had one not heard and smelled the presence of horses inside, he might think they were behemoth warehouses for some Detroit manufacturing plant. Through the huge sliding doors he could see horses mingling about, some being led to or from wash racks, others in cross-ties. As he walked in, he was overwhelmed by the hum of whirling fans, tied onto every stall. Brad wondered that the sheer number of fans did not blow the building's electrical circuits. Considering the number of horses housed within, there was surprisingly little stomping about and snorting going on. It was just too hot.

And something else really took Brad's breath away. The stall areas were absolutely beautifully decorated! Canvas curtains with tailored valances encircled each stall. Anywhere from four to twenty stalls would be draped in each farm's logo colors, and the farm name was brightly embroidered in six-inch letters on the fabric. Landscape timbers outlined artificial gardens filled with tan bark, cedar shavings, or white rock. Potted bushes and flowering plants finished off the effort. Behind some of the curtains there were no horses. Maybe they were set up to hold tack and equipment, or to be used as a dressing room for the exhibitors. Some had cots for the barn help.

All the farms had photo displays of their winning horses and riders either hung handsomely on their drapes or arranged on tables that were also laden with candy dishes, farm brochures, and business cards. Every so often Brad noticed a video playback television replaying a recent class. And all the farms had their three-and-a-half days' worth of ribbons streaming from their curtain valances. These ribbons were an astonishing two or two-and-a-half feet long with three beautiful streamers. Championship ribbons had six-inch wide rosettes and tri-colored streamers. In contrast, Brad's two yellow ribbons earned earlier that day seemed pretty insignificant. Mr. Wheaten's comments about this being out of his league began to sink in. Observing the All-Morgan, Brad began to get a feel for the road that lay ahead of him. And he knew he wanted to walk, or rather ride, that road!

"Hey, hey, hey! Who goes there?" chimed a very familiar voice. Brad turned to find Cindy Ramsey striding toward him, her hand out to shake his. She certainly had been raised around businesspeople and showpeople, he thought.

"I never thought I'd see you here," she offered cheerfully. "Who came with you?"

"Oh, nobody. Gary Shortner told me about it so I thought I'd come down and check it out."

"Well, I'm so glad you did!" Cindy responded with obvious enthusiasm. "C'mon over to our stables and meet my folks."

Cindy led Brad through aisle after aisle of beautifully decorated stabling niches. Dozens of tired horses munched quietly on hay, thankful for the breeze afforded by their fans. Brad wondered at the coincidence that Cindy came upon him so soon after his arrival. She must have been wandering around chatting with everybody. As they walked, Cindy commented about this farm or that. It seemed she knew something interesting about each of them. She knew all the trainers and grooms by name and most of their dogs. One farm had a basket of puppies looking for homes. Another had barn hands arguing about a certain procedure. Yet another had two women gossiping about something official that, to them, didn't seem quite fair. Brad absorbed all the social hubbub of the barns as he followed Cindy. They left one barn, crossed a wide drive area and entered another steel building. Four horses were lined up in an indoor wash rack. A half dozen people, nearly as wet as the horses, were sudsing them up or just cooling them down. Beyond, were more stalls, and more stalls. Finally, they came to the black, red, gold, and white of Ramsey's Riverside Stable. Ramsey's effort took up the entire southwest corner of the building. Between their horse stalls, tack stalls, and cot rooms, they must have consumed sixteen stalls. Cindy took it all for granted. Brad attempted to take it all in stride.

Bill Ramsey burst around the corner. A puff of cigar smoke trailed behind, filling the air with its odor. The sudden flurry of commotion took everyone by surprise. A woman was practically jogging to keep up.

"First place, Linda, first place. Not Reserve Champion. I want Grand Champion. Do you hear?" Bill Ramsey boomed. "We are going home tomorrow with nothing but Grand Champion. Rocky won't let me down, and neither will you!" Then he added with emphasis. "Right?!"

Linda Cramer, Riverside's head trainer, scrambled to regain control of the conversation. "I just said he seemed a little off his feed this afternoon," she quipped.

"Well, you tell that horse this is not the night to be off his feed! I've got to find McMichael and nail down that breeding contract before tonight. If he bests me in the ring . . . if, I said, which you will see to it he doesn't . . . if he bests me in the ring, he'll up his stud fee before we make it back to the barn."

Linda threw up her arms in exasperation. Why, she asked herself, did she even mention it? Bill Ramsey wasn't interested in hearing about possible problems, only real ones, and then, only after they'd been solved.

Mr. Ramsey strode out as quickly as he had walked in. Cindy stepped forward to conspicuously block his path.

"Dad, this is Brad Bateman, the boy I mentioned." Bill Ramsey barely skipped a step as he stuck his hand out to shake Brad's.

"Nice to know you, kid, I'm not hiring." And he and his cigar were gone.

Brad wasn't quite sure what had whizzed through, but Cindy knew. That was her father. Always hustling, never second guessing himself, usually winning and cussing when he was not.

Cindy turned to Brad matter-of-factly and shrugged her shoulders. She tried to cast off that veil of dominance that was Bill Ramsey.

"Did you tell your father I was looking for a job?" queried Brad.

"Of course not. I told him I met you and Burgie at the open shows and had invited you to a youth club meeting."

"Then why did he say he wasn't hiring?"

Cindy sighed. "Because he rarely listens to me. C'mon. I'll introduce you to Linda and Rocky."

They found Linda Cramer examining the inside of Rocky's mouth. Her left hand was wrapped snuggly around a long, fat tongue held out and to the side of the horse. Her right hand was poking around inside. She was hoping a sharp tooth had him off his feed and not some abdominal problem.

Brad gave the jet black gelding a thorough visual inspection. He was taller than Burgie and Pogie, and held a stately air about him, even with Linda Cramer poking around inside his mouth. Maybe it was the length and arch of his neck that gave Rocky that aristocratic appearance. Whatever, Brad liked what he saw.

"Brad," Cindy interrupted his thought. "This is my riding instructor, Linda Cramer. She's Dad's head trainer and also handles most of the bookkeeping for our farm."

Linda offered an earnest smile. "Hi there, Brad. They keep me pretty busy, that's for sure. I've been begging for an assistant for the last three years! Are you the same Brad Cindy's mentioned from the summer shows?" Brad was pleased to hear his name had crossed Cindy's lips more than once.

"Yes. Glad to meet you." He wasn't sure what else to say.

"You're riding that mare from McMichaels,' aren't you, the one that went through an auction?" Linda continued, "That Burgundy Delight?"

"Yes. Burgie. She's mine. I own her now." He was surprised that Linda would know of the horse. In fact, he was constantly surprised at how much all these people knew about what was going on at everybody else's barns. It was obviously a tight network of friends and enemies, colleagues and competitors.

"She's a nice horse," Linda continued.

"Thanks, I think so."

"Bet Evan McMichael was fit to be tied when his dad decided to push her through the auction."

"Why do you say that?" Brad ventured. "Didn't she belong to one of their customers? That's what we were told."

"Oh, yeah," replied Linda casually as she stepped away from Rocky and motioned the kids out of the stall, "but Evan worked that horse since she was a foal. Took first place in the Futurity when she was just a weanling. Had her in the ribbons ever since."

Brad was silently surprised and impressed. This was his horse she was talking about.

"We trainers aren't supposed to get emotionally attached to our horses, you know. But every once in a while one comes along, like Rock-N-Roll here, that you just can't help but love. I heard Dee Dee was Evan's favorite."

Evan's favorite? Brad wasn't sure how to respond to this. *And Dee Dee? That's not my horse,* thought Brad. *She doesn't look like a Dee Dee. Burgie looks like a Burgie!*

"Well," concluded Linda matter of factly. "Tonight will come, tonight will go. A few will become state champions, most will not. I'll live through it. And," she continued as she gave Cindy a big sisterly squeeze on the arm, "so will your father. Now you kids go enjoy yourselves. And, Cindy, my heart will be in your pocket for the youth thing." Cindy gave Linda Cramer a big hug, suitable only for those one really loves.

"Thanks, Linda. Like you say, it will all be over tonight."

Brad and Cindy strolled slowly through the barns. Cindy offered a little info here, a tidbit there, about various horses and their owners or riders, and how they had fared well, or not so well, so far. She described dozens of halter classes divided by sex and age of animal, and multiple dozens of riding classes: western might be western pleasure or stock seat equitation, or reining. Hunt seat might be performance on the flat or over fences, plus hunt seat equitation. Dressage was performed at various levels. And driving could be two-wheel pleasure or four-wheel park, roadster to bike, or the historical Americana class; plus two-horse or four-horse carriage driving and performance on the obstacle course. English pleasure was actually divided into two levels of animation: the mid-stepping pleasure or the high-stepping park horses, plus saddleseat equitation. Also, many of these classes were divided into groups according to the age of the rider or driver and whether they were an amateur or a professional. To a beginner, it could be incredibly confusing. Brad found it interesting how a diverse group of horse enthusiasts could take one little Morgan horse and develop such an elaborate show of talent to fill everyone's needs and desires. When he voiced this observation to Cindy, she added with a chuckle, "This is just the people on the Morgan circuit. When you add all the other breeds, it becomes huge, monstrous, overwhelming, never-ending." As the two teens walked away, they began to compete quickly to see how many other breeds they could include.

"Quarter Horse," said Cindy.

"Appaloosa," said Brad.

"Arabian and Tennessee Walker," added Cindy.

"Thoroughbred, Paint, and Pinto," continued Brad.

Their chatter continued across the drive between the buildings. "Palomino, Saddlebred, Standardbred, Paso Fino, and Peruvian Pasos. Plus the big breeds: Shire, Belgian, Percheron, and Clydesdale. Oh, and, the ponies: Welsh, Shetland, Hackney, POAs . . ."

They were still rattling off breed names, chastising each other if he or she offered a name more than once, when they collapsed at a table in the concession area. The lunch counter was tucked under the bleachers at the southeast corner of the coliseum. There was easily room for twenty or so tables and a windowed counter with two people wiping down pop machines.

"I'll buy you a Dew." Brad stood and reached deep into his pocket for his wad of rolled-up ones.

"Make that a Diet Coke and I'll accept," Cindy answered graciously. With a smile, Brad sauntered up to the concession window. Cindy watched him intently, knowing so automatically and matter of factly that she just plain liked this guy a lot. A lot! It just felt like he was supposed to be in her life. He was casual, easy going, with a genuine interest in horses, which tends to be rare among boys who were not raised around them. She watched him closely as he returned with the two soft drinks. He never let his eyes leave hers, using his feet to push wire-legged chairs aside here and there as he wove his way through the empty food-concession area. He sat across from her and slid the Coke across the surface of the small, Formica-topped table.

"So, why . . . " she began.

"So, tell me . . . " he began. They both laughed and said simultaneously, "Sorry, you first." They giggled again and he waved for her to speak.

"So, why have I never seen you around before?" she asked. "You must be new to horses, or at least Morgans, because I've been around this stuff forever."

Brad wondered what Cindy might think if she knew his only horse experience was at an auction barn. He suspected a lot of big show people held discriminatory views toward auction horses and auction barn people, but Brad cared a lot for most of the people who comprised the aura of the auction barn. He told Cindy, with much color and detail, how he came upon the Wheatens years ago.

"My family was new in Linden. I was out bicycling, exploring around my home one day when I found this rather deserted looking set of barns. I parked my bike in some bushes and was investigating what I thought, at the time, might be some totally abandoned barns and outbuildings. Well, I found a couple horses in a dirt pen that were struggling to reach the grass under the fence. So, I started pulling grass for them when Old Man Wheaten caught me. I thought he'd get me for trespassing so I scrambled for my bike. Instead, he grabbed me by the arm and before I knew it, I had a pitchfork in my hand and was helping him muck out stalls. I went home that day with ten bucks in my pocket and have been working for them ever since."

Cindy asked how Burgie fit into this story, but Brad said, "Oh, there's not time to tell you that now. What's this youth thing your trainer was talking about?"

"Oh, that. It's the State Youth of the Year competition. No one ever expects to win because the contest categories cover so much information. But we all hope to win in at least one of the four areas and, of course, someone will win the overall high points for all four areas. They get to represent the state at the World Championships in October, and if you win overall at the World, then the American Morgan Horse Association will pay your way to a foreign country of your choice. While you're there, you get to represent the American Morgan Horse to the horse clubs in that country.

"Sounds cool," mused Brad, "You ever been overseas?"

"Nope. How about you?"

"Nope. Didn't I hear the Morgan Horse breed started here in the States?"

"Yes, in 1789, the same year George Washington became president," tutored Cindy. She thought it fun to be able to relay a little of what she knew about her favorite breed of horse. "There's a kids' book called *Justin Morgan Had a Horse* that tells a pretty accurate history, and Walt Disney made a movie by the same name. It's pretty old but a few video stores still have it."

"So, where can I go to get some real information about Morgans?" asked Brad. "I mean if I don't want to watch a kids' movie?"

"Easy," Cindy beamed. "I'll loan you my copy of *The Morgan Horse* by Jeanne Mellin Herrick." Cindy relished the thought that loaning the book would give her a reason to see Brad again.

"Back to this youth thing," Brad interrupted. "You said there are four test areas."

"Yes," Cindy explained. "The first is a written test covering breed history, basic horse care, health care and reproduction, and tack and equipment." Brad set his chin in his hand, elbow on the table, and raised his eyebrow with interest.

"You know," Cindy added, "just like a school test: multiple choice, fill in the blanks, true/false, and matching."

"So what are the other three parts of the competition?" Brad encouraged Cindy to continue.

"There's a judging competition where they bring four mares and then four geldings into the ring and we have to rank their body conformation from best to worst."

"Well, how can they grade you on that?" Brad asked. "Isn't judging subjective?"

"Yes and no," responded Cindy, enjoying owning this little bit of authoritative knowledge and having someone upon which she could bestow it. "There is an ideal Morgan type against which all judges line up their winning choices. But you're right, subjective preference on the part of the judge creeps in there, too. In the youth contest, we're not graded so much on *how* we place the winners as much as *why* we placed them the way we did."

"Oh," summarized Brad. "So, it's in the contestant's best interest to document in writing what they see in each horse."

"That's right," Cindy concluded. "And by reading what the kid writes, the graders can tell how much she or he knows about ideal Morgan type: eyes, crest of neck, angle of shoulder, and stuff like that."

Cindy stopped talking because Brad was staring at her, smiling. She squirmed slightly in her chair.

"Are you enjoying this?"

"Yes," he said. "So, what are the other two areas?"

"Oh," Cindy got her mind back on track. Brad kept smiling at her so it was hard to concentrate. "There's a pattern ride and a speech."

"A speech? Yuck," concluded Brad, "What's the pattern ride?"

"Both the speech and the ride are predetermined," Cindy explained. "This year's topic is 'Morgans in Your Community.' We were supposed to write a paper on how one can use Morgans to do community service. The pattern was posted on the bulletin board by the show office last Wednesday so we all had time to memorize it and practice."

"Are you done with all four parts?" asked Brad earnestly, his smile fading.

"Yup, and thank heaven," replied Cindy. "I did the written test Wednesday morning, the judging Thursday afternoon, the speech last night, and the pattern class this morning."

"I'm sorry I missed them," Brad replied rather seriously.

Cindy found his earnestness exciting. She felt a tingle in her tummy. "I'm glad you weren't here."

"Why?" pressed Brad. "I would have enjoyed being part of all that. You should have told me at the last open show. I would have come down here to watch."

"I didn't even know you." She corrected herself. "Don't even know you." Cindy found herself staring at the table, surprised at her own shyness.

"Well, you know me now," Brad said softly. Cindy wondered why Brad seemed so confident. It had been he who was reserved when she approached him at that last show. *I was the one who had to introduce myself!* she thought.

"So, why didn't you call me?" Brad asked. "You said you were going to call about this month's youth meeting."

"Yeah, well," Cindy hedged. "I forgot the meeting was going to be held down here, and . . ."

"And you didn't want me down here." Brad quietly finished her sentence.

"It wasn't that I didn't want you here," defended Cindy quietly. "And, besides, I'm glad you're here now."

"I am, too. And, hey! Let me tell you about my morning." Brad cheerfully boasted in an obvious effort to change the subject.

"Did you do the Boots 'N Spurs Show?" asked Cindy.

"Yes, and we brought home our first third-place ribbon, two of them, in fact. Mostly because you weren't there."

Cindy ignored the last part of his comment.

"Cool!" she said, and turned her attention to the sound of men talking as they came around from the south side of the arena. Mr. Ramsey, cigar still hanging from the corner of his mouth, was in a heated debate with Joe McMichael—something about a white spot above the knee on one of McMichael's yearlings. Without interrupting his stride or the waving of his arm, his voice boomed, "A rule is a rule and rules aren't supposed to be changed." Cindy watched him cast a sidelong, curiously disapproving glance toward Brad. She caught her breath and then let it relax as her father continued past them and disappeared from sight through the east door.

20

For a fee, training stables could have a section of coliseum bleachers reserved in their name. The show committee would print a nice banner that stated the stable name. It was one more way for the show to support itself and it offered the friends, families, and clients of each stable a specified gathering place. This was much easier than searching the stadium for familiar faces at the start of each session.

Cindy invited Brad to sit with her family in the section marked RAMSEY'S RIVERSIDE STABLES. Throughout the evening, he was able to visit with Rita Ramsey, Cindy's mom, a gracious woman who seemed to enjoy his company. It appeared to him that she was not particularly interested in what was going on in the ring, nor in much of the stable's business talk that was going on around them. She asked Brad about his family and his school; things that were easy to talk about. Brad was glad she was there.

Neither Bill Ramsey nor Linda Cramer spent much time in the stands. For that matter, neither did Cindy, but she had suggested that Brad not hang out in their stabling area while Bill and Linda were supervising the night's performances.

"It can get pretty hectic back there, if you know what I mean," she had cautioned.

What little Brad saw of Mr. Ramsey gave a clue to the kind of man he was. Whereas his own dad was kind of a quiet, steady guy, Bill Ramsey was boisterous and erratic. One minute he was joking and slapping colleagues on the back, the next he was waving his cigar in the air, screaming orders or opinions at people who neither deserved nor needed that kind of pressure. But Brad also could easily tell that Bill Ramsey loved his horses, loved the spectacle of the show ring, loved the pressure of competition, and loved his daughter.

In the bleachers, Brad was sitting ten feet above a conversation between Bill Ramsey and Evan McMichael. Brad immediately recognized Evan as the man who had delivered Burgie to Wheatens' Auction Barn seven months earlier. The men appeared to be enjoying a bantering conversation about which farm had taken the most or the best ribbons thus far.

As Evan turned to go on his way, he said, "Yeah, but our boy, Andy, will clean up on the Youth of the Year."

Ramsey immediately wiped the smile from his face and retorted sharply, "My daughter's got it in the bag!" Evan stopped and turned on his heels, once again facing Cindy's father.

"What makes you so sure, Ramsey?"

"Because I know my daughter!" boasted Bill Ramsey. "I raised me a tough cookie. She's a showman and a true competitor. This is all about winning and she'll handle it just fine."

Evan just waved his hand away in cordial disagreement and wandered off. Brad sat wondering what it must be like to live with such a demanding and expectant man. He wondered how Cindy felt about it, or if she thought about it at all. In the show ring, at least, she certainly appeared to live up to his expectations.

The Saturday evening championships at the Michigan All-Morgan Horse Show began with a youth color guard. Four riders, two western and two English, entered the ring with huge waving flags on long poles. The poles were held at arm's length, their bottoms resting in stirrup cups near the riders' feet. The riders performed a simple but meticulous synchronized riding pattern, first to the "Star Spangled Banner" then, with respect for the competitors from across the bridge to "Oh, Canada." There was a U.S. flag, a Canadian flag, and a State of Michigan flag. The final flag, a royal blue, was emblazoned with the ornate logo of the American Morgan Horse Association. When the young riders left the coliseum, the evening's judges were escorted to the island stage at center ring and introduced to the audience.

After the third class of the night, the announcer asked that all youths who had completed the Youth of the Year competition please come to the center of the arena. Brad was surprised to see the teens and pre-teens wearing, not riding clothes, but rather dress attire. A few of the girls even stepped gingerly across the soft, dirt arena in low-heeled pumps. Brad recognized the girl who rode the big red horse with the white blaze at his open shows as one of the group.

Cindy walked gracefully to center ring in a royal blue mid-calf shirtwaist dress with a western yoke. It was trimmed in gold chord and western studs. A gold-colored western buckle adorned her matching belt. The blue of her flats matched perfectly. Her hair was pulled back on the sides and held up with a royal blue and gold hairpiece. The bulk of her silky brown hair lay smoothly down her back.

She's absolutely beautiful, thought a mesmerized Brad, just as she caught his eye and flashed a hopeful smile.

Six pre-teens and nine teens competed in the two divisions. After naming the winner in each of the four junior contest areas, the announcer named the top point winner of the Junior Youth of the Year award. A youngster from Davison received a plaque and an engraved silver cup, plus a gift certificate from a tack shop.

The announcer then turned his attention to the senior division contestants. He congratulated all of them on the efforts in the contest and their dedication to the Morgan Horse. As in the junior division, he asked that the audience give the entire group a round of applause. He then individually read the name of the winner of each of the categories. As the names were read, the winner stepped forward to receive a rose and a silver cup. Brad did not recognize the girl who received the cup for the written examination. Cindy graciously accepted a rose and silver cup for her and Pogie's flawless pattern ride. Andy Prescott took home the cup for both the public speaking and the judging. Brad assumed it was the Andy from McMichaels' Stables, and his heart sunk as he sensed the disappointment that Cindy must have been feeling at that very moment.

"And now, ladies and gentlemen, we are proud to introduce to you, the overall high point winner of the senior division Michigan Justin Morgan Horse Association Youth of the Year competition. He or she will represent our state club at the World Championships to be held in Oklahoma City this October. Ladies and gentlemen," the announcer continued, "Miss Cynthia Ramsey, your High Point winner!" Brad would later learn that, although Andy scored highest on his speech and his judging, and third on his pattern, he had been totally unprepared for his written test. Cindy had scored second on her written test, third in judging, and third on her speech, giving her the high point total.

The show steward held a beautiful plaque and a huge perpetual trophy. Her name would be added to the trophy and she would be able to keep it in her home for the next year. It would then be passed on to next year's winner. Before stepping forward to accept her plaque, Cindy turned to Andy Prescott, and extended a congratulatory handshake. He passed the handshake and, instead, gave her a big kiss on the cheek, much to the crowd's delight. A showman, for sure, thought Brad from his place in the stands.

Later in the evening, with a radiant Cindy at his side, Brad stood near the half-wall chute at the entry gate as Linda Cramer boldly trotted Riverside Rock-N-Roll into the arena. It was the Park Saddle Championship and Rocky would take home the reserve award. The championship was awarded to McMichaels' Jay-B-Boy, owned and ridden by Andy Prescott's father.

An hour later, Brad and Cindy sat in the box seats, along with Cindy's mom, for the final class of the evening. It was nearly eleven o'clock and for most people in the stadium, a long, long four days was drawing to a close. Still, the excitement of the final class, the Park Harness Championship, had the crowd on its feet. Linda Cramer hugged the ringside, calling to Bill Ramsey, coaching him through this final feat. Rock-N-Roll pounded vibrantly around the mammoth arena. Mr. Prescott was out there, too, with Jay-B-Boy strutting his stuff equally well. Brad had never seen horses lift their legs so high or extend them so powerfully. They somehow reminded him of pistons pounding up and down as they fueled a giant engine. In the midst of the excitement, with the crowd whistling and cheering the horses on, Brad reached for Cindy's hand and squeezed it in anxious anticipation. He released the squeeze, but she held on. Their eyes met quickly; then with fingers entwined, they jumped to their feet and screamed with elation as Rocky took the Michigan All Morgan Horse Show Park Harness Championship, claiming this most elite award for Bill Ramsey's Riverside Stables.

The entire Riverside team—Linda Cramer, along with her grooms, barn hands, and exercise boys—gathered outside the east door in the cool night air. Standing between the coliseum and the stall barns, they stripped a sweating Rocky out of his harness and steeped congratulations on each other and themselves. Bill Ramsey left the rig to accept a cigar from Joe McMichael and Mr. Prescott. Rita Ramsey watched quietly as Brad slipped away to a pay phone to call home. A good boy, she thought to herself.

Linda led Rocky to the barns, tri-color ribbon gracing his neck and rippling over his shoulder. The barn crew rolled the four-wheeled viceroy, piled high with harness parts, towels, and brushes, behind her. Cindy, still in her royal blue dress, wandered over to the pay phones at the south end of the coliseum. She played with the material of Brad's left upper shirt-sleeve as he cleared a late night arrival home with his folks. He set the receiver in its cradle and gazed quietly into Cindy's eyes. The entire coliseum had become amazingly quiet. Beyond the bleachers, the low drone of a tractor was grading the dirt, already in preparation for the Arabian horses that would be arriving for the Michigan All-Arabian Show in three days. The sound of people gathering outside the north end doors for the exhibitors' party seemed a million miles away.

With his right hand still on the telephone, Brad's left arm reached around Cindy's waist and drew her slowly toward him. Rising on her toes, she stepped readily into his kiss. It wasn't an uncertain kiss, a first date, first kiss, kiss. It was an "I love you and I know I love you" kiss. Brad released his hold on her waist ever so slightly and Cindy stepped away. Leaving the telephone behind, Brad ran the back of his fingers gently down her cheek.

"Congratulations on an absolutely wonderful evening," he whispered.

"Thank you for being part of it," she whispered in reply. Hand in hand, they joined the exhibitors' party and two hours of music and dancing.

BOOK TWO

21

When Brad and Pat unloaded Burgie at the Thornhollow Troopers 4-H Show in early August, everything was different. Now, Burgundy Delight did not seem too big a name for a horse. With the All-Morgan etched in his memory, Brad was determined that Burgie would feel a different person, a new person, a more confident and driven person, on her back from now on.

"Did you know you were Evan McMichael's favorite horse?" Brad had asked her during a recent grooming. Burgie twisted her head sideways in an attempt to chew on her cross-tie, but ignored his question. "Linda Cramer said McMichaels were planning on showing you park saddle and park harness." Burgie continued to play with her cross-ties. "And here I am showing you in country shows. You deserve better than me, Burgie Girl." Brad let his brush drop back into its box. He pulled a carrot from his hip pocket and held it firmly, forcing Burgie to take a bite, rather than inhale the entire carrot.

"This I promise you, Burgie," he whispered to his disinterested horse, who was now searching for another carrot. "I am going to become the person who deserves you. And next year, you and I will take the All-Morgan and Evan McMichael by surprise. What do you say about that, girl?" But Burgie had returned to playing with her cross-ties.

Now, today's open show took on new meaning for Brad. It wasn't just showing Burgie, enjoying the day, and trying to better the performance since the last show. It was serious preparation toward his participation in next year's class A Morgan circuit and he had his strategy planned.

Today would be his last open show for this year. There was one more show in the summer schedule but it conflicted with the ten-mile Bobby Crim Road Race up in Flint. After the Bobby Crim came the annual Morgan Youth Club field trip to Cedar Point. Brad was looking forward to an entire day with Cindy at the amusement park in Ohio and the long bus ride to and from.

But here was where his strategy got serious. After spending the evening at the All-Morgan championships, Brad had poured his heart out to Dorie Wheaten. Sitting in the dreary office of the auction barn, she shared all his excitement for the aura and competition of the big show. She asked who won the park classes as if she might recognize their names.

"And what about Cindy?" Dorie asked with a soft smile. "I suppose she was there, too?" Brad couldn't hide his attraction to Cindy Ramsey, but he shared fewer details about that part of the evening with Dorie.

"I've got to show Burgie at the All-Morgan next year, Mrs. Wheaten. I've got to do it for me, and for Burgie. Even if she doesn't know she deserves it or doesn't even care, she still does deserve her day at the coliseum."

"I agree with you, Brad."

"You do?" he said excitedly.

"Yes, I do, but you two have a lot of work ahead of you. And you can't do it on your own."

"Why not?" Brad asked innocently enough.

Dorie continued thinking out loud. "You can't afford a trainer. . . . "

"A trainer?" Brad responded in surprise. "No way, Mrs. Wheaten. I'm going to do this on my own!"

"Can Cindy help you?" Dorie asked.

"No!" Brad insisted emphatically. "This is my baby. I want to do it on my own." Dorie Wheaten shook her head quietly at the naiveté of her young employee. How did he expect to compete with those big stables with all their years of professional experience?

"Well, you learn quickly enough," she admitted. "I'll tell you what. Let me make a couple phone calls. I'll see what we can arrange."

"Arrange what? How? Who are you going to call?" Brad was perplexed, but Dorie just smiled her usual reassuring smile.

"Give me a couple days, Brad," was all she would say.

So, today, he was unloading Burgie and tacking her up for his final summer show. It had been a week and Dorie had not mentioned anything about her mysterious telephone calls. Pat was brushing the hairs smooth in Burgie's mane and tail.

"So, let's suppose, Brad, that Mrs. Wheaten didn't exist," she prompted.

"Why?" he asked.

"What, then, would you do to prepare yourself for next year's shows. Have you thought about that, or are you letting the hope of Mrs. Wheaten's help keep you from thinking on your own?"

Brad tightened his saddle into place and looked straight at Pat. "That's what I don't like about you. You're always thinking." He pulled on his derby and gloves and rode off to the warm-up ring.

This was a good-sized show. The weather was great and a lot of riders were entering extra shows and extra classes in a last ditch effort to earn points toward seasonal open show high point awards. Cindy Ramsey, however, was not showing today and Brad really missed her. It was policy in Bill and Rita Ramsey's house, that for two weeks each August, after the All-Morgan, and two weeks in late January were devoted to private family vacation time. Cindy had gone with her folks to visit relatives on the west coast.

Brad and Burgie showed exceptionally well, garnering another sixth in equitation and third in performance, even with the bigger crowd—fourteen riders in each of his classes.

On the way home, Pat and he continued their conversation from the morning.

"As a matter of fact, Pat," Brad said, "I have thought about my options and I've talked to my dad about it, too." Pat listened with interest as he continued.

"Dad said something really interesting. He said, 'Brad, you'll be the same person five years from now that you are today except for the people you meet and the books you read.'"

"Say that again," queried Pat.

Brad repeated, "You'll be the same person five years from now that you are today except for the people you meet and the books you read."

"Hey, I like that," said Pat.

"Yeah, well anyway, yesterday, I went to the library but couldn't find anything really specific on horse training. Mom said I should ask Cindy when she gets home because she probably has some books I could borrow." Pat agreed with that idea.

"So what about this 'people you meet' thing?" She asked. "Can the people at these shows help? What about Cindy? You just said that what you saw about her dad's place while you were at the Detroit show was pretty impressive."

"Well, you're sort of on the same train of thought as me," Brad continued. "I can't afford to put Burgie in training at a place like Ramsey's and, besides, I don't want to. I want to do as much of this as I can by myself. And," he added, "they're certainly not going to give me any training secrets for free."

Pat looked confused. "So, what are you going to do?"

"Easy. I'm going to hire myself on as barn help and then learn by observation."

"You mean you're going to leave the Wheatens?" Pat was really shocked at the prospect. "Who will I run with? I've grown used to having you around." Pat feigned a pout, but there was some truth in her teasing.

"Oh, I'll still keep Burgie at Wheatens'. I'll have to pay board but I'm sure they will let me keep her stall."

"So, are you going to ask for work at Cindy's dad's?" That made sense to Pat.

"No," Brad said emphatically.

"Where, then?" asked Pat.

"McMichaels'," beamed Brad.

"Isn't that where Burgie came from?"

"Yeah, but they won't remember me. I mean, they won't recognize me from that one day when Evan trailered Burgie over for the auction—and I don't plan on reminding them. I'll just play dumb and do a good job. Get to know their blacksmith and their vet. Just watch them working their horses as much as I can. I'll learn by observation."

Pat was impressed with Brad's plan.

"Boy, this last year of school is going to be hard on you. How are you going to handle the load?"

"Well, I don't have much choice," replied Brad. "Mom and Dad said one D will cost me my job and two will cost me my horse. So, I guess I'll be burning the night oil, but it'll be easy."

"You call that easy?" questioned an amused Pat.

"Yup."

"How do you call that easy?"

"It's easy because, like I said, I don't have a choice. There won't be time to ask myself whether I want to shoot hoops or do a term paper. Because I'll know I only have time for the paper."

"Well, let me know how I can help," Pat said earnestly. "I want to see you competing in the All-Morgan next year." Pat continued, "So when are you going to McMichael's?"

"I don't even know where they are," responded Brad. "They're not in our phone book, I checked last night. I'll have to ask Mrs. Wheaten."

"What do you think Mrs. Wheaten will say when you tell her you can't work for her anymore?"

"Dunno. I guess I'll find out tonight."

As soon as the kids returned to Wheatens', Pat excused herself, hopped in her car, and headed home. Brad backed Burgie from the trailer and walked her to her stall. He pulled off her shipping boots, checked her water, and tossed her a flake of hay. He had backed the trailer up to the spigot and was hosing down the floorboards when Mr. Wheaten came out from behind the barn. Brad thought he looked even more weary than usual.

"Hey, boy, just the guy I was looking for." Mr. Wheaten stopped for breath after every few words. Brad worried for Chuck Wheaten. He had never seen anyone have a heart attack before, but wondered whether this tired auctioneer might, one day soon, have his first.

"We're losing the foundation on the back wall," panted Mr. Wheaten. "It's been leaning for years, but now it's just giving way. I'm afraid if we don't do something about it, we'll lose that whole section. With this bad back, there's no way I can repair it my myself." Brad turned off the water and wound up the hose as Mr. Wheaten continued.

"Between your young back and my old brain, I think we could handle the cement and block work." Brad listened intently.

"Think you're up for a big job?" asked Mr. Wheaten.

"When are you thinking of getting started?" Brad queried.

"Well, seems to me you got school starting in another month, and winter setting in pretty quick after that. If we can get the bulk of it done in August, it'd be right good." He hesitated, hating to humble himself, then continued. "It's a big job, boy. Will take some long hours. Don't know if I can pay you right up front. . . ."

Brad finished Mr. Wheaten's line of thought. "Might have to wait 'til near October when you sell off some of the summer riding stable horses?"

Chuck Wheaten asked, "Is that all right with you?" To himself, he mumbled, *No one should be this old and not have a cash reserve. Living hand-to-mouth; that's what it's called.*

Brad's brain was whirring. This might fit in perfectly with his plan, but first, he needed to talk to Dorie and his folks.

"Can I let you know tomorrow, Mr. Wheaten? I mean, I do want the job, but my folks are planning to go up to Houghton Lake for a couple weeks and, with this being my last summer before graduation, they want me with them. I'll talk to them tonight. Okay?"

"Okay," Chuck replied and softly slapped his palms on his belly. "I like you, boy," he added as he turned back into the barn.

"What's that, Mr. Wheaten?" Brad called after him.

"Nothing," answered Chuck as he disappeared from sight.

Brad pondered Mr. Wheaten's offer and wondered where he might find Dorie. He hopped in the cab of Wheatens' truck and towed the horse trailer over to the fencerow. Wheeling the rig around, he deftly backed it up to the fence. Once unhooked, he drove to the front of the auction barn. He could see Dorie through the office window, reviewing a pile of papers on her desk. She looked up when Brad entered the room.

"Oh, just the man I want to see," she said cheerfully. "Grab a chair."

Brad pulled a chair near the desk and made himself comfortable, as Dorie searched through the mound of paperwork.

"Here it is," she said as she retrieved a small slip of paper and handed it across the desk. Brad took the sheet from her hand. It contained only a telephone number.

"I took the liberty of calling a couple of big stables for you," she began. Brad looked at her and the slip of paper inquisitively. She continued. "Joe McMichael was the first to say he could use a general handyman this fall. Mostly stall cleaning and manure spreading, but maybe some odd jobs, too." Brad didn't follow Dorie's line of thought and couldn't hide the puzzlement on his face.

"Gosh, Mrs. Wheaten, are you telling me I'm fired?"

"No, no, Brad. You could work for us forever as far as I'm concerned. But remember our conversation last week, when you said you wanted to work Burgie on your own?"

"Well, of course I do," returned Brad.

"Seems to me," continued Dorie, "that you're going to need help from somewhere, and a lot of it. If you won't, or can't, hire a trainer, then I figured you'd need to somehow get close to one."

Brad was amazed. This was exactly what he had been thinking. He had come up to Dorie's office hoping to get McMichael's telephone number and address. Now, he was getting those, plus a referral.

"Mrs. Wheaten," Brad asked with some hesitation.

"Yes?"

"Did you tell them I have Burgie?"

"No, I didn't, Brad. I figure that's your business, not mine."

Brad pressed the issue.

"Do you think Evan McMichael will remember me from the day he brought Burgie here for the sale?"

"I doubt that, Brad. Evan had a lot on his mind that day. When I talked to him on the phone yesterday, he never asked what became of Burgie."

"Good," replied Brad. "I don't want them to think I'm spying on them while they're training their horses."

Dorie smiled slyly, "Oh, but you are, Brad! But I don't think Joe and Evan McMichael will worry about any of their stable help stealing their training secrets."

"Why not?" questioned Brad defensively.

"Because knowing how to do it and being able to do it are two different things. Understanding horse behavior and horse-training techniques is just one part of the process." Dorie continued, "A great trainer knows the heart of a horse and rides from the horse's heart. He intuitively knows how to turn a good horse into a great horse."

Brad pondered Dorie's commentary.

"Maybe," he mused, "the horse is already a great horse, but average people can't see its potential. A good trainer, however, might have the eye to see the promise in the untrained animal."

Now Dorie pondered Brad's summation. "So, you're saying they get more winners because they know what to look for in the first place."

"Right."

"Well, I'm sure that's got a lot to do with it." Dorie smiled. "One way or another, you've got a lot of catching up to do before you go in the ring against the McMichaels. Brad," she added earnestly, "I'll do everything I can to support your effort, even if it means encouraging you to leave the auction barn. I want to see this happen for you."

Brad stared at the telephone number in his hand. "I really appreciate this."

Dorie responded without hesitation. "You've been the best young worker we've had here. You're a hard worker, independent, and dependable. Chuck and I have never had to follow up to see whether you're getting a job done, or done right. And, we've never had to worry whether you were going to show up for work." Dorie continued, "It's not hard to give a recommendation to an employee who has earned it."

Brad glanced at Dorie and back at the paper in his hand. Sometimes it's as uncomfortable to accept a compliment as it is a complaint, and Brad shifted in his seat.

Dorie continued, "Brad, I think it's your dependability and quiet determination that has gotten you this far. It will serve you well when you take Burgie onto the class A circuit next spring. She's going to need that kind of effort if she's going to be a consistent and dependable performer. But," she added with quiet resolution, "there's something missing."

"I know," mused Brad in response.

"What do you know?" queried Dorie.

"I know what's missing," said Brad.

Dorie just waited, staring at the boy. Brad stretched his legs out in front of him, raised his arms tight above his head in a huge stretch, and then relaxed again, as if to say he needed to draw this conversation to a close.

Dorie pressed, "What do you think I was going to say?"

Brad learned forward, put his elbows on his knees, and looked straight at Dorie. "You were going to say the missing element is that I won't know how to light a real fire under her. That I'm not a dynamic person."

"And how do you mean?" coaxed Dorie.

"Being on the edge," continued Brad. "I've seen it in the ring. The best English pleasure horses are vibrant; the park horses even more so. I'm a quiet, observant kind of guy and you're wondering how I'm going to put a spark in her if I'm not really very aggressive."

Now Dorie knew she and Brad were talking at the same level. She pondered her response carefully, knowing what she said could make or break the boy's effort in this all-important endeavor. "Brad," she began, "it's your solid dependability and consistent determination that has gotten you this far. Third-place ribbons your first year out, with no prior show experience and no help from professional trainers, is an honor for which you should be proud. And I bet you do have a burn in your belly to take Burgie to the Morgan championships. Maybe, even the world championships the year after. I just think Burgie might need sixty days in a show barn to give her that edge before the season opens."

Brad stood to leave, not wanting to contemplate that suggestion right now. "Hey," he said, "I almost forgot why I came by in the first place."

"What's that?" asked Dorie.

"Well, Mr. Wheaten's talking about this foundation job. Do you know about it?"

"Some," said Dorie. "I was looking at the blocks yesterday with Chuck. They're really buckling under that back hip, and we can't afford to lose those ten back stalls."

"Well, I've got a proposition to offer," Brad continued.

"Go for it," quipped Dorie.

"If I get this job at McMichael's and don't want to tell them I have Burgie, then I need to keep her here."

Dorie listened and mused. "I suspect Chuck will want a hundred and fifty a month for her stall and feed, maybe more if you want the boys to clean her stall along with the others."

"No, I'll take care of her stall." Brad did not add that he wasn't exactly impressed with the effort the other boys put into their stall cleaning. "But how about if we keep a running tally of my pay for the foundation work and we can just take it out in board for Burgie?"

Dorie didn't know that Chuck had already admitted to Brad that they were strapped for cash. However, she was sure Chuck would agree to this proposition.

"It's a deal," she smiled. "Now go call Evan McMichael."

Brad got almost to the minivan before a final question hit him. He jogged back across the porch, into the barn foyer, and Dorie's office.

"Hey, if you didn't tell Mr. McMichael that I have Burgie and want to spy, why did you tell him I wanted to leave here and apply for a job with them?"

"Oh, that was easy," Dorie explained. "Evan called here about some extra hay they wanted to sell. He wondered whether that was something we could move through here. During our conversation, he was complaining about not being able to get or keep enough good help. That gave me an opening. I told him we had a fair number of boys going into the winter with us and one, in particular, who had two years with us and was very dependable."

Her smile got bigger. "So he said as a joke, 'Can I steal him?' and I said, it would be unfair of me not to pass his offer on."

Brad was satisfied with her explanation but another question lingered. "How did you come to know the McMichaels?" he asked.

"Oh, Joe and we go way back," Dorie mused. "He called this week and asked Chuck if he might want to do some horse hauling for them. They do the sunshine circuit through Texas, across to Alabama, and into Florida during the winter and are short on drivers for the big rigs."

"Is Mr. Wheaten going to do it?" asked Brad, wondering how the auction barn would survive without him.

"Oh, no," said Dorie. "Chuck hasn't kept up his trucker's license and isn't interested in working for the McMichaels." Her voice trailed off somewhere else, maybe to another time but then came quickly back. "He likes to work for himself," she said with a failed attempt at being cheery. "Get out of here now; I've got bookkeeping to do."

Dorie Wheaten sat at her desk and watched through the window as Brad drove away, but she didn't go back to her books. Her mind slipped away, twenty-five years away, to a time when she and Chuck, and Joe McMichael were all younger. . . .

22

August was an all-consuming month. There never was a Bateman family trip to Houghton Lake. That was just a ruse to put Mr. Wheaten off until Brad could talk to Dorie. Cindy, however, had gone out west for the first two weeks of the month, leaving Brad plenty of time to dig into rebuilding the foundation on Wheaten's barn. After setting roof supports with six-by-six upright beams, and leasing a Bobcat to dig out the old foundation blocks, Brad set to work sledgehammering and yanking out the broken cement. He was amazed to find a mammoth base of large boulders below the crumbled blocks.

"Who built this barn?" he exclaimed.

Chuck laughed gruffly and spit to the side as he helped as much as his back would allow. "This here part of the barn is a hundred years old," he boasted. "They knew how to set a barn in those days. Bet those boulders go a good three or four feet deep."

"Is that for drainage?" asked Brad.

"Yup. They didn't mess around if they knew they were gunna have livestock in here."

Brad pondered such an effort made a hundred years ago by men who were long since dead. He stared at the hand-hewn overhead beams as if seeing them for the very first time, and gained a whole new respect for the ancient building. Suddenly, he felt he was one of those men who had built this mammoth structure so long ago. He wasn't just saving a crumbling wall; he was preserving a masterpiece.

Brad went about his work with a new and different vigor. On the way home, he stopped at the small Linden Library and scoured the shelves for books on old barns. With the help of the computer files, he found a couple of books. One was a picture book of New England barns and another's topic was the general construction of modern outbuildings. Not exactly what he was looking for, but he took them anyway. At the librarian's desk, his eye caught a display book propped on a tripod, "Pictorial History of Linden," published by the Linden Historical Society. Brad leafed through the pages and saw a lithograph of a community barn raising. He added the book to his stack and headed home.

Every afternoon, when he stepped from his mom's van, Brad's muscles would call out to him viciously. The drive home from the cement pouring and block setting was just long enough to let the stiffness set sorely into his lower back, his thighs, and his neck. Upon arriving home, the hottest of showers was always his most cherished friend. But after dinner, when the air began to cool, Brad would head back to the barn to work Burgie. Often it was just a trail ride through the woods, across fields, or down the country road. He knew keeping miles on her would keep her fit and solid through the winter months.

Only on Mondays did Brad not ride. He chose Monday as Burgie's day off because, when school started, that would most likely be his busiest day. His senior class schedule had been set before school let out last June. At the insistence of his parents, he maintained his college prep curriculum with Algebra III, Life Sciences II, and Advanced Composition. However, his electives were his choice and he added two more building-trades courses: Electrical Science and Computer-Assisted Architectural Drafting. He had scheduled study hall as his sixth hour.

☆   ☆   ☆

It was well into the second week in August before Evan McMichael could schedule Brad for an employment interview. The older McMichael was out of town negotiating sales and purchases of horses for a number of his clients. Brad was to meet Evan at eight o'clock in the evening. He wasn't sure what to wear for the interview; after all, it was primarily a stall-cleaning job. He decided on clean jeans. He bypassed a T-shirt, truly appropriate for stall cleaning on a hot August day, for a short-sleeved plaid cotton shirt. It had been a Christmas gift from an aunt and he didn't like it and rarely wore it, but it seemed just neat enough for a manual labor job interview. He also decided to wear his leather hiking boots but took his rubber muckers along just in case.

McMichaels lived in Northville, more than a half hour away. Brad would have to figure the extra time and gas money into his budget. As he reeled the minivan around the corner onto Horrigan Road, he slowed to read the house numbers. A thousand digits off, he knew he had about a mile to go. As he approached the McMichaels', he didn't need the address to clue him in. Ahead, he saw what appeared to be miles of white fencing looming up to greet him. Each side of the drive was graced with a chest-high white brick pillar, flat on top supporting concrete lions, also painted white and sitting royally. Brad wondered whether the big cats were there to welcome visitors or guard the house. Beside one of the pillars was a large sign, suspended by chains on its own wood posts. The sign was gray, black, and royal blue. In bold letters, it said, McMICHAELS' TRAINING CENTER. Beneath that it said American Morgan Horses. And, still below that it said Training, Breeding, Sales. Finally, in smaller letters but no less impressive, it said, Standing at Stud: Moriah's Black Magic. Brad remembered admiring the handsome stallion as he stormed the ring to win the Junior Park Harness Championship at the Michigan All-Morgan. He must be one of their up-and-coming stars, thought Brad as he pulled into the drive.

There were no buildings in sight as Brad idled his van up the winding tree-lined drive; only paddocks on either side of him, each sporting a few horses. The drive went over a small rise and, as the minivan reached the crest, two barns, two houses, and a huge steel building with long hip additions stretched off to his right. Beyond that, the blacktop drive wound around a curve, through a woodlot, and disappeared.

Brad passed the first house, a neat brick ranch, and parked near the first barn. It appeared to be strictly for equipment. There were two baling elevators, a grain grinder, a number of galvanized steel water troughs, and three red pipe-iron hay feeders. Shelves and hooks on the wall held rubber water buckets, hoses, and containers of various sizes and shapes. A corner harbored shovels, rakes, and pitchforks. Brad pondered what he saw. It was all physically too far away from the horse barn. He guessed that this must all be extra stuff in storage for future use.

Brad wandered across a drive, large enough to house a semi-truck cab, a fair-sized stock truck, and two horse trailers. All these vehicles had the McMichael name painted ornately on their sides. Brad recognized the van that delivered Burgie to him nearly a year ago.

The second barn was a handsome, well-maintained gambrel roof structure. Its hayloft, with its high exterior door swung open, billowed with fresh green, newly baled hay. Late second or early third cutting, thought Brad. The sound and smell of horses lured him inside. The cool paved center aisle cradled huge, double-size box stalls on either side. Every stall—Brad counted eight— housed a lactating mare with a foal at her side. They had apparently been brought in from the day field not long ago, as Brad noticed water buckets filled to their brim with clear, clean water and corner racks filled with sweet-smelling hay. Most of the mares were more interested in their dinner than in Brad. The quiet munching gave the barn a most welcoming aura. Down at the far end, one mare kicked at her stall wall, disrupting the otherwise peaceful nursery. Brad dallied to check out the foals. Some were bay and some chestnut, most with some sort of white facial marking—a star or strip, a snip on the nose, or some combination of these. A few sported white socks or stockings on one or more leg. All of them had the curliest tails, short and sweet, flicking up and down and to and fro as they suckled warm milk from their dam's bag, or competed with her for a sprig of hay. Tiny, curly mane hair sprouted upward from their necks. Most looked at Brad with timid curiosity but did not venture away from their dams. One, however, a little chestnut with two low white hind socks and the most curious of facial markings, ventured boldly toward the front of his stall. He had a huge white star, diminishing into a curved white strip at its bottom. Brad thought it looked like a big comma . . . a comet . . . a shooting star. "Comet" was not at all shy. He stuck his furry muzzle between the stall bars, his head rolling and body wiggling, trying to introduce himself. Brad reached through the bars to pet the little fellow between the eyes. Comet, however, wiggled his head, stretching his flapping lips to the hem of Brad's shirtsleeve. Brad slid his hand down Comet's face and playfully squeezed the bottom of his chin. "Ouch!" Somehow, Comet had managed to wiggle just right and chomped down hard on Brad's fingers.

"Man alive!" gasped the startled teen. "You've got teeth!" Upon closer and more careful inspection, Brad discovered that this little colt had a mouthful of surprisingly large incisors. He guessed this baby to be no more than three months old simply because he knew that most pleasure horses foaled in the late spring. "How does your mother allow you to nurse?" Brad asked Comet emphatically. Comet's dam pulled her head from her hay rack and turned to look at Brad with weary resignation. It was as if she were saying, "Yeah, buddy, I agree with you!"

"Don't worry. We'll be weaning these foals soon."

Startled, Brad turned to see Evan McMichael leaning against one of the stalls.

"I'm sorry," ventured the still startled teen. "Should I not be in here?"

"You're fine. I just came over to see what this here mare was fussing about. I could hear her kicking her stall way over from the other barn." The mare in question stood quietly under the watchful eye of the younger McMichael, as if saying, "Who? Me?"

Evan walked near to Brad and joined in playing with the frisky Comet. "Actually," Evan continued, "these young'uns show their teeth before they're a week old. You'll catch them stretching for grass in the field on their third or fourth day."

"How long do they nurse?" asked Brad.

Evan pondered his reply. "Oh, as long as their dam will let them, which is a good year, if we don't intervene. We usually wean them at about four months. Sometimes sooner," he added, "if the mare is getting ribby, having trouble holding weight." He motioned up and down the aisle with his hand. "Most of these mares are already re-bred for next spring."

Brad raised his brows with interest, and then said, "I like this little fellow. Is he yours?"

"Oh, no," answered Evan. "Did I hear you call him Comet?"

"Yeah," Brad rubbed Comet's forehead. "Doesn't this look like a shooting star?"

Evan mused, then replied, "Shooting Star. I like that. I'll have to mention it to Mrs. Prescott. This here's Andy's new foal." Motioning to Comet's dam, he added, "Brandy, here, is Mrs. Prescott's favorite mare. She said she's keeping this foal for their boy, Andy. He's about your age. A good kid. You'll like him."

At this, Evan stuck out his hand to formally meet Brad, "You must be the kid Mrs. Wheaten sent over. I'm Evan McMichael. My dad, Joe, and I co-own the training center. Stan and Judy Prescott own the farm."

Brad returned Evan's handshake. He didn't understand how one family could own the business while another family owned the farm. He made a mental note to ask his folks whether they could explain. More importantly, thought Brad, it was obvious that Evan did not at all recognize him. *I must have been a total nobody the day he delivered Burgie,* he concluded. Which was exactly what he had hoped.

"Yes, I'm Brad Bateman," he responded out loud. "I understand you've got some stalls to clean." Evan turned to walk away and motioned for Brad to follow.

"Well, not quite yet. We're losing two good helpers in September. Sue's leaving right after Labor Day. She'll be taking an overload at Washtenaw Community. Her folks say they'll pay her tuition, but they want her studying, not working. Skip won't be leaving 'til mid-month. He's pre-vet over at State and they start later." He turned to Brad, "Are you a college fellow?"

"No, or not yet," Brad answered, a bit surprised by the question. He was tickled that Evan thought he looked old enough. "I'm starting my senior year at . . . high school," he finished. He decided not to say Linden High because he didn't want Evan wondering why he was willing to drive so far for a stall-cleaning job. After all, there were a million fast food restaurants looking for dependable help between Linden and Northville. To quickly change the subject, he added, "How many stalls do you have here?"

"Fifty-two," Evan said matter-of-factly." Forty in the main barn, eight here in the foaling barn, and four in a side barn."

"I guess I had noticed another barn," Brad responded, carrying the conversation along as they continued toward the huge steel building.

"It's a transition barn. All new horses coming on the premises are kept there until we're comfortable moving them in with the others. Even if their papers indicate they're up on their shots, we don't want to risk bringing in any contagious diseases."

Brad nodded in agreement but thought how dozens of strange horses were mingled together every weekend at Wheatens' barn—and Dorie never asked at the registration window whether they're up on their shots. Brad was already getting an education and he had not yet even been offered the job.

Evan strode through a wide-open slider, but Brad couldn't help but stop long enough to let his eyes consume what was before him. All the way down his right, for a hundred-and-twenty feet, stretched twenty box stalls. They graced both sides of a wide cement aisle, impeccably clean and well lit. Brightly painted blue and gold tack trunks dotted the aisle in front of some of the stalls. Three quarters of the way down, a bay gelding stood patiently in his cross-ties. A middle-aged woman rummaged noisily in her tack trunk, searching possibly for a favorite body brush or mane comb.

Ahead of him, on his left and perpendicular to the stall hip was an extensive expanse of glass windows. Behind them, Brad could see a darkened room but light from the huge arena before him cast shadows through the window, illuminating the couches and lamps of a comfortable observation room. The bright red and blue lights of a Pepsi cooler added a glow across a handsome table. An impressive room for a barn, thought Brad, and Mountain Dew on site! What more could a kid ask for?

On the far side of the arena, an open slider exposed darkness beyond. It was obvious to Brad that an identical set of twenty stalls filled the far hip. A lone horse was working in the arena. Its chestnut body was encumbered with what Brad would later learn was a bitting rig. It looked somewhat like a lightweight buggy harness but with no buggy behind. From the bit on the horse's bridle, two long lines extended through rings on the body harness. The near line extended twenty feet across the arena, its end resting in the left palm of a young man, possibly in his early twenties. The right line, on the far side of the animal, came around the horse's hip, across the twenty-foot expanse between horse and handler and found its home in his right hand. The horse's head was set high and steady, its nose tucked, causing an elegant arch in the crest of its graceful neck. A light set of weight chains encircled each hoof, and white rubber bell boots were strapped on the horse's front feet. The handler clucked to the horse, encouraging it to continue a 40-foot circle to the left, around his own body.

An advanced form of lunging, thought Brad. Rather than loose and relaxed, this horse was being asked to maintain a collected, steady working trot. He made an immediate mental note of the apparatus in hopes that he could duplicate its parts back at Wheatens' barn.

Brad followed Evan as he continued toward the dark hip at the far end of the observation room. The glass windows stopped thirty feet before the end and the solid wall sported a wood slider. As Brad neared, Evan slid the door along its top rail and reached in to flick a light switch, exposing a neat and well-stocked equipment room. There were wheelbarrows and muck baskets, a garden tractor with a pull-behind wagon, and stacks of clean rubber water buckets. The walls were lined with hooks supporting forks, rakes, and brooms. It was apparent to Brad that the entire operation was designed with efficiency in mind. Here, the buildings had been built to support the business. It was so unlike Wheaten's, where a business had been squeezed into available buildings.

"This is where you start," said Evan. "Dad said that if you're coming here with a recommendation from Dorie Wheaten, then we can trust you know how to use your noggin. But I gotta tell ya," he added, "we do things different here so let me give you some tips."

As he talked, Evan turned off the light, stepped away from the equipment room, and slid the door closed. Brad followed him to the darkened doorway ahead. Soft streams of light from the setting sun filtered through small barred windows in each stall. It cast an eerie look down the long aisleway and Brad could see that it was, in fact, a replica of the opposite side of the barn. Even though the light was dim, the familiar smell and sound of horses made Brad feel right at home.

Evan switched on the overhead lights. The horses in the near stalls squinted and blinked as their eyes adjusted. The two men walked the length of these twenty stalls, again ten on each side, as Evan continued his instruction.

"How often are the stalls picked or cleaned at the auction barn?" he asked.

"Well," said Brad, "the horses are all run through the auction on Saturday night and after they're sold, a lot of them are left in their stalls until Sunday, or sometimes Monday. So, I come around on Tuesday and Wednesday and clean all the stalls right down to the dirt. We kick a bale of straw open in each one and the new horses begin to arrive on Thursday and Friday. Then we start all over." He added, "I see you don't use straw here. Are those wood chips I'm looking at?"

"We use baled shavings," Evan answered. "They're kept in a semi-trailer behind the barn. I'll show you where later." Then he explained, "We don't scrape our stalls out once a week. We pick them twice daily. You'll be responsible for the twenty stalls on this side, plus the four in the transition barn. Plan on an hour and a half in the morning and a couple hours at night. We'd like you here all day on Saturday to help with odd jobs and you've got Sundays off. Can you handle that?" he concluded matter of factly.

Brad had not anticipated a morning schedule. He knew immediately he would have to switch his study hall to first hour, plus he'd have to figure on gas money for two trips a day. The thought crossed his mind that maybe the job wasn't worth the effort, but he decided he'd have time to decide that later.

"Yes, I can handle that," he answered.

"Good." Evan reached out to shake Brad's hand to seal the deal. "Six bucks an hour and we'll expect to see you here by six A.M. the first Tuesday after Labor Day."

As Brad headed for his van, he turned back to Evan. "Just out of curiosity—how do you know Mrs. Wheaten?" he asked.

"I don't," Evan replied. "I met her just once when I delivered a horse to her barn, but I guess my father knows her. He said they went to high school together." With that he waved goodnight and headed for the smaller of the two houses. Brad could see a woman, presumably Evan's wife, holding the front door open. A toddler was wrapped around her leg.

23

The following Friday night, Cindy Ramsey couldn't wait for the plane to land at Detroit Metropolitan Airport. Two weeks with west coast relatives had been two weeks too long. There were no teens out there so her time had been spent visiting with older women about things that did not interest her at all. Sometimes, she had wandered off on her own, discovering a shopping place or a beach to roam. Now, she couldn't wait to get home to see Pogie and call Brad.

She was disappointed to learn Brad could not see her right away Saturday morning. He planned on watching a buddy, Pat Spielman, run a road race up in Flint. He asked if there was a chance she could come up and join them for the fun and festivities but, as she expected, her mom said it was too early in the morning for her to be gallivanting across the state the very morning they returned from vacation. It was true she'd have to leave the house by five in the morning to be at Brad's on time to drive together into Flint, but what's the diff, she wondered. Five A.M. starts were routine on horse show days. Cindy shook her head, wondering how parents came up with the crazy dictates that only served to slow down ambitious teenagers.

Still, Brad and Cindy agreed to go to a movie on Tuesday night and spent the rest of their telephone chat discussing the youth club's upcoming trip to Cedar Point Amusement Park. The call did not last as long as they would have liked. Long distance by phone can put a real damper on a budding relationship. They both went to bed that night dreaming of Tuesday night at the movies, and then a full day together at Cedar Point the following weekend. The youth group planned to spend the entire day and evening enjoying the rides. When one adds the three-hour bus trip each way, that would mean Cindy and Brad would spend sixteen nonstop hours of fun together.

24

It was five-thirty when Pat Spielman rolled out of bed Saturday morning. After downing a bagel and a single cup of strong coffee, she waited for the sound of Brad's van. She had not been excited about having Brad pick her up at her house, but he insisted it would make her morning easier if she didn't have to find a parking spot when they got to Flint. She heard the van pull into the drive and slipped out, locking the door behind her, not waiting for Brad to meet her at the door. She tossed her gym bag on the floor and slid onto the passenger seat. Brad couldn't help but notice that the house was dark. There appeared to be no life at all stirring beyond the home's stark windows. He could not imagine, for the life of him, how Pat's parents could be sound asleep on the biggest morning of their daughter's life. He thought it best not to ask. Instead, he leaned over, planted a secure kiss on her bare left shoulder and swung the van into reverse. As he backed into the street, Pat asked with surprise, "What was *that* for?"

"It's a good luck kiss from Burgie, who happens to be very upset that we didn't invite her along."

"A kiss from Burgie? I'll tell you what, Brad Bateman. If I win this race, I'd better get a kiss from you!"

"I'll make you a deal," he offered. "If you even finish the race, just make it over the line, I'll give you a kiss and take you to lunch."

"That's a deal I'll accept," said Pat. Then she added with emphasis, "And I do plan on making you pay up."

Brad delivered the young runner to the community college parking area, which had been designated for the start of the race. As Pat headed toward the registration banner, Brad was surprised at how quickly she was consumed by the crowd. There were thousands of people in town to run the Crim, plus all their family and friends. Local people, many of who thought the Crim was the run of their lives, were on hand, plus hundreds of people from all across the nation who would chalk the Crim up as one more qualifier in preparation for future twenty-six mile marathons. Still others had arrived from numerous foreign countries—serious life-long runners and Olympic contenders.

Even with the depth of mission placed upon this road race by so many serious competitors, it did not dissipate the light-hearted festivities that surrounded the entire event. There were mini-runners, stress walkers, and wheelchair contenders, all of whom took their divisions seriously. Then there was the teddy bear run for the little kids, and barbecues, street music, face painting, and activity tents throughout the downtown area.

Upon losing sight of Pat, Brad decided to re-park his van downtown, nearer the finish line, and find a place to stand where he would, hopefully, see her cross the finish line. He had considered positioning himself somewhere along the ten-mile raceway, which wound its way from the college, through the numerous surrounding residential neighborhoods, past a city golf course, until finally ending on Saginaw Street in the heart of the city. However, the crowds were gathering quickly and he didn't want to risk losing a position near the finish line.

At eight A.M. sharp, the first round of runners hit the street. Forty minutes later, Pat was nearing Bradley Street. She had held her own extremely well for the first six miles, then she turned onto the hills of Bradley Street. To any non-runner, Bradley is just a pretty area in a quiet neighborhood, nestled between one of the nation's first General Motors manufacturing plants and the McLaren Regional Medical Center. However, for the Crim competitors, the three graceful hills of tree-lined Bradley Street loom up like the back of a mean and spiteful serpent. It calls out to and entices the tired runners, *Come, lay on me, collapse on my beautiful green lawns, end your racing career here with me.* Only the lean of muscle and brave of heart survive. Those who chose to see the three consecutive hills as an enemy would surely succumb to them, but Pat was not one of those. She stared at the pavement directly in front of her. Her feet hit the concrete, one then the other, one then the other. She dared not look at the rise and fall ahead.

Come into me, you spiteful serpent, she thought. *I am melting into you. We are becoming one and together, we will roll to Court*

Street and be done with it. A few minutes later she found herself rounding the corner and leaving the serpent behind. She passed the eight-mile marker, painted boldly in blue on the pavement. Crowds of friendly homeowners held paper cups of water in outstretched arms so runners could grab them without slowing down. Pat splashed her face with the warm liquid and threw the empty cup to the ground, trampling dozens of other cups from runners, mostly men, who had gone before her.

She had two miles to go. She had survived Bradley Street, but now she "hit the wall." Only a runner who has pushed herself beyond her own belief can describe "the wall." It's not really there but it's definitely there—unrelenting and impenetrable. It is the point where even the best runners can fail. Their bodies aching, their brains numb, they just can't find the reserve energy to finish. Pat was at that point. Her sides ached; her stomach was sick, her head was light.

Suddenly, she heard a snort, a sound so alien to the city. Could it have been a dog that barked? Then she heard the clink of steady hooves chink-chinking on pebbles on a country road. Her feet continued to hit the pavement one after the other, one after the other, as she searched for the source of the sounds. Bbllt, bbllt, bbllt, bbllt. It was the steady exhalation of breath from Burgie's huge nostrils as she trotted, leg-for-leg in time with Pat. Pat was no longer on Court Street. Her mind was on her favorite country road with Burgie and Brad right at her side. The sweaty smell of horse flesh filled her head and the hooves continued their chink-chink as the motion of the horse carried her mind, her legs, and her spirit across the ground.

Just as suddenly, Burgie was gone. Pat was astonished to find she was rounding the corner and heading north on the historic red brick of Saginaw Street. The crowds were cheering as their favored runners appeared before them. The noise of the people, jubilation of the human spirit, entered her body and carried her toward the finish line. Did she do it? Had she done it? The crowd and the noise turned to a blur and she felt herself collapsing, falling, falling, and floating into space. Her mind was drifting into infinity; her battered body was nonexistent. A meteor or a star flashed before her. Later she would learn it was the bright blast flash of a newspaper reporter's camera.

25

"Hi, Cindy!" It was Sunday morning and Linda Cramer was rolling a small grain barrel on two wheels down the aisle at the Ramsey Stables. At each stall she'd stop and shovel a scoop of sweet feed through the stall bars to a waiting grain bin. "I wondered where you were yesterday."

"I was out here around nine o'clock," Cindy replied, giving Linda a warm embrace. "Mom and I went school shopping. We didn't get home until late." She added, "You took good care of my Pogie while I was out west. He acts like he didn't even miss me."

"He did just fine," laughed Linda. "And you're right. He didn't miss you one iota. Probably enjoyed his vacation, too, lying around doing nothing."

After a friendly conversation and the meting out of an entire bag of carrots to her favored horses, Cindy wandered back up to the house. She had hoped to see Brad soon after her return from the west coast, but yesterday he was consumed with his buddy's road race and today he planned to spend the entire afternoon finishing up the foundation repair at Wheatens'. He had feared that, if he didn't get the job done this week, he might not be able to get away for the Cedar Point trip.

Cindy dallied around the kitchen, snooping for something good for breakfast. Bypassing the various boxes of cereal, she finally settled on a banana and two pieces of cinnamon toast. She set her plate across from her mom and went to the refrigerator for a glass of milk. A small red corgi pup scampered after her socks, begging for attention.

Mrs. Ramsey was buried behind the Sunday edition of the *Ann Arbor News.*

"Say, didn't you mention that boy of yours was at the race in Flint?" she asked, cup of coffee in one hand, paper in the other.

"Yeah, why?" responded Cindy as she plopped onto her chair.

"Because this looks just like him," said Mrs. Ramsey as she handed the sports section to her daughter. Cindy stared in disbelief. There on the front page was her Brad, planting a kiss on the exhausted body of a very female runner! The caption read, "Pat Spielman, 16, of Linden, collapses in the arms of friend, Brad Bateman, 17, also of Linden, after winning the Women's Junior Division of Saturday's Bobby Crim Ten-Mile Road Race in Flint." Cindy's stomach turned somersaults.

"I thought Pat was a guy," murmured Cindy out loud. Her mom looked over her section of the paper.

"Looks to me like she's more than just a girl. Looks to me like she's a girlfriend," observed Mrs. Ramsey.

Cindy couldn't take her eyes off the paper. She really had not known Brad for very long. Had she jumped to conclusions because of their wonderful evening at the All-Morgan? The cinnamon toast no longer appealed to her. Cindy rose from the chair and headed for the door, paper still in hand.

"Cindy, please come back and put your dishes in the sink," chided Mrs. Ramsey.

The despondent girl turned and stared at her mom. Blankly, she returned to the table and, without responding verbally, dropped her plate, toast and all, into the sudsy dishpan. Rita Ramsey watched with quiet contemplation.

"Honey," she asked. "Do I sense there's a little more to your relationship with this boy than I might have thought?"

Cindy left the kitchen. "Probably not," she mumbled as she headed for her room.

26

Mr. Wheaten and Brad did not finish their block work on Sunday, but by sundown on Monday they had completed all but the cleanup. They stood back in the dusk to admire their work.

"I can't believe it's done," said Brad, shaking his work-weary head.

"Well, my back's telling me it's done. And I'm done!" added Chuck Wheaten. "My back's saying, 'You go get yourself a cold beer, Chuck Wheaten.' That's what my back's saying." Then he added, "You want a beer, kid?"

Brad ignored the offer. Instead, he suggested, "How's about we clean up the mess on Wednesday?"

"Sounds fine to me," said Chuck as they wandered around the front of the barn.

"Good," finished Brad. "Then with all due respect, you can expect to see neither hide nor hair of me tomorrow. I'm outta here."

Chuck put his hand on Brad's shoulder as they walked. "I enjoyed working with you, boy," he said. "Dorie tells me we're losing you to the McMichael's this fall."

"That's right, Mr. Wheaten. I'm hoping to pick up some training tips while I'm over there."

"Dorie didn't offer?" Mr. Wheaten asked.

"Offer what?" queried Brad.

"Oh, nothing. So yer goin' for the big time, are ya?" Chuck shook his head. "Waste of time 'n' money if'n ya ask me," he added.

Brad didn't respond to Mr. Wheaten's comment. He just slid slowly into his van and drove home, exhausted.

The Bateman house was like a tomb Tuesday morning. As the world went about its usual daily business, Brad slept the entire day away. His alarm, set for ten o'clock rang, but a sleeping hand reached up, turned it off, and returned to blissful oblivion. The phone rang a few times down in the kitchen, too far away to jar the spent boy awake. No one picked up and the answering machine clicked on. Mrs. Bateman's voice would rattle on in the empty room, "Hello, you've reached the Bateman's. We're not home but if you leave a message . . ." Some callers did, and some did not, but Brad dozed on. Eleven o'clock. Noon. One o'clock. His work-weary body was mending and rejuvenating itself from the inside out. At three in the afternoon, Mrs. Bateman returned home. She did not find a note on the kitchen counter and assumed Brad must be home. A quick survey found him still in bed, belly down, the quiet radio playing in the background. Mrs. Bateman just shook her head and went back downstairs. She knew he deserved a total veg-out day even though she thought she remembered his having an evening date arranged with that young woman who showed horses with him.

At five-thirty, Brad slipped out the back door to head to Cindy's. As he left, Mrs. Bateman called after him. "Hey, Brad, did I get any messages today?"

"I dunno," he called back. "I never heard the phone ring." With that, he was gone.

As Mrs. Bateman watched the van pull away, she glanced at the answering machine and saw the red message light blinking. She pressed the replay button. There were two hang-ups. The third caller left a message.

"Hello? Brad? This is Cindy. I don't think I can go out tonight. Um, well, I think I'm not feeling well. Well, anyway, I'll see you later." Click.

Mrs. Bateman listened to the message a second time. "Sounds to me like she's hedging," she mused.

☆　☆　☆

Brad pulled the slip of paper from his glove box as the van whizzed down the expressway. A quick glance and he was sure he'd have no trouble finding Cindy's house. Although they had spoken briefly by phone last Friday upon her return home from vacation, this would be the first time he'd actually see her since the All-Morgan. He had so much to tell her about decisions he had made, and the part of the plan that he had already set in motion.

As he turned onto Cindy's road, he glanced once more at the paper to confirm the house number. She had said it would not be hard to find: "Watch for a big woodlot on the right, then a paddock with a black fence and a buggy path along the inside of it, then our drive."

As Brad pulled into the drive, he saw her red brick and white wood two-story home on his left with an attached three-car garage along the backside of it. Not far beyond was a huge, white metal horse barn, obviously large enough to accommodate an indoor arena. It was clear that Mr. Ramsey loved his horses, having built his barn so close to his house. There was no lawn between the gravel drive and the barn; just a neat garden area filled with white rock and big black planter boxes brimming with bright red geraniums.

Brad parked in front of the garage and knocked at the back door. Through the screen door he could see over the kitchen table and into the dining room. A yappy corgi was the first to reach the door, announcing his arrival. Brad waited for a long time, but no human answered his second knock, nor the pup's persistent barking. He turned to look around the yard. Rock-N-Roll grazed quietly in the front paddock, but there was no other sign of life. As he wandered past his van and toward the barn, he heard the sound of people and animals inside.

Linda Cramer was working a very young horse in the center of the arena. She had it on an extremely short lunge line and was encouraging it to circle her. The yearling appeared to be more interested in playing with her than in obeying. An older man, maybe in his sixties, was tinkering with the engine of a fair-sized garden tractor in front of the stalls. The wagon it had been pulling was partially full of manure. Cindy was nowhere in sight. Brad watched Linda Cramer quietly, not wanting to intrude. After about five minutes, and some small measure of success, Linda congratulated her yearling with a fond petting about its face. She turned to return the colt to its stall and noticed Brad standing quietly in the doorway.

"Well, hi there, Brad," she offered with kind but reserved friendliness.

"Hi, Linda." Brad sensed her reservation and began to feel just a little uncomfortable. "Cindy's expecting me, but no one seems to be up at the house."

"Oh?" Linda responded, with an obvious hesitation that left Brad definitely uncomfortable. "She was out here a little while ago, grooming Pogie. She didn't look like she was planning on going anywhere."

"Gee, I don't think I have the wrong night. I'm sure we agreed on Tuesday."

Linda acted like she didn't know how to respond, and Brad wasn't sure what he should do. Finally, Linda offered, "Listen, why don't we go to the office and get some paper. You can leave her a note."

"Yeah, I guess I can do that." Brad was crushed. He had so looked forward to tonight. Cindy had been home from vacation for four days. Hadn't she missed him? How could she forget tonight? He was positive he did not have the days confused.

The horse trainer watched Brad scribble a brief note. She could tell he was trying to hide his disappointment. Linda knew what was going on between the two kids because Cindy confided in Linda about everything. When it came to really personal stuff, Cindy told her riding instructor more than she told her own mom. Linda was less judgmental so Cindy found her a safe haven for female problems. Now, though, Linda was wondering why Cindy had not been polite enough to call and cancel tonight's date with Brad. She decided to venture out, just a little, and gather information.

"I hear you have a friend who's a runner."

"Yeah," said Brad. "Pat Spielman. She ran the Crim up in Flint last Saturday. Took first place in her division. It was great." Having something to talk about broke the silence that hung over the office and Brad relaxed a little. He welcomed Linda's hospitality. "We even got our picture in *The Flint Journal*," he added with a tenuous grin.

Linda pondered his quite descriptive response. He obviously was not hiding the fact that this girl was a fairly close friend. She decided to venture a little further.

"Are you a runner, too?"

"Heck, no," laughed Brad. "That sport's for masochists! I'm like you. I'll take a horse's four legs over my own two any day."

Yep, thought Linda to herself. I like this kid. She decided she was going to get all the facts.

"I'm really sorry that you came all the way down here for nothing. You must have a little time on your hands, now. I'd love to hear about the race." She motioned toward a short sofa and then sat herself in the chair beside the desk. Brad accepted her offer and sat on the edge of the sofa, his elbows resting on his knees.

"Well, I'd like to tell you it was great but actually for me, it was a lot of standing around eating hot dogs and hoping I'd see her cross the finish line. But," he added, "it was worth it. To see her coming down Saginaw Street was awesome. I was so impressed."

Linda formulated her questions carefully, not wanting to sound as if she were prying into business that was not hers to know. "So tell me, Brad. If you're not a runner, Pat must be a friend from school?"

"No. I go to Linden High. She attends Lake Linden. They're two different districts." Brad explained how Pat and he met on the road and trained together throughout the summer. How she supported him during the early summer shows, teased him about being consistently beat in the ring by Cindy, encouraged him to get to know Cindy better, and appreciated him being there for her at the Bobby Crim.

Linda Cramer listened with increasing interest as Brad described how Burgie's cross-country trotting served as a pace setter and distance encourager for Pat. "She may not like horses, but she sure loves Burgie!" he concluded with a grin. "And," he added, "I wish you and Cindy could have been at lunch when she described how she was sure that Burgie was actually with her for the last two miles of the race. Man, it was a goose-bump story."

By now, it was clear to Linda that Brad was a just plain good kid and that Cindy had expended a lot of emotional energy jumping to conclusions. She would have to see what she could do to clear up this silly misunderstanding.

"I saw the picture in the paper," she said.

"Really?" Brad asked in surprise. "I didn't think the *Journal* came this far south."

"Surprise, surprise," responded Linda. "It was in the *Ann Arbor News.*"

"Really?!" gasped Brad in gleeful amazement. Suddenly, his face went ashen and he stared bug-eyed at Linda.

"So is that why Cindy stood me up tonight?"

"I'm afraid so," she responded gently. For a moment they just looked at each other, contemplating the situation.

Finally Brad said, "Well . . . will you please tell her I'll call her later tonight?"

Linda started to answer, but before the words passed her lips, a quiet voice came from just outside the office door.

"I'll tell her," said a meek Cindy. Brad and Linda looked to the door in surprise. "And I'll tell her to listen," she added.

"Cindy!" Brad jumped to his feet as the remorseful girl entered the room.

"I am so sorry, Brad. Sometimes I can be so dumb. I got my undies bunched because after being out of town for so long, I was jealous that you spent my first day home with some other girl."

Brad looked at her helplessly. "I could hardly change the date of the Bobby Crim," he said with a cringing smile.

"I know," said Cindy. "As Linda would say, I wasted a lot of time and energy jumping to conclusions." Brad glanced at his watch.

"We still have plenty of time for dinner and a movie," he said.

"I'll need to change my clothes. Will you wait?" Cindy asked.

Linda decided it was high time she squeezed out of the office. "I need to see whether Herm's got that tractor fixed," she lied. As she excused herself and slipped past Cindy, she heard Cindy ask, "Is Pat the girl who is always showering with us at all the summer shows?"

27

If ever a wonderful day starts and ends too quickly, that was the case on the following Saturday. At seven in the morning, about fifty kids plus a few chaperones clambered aboard a chartered bus and headed for Cedar Point. Half the crew slept all the way to the amusement park. The second half chattered so loudly that one would wonder how the others could sleep.

By ten o'clock, the group burst through the park's entry gate in excited anticipation.

"Hold up," said Mrs. Prescott, one of the volunteer chaperones. "Everyone check in at the giant ferris wheel at two o'clock and at six. And be at the bus promptly at ten tonight. Not tomorrow night. Tonight! Kids younger than fourteen stay here until we organize chaperone groups. The rest of you can go."

With that, Brad and Cindy headed for the Demon Drop with a small group of friends. These were new friends for Brad; some he had recognized from the summer shows, others he did not. One in particular was Andy Prescott. Brad had seen him show at the All-Morgan and knew that Andy's parents owned the farm where he would be working in September. Andy was boisterous and good-natured. He was a tease with a real sense of humor and the perfect kind of guy to have along at an amusement park.

By two o'clock, the teens had hit every fast, high, scary, wiggly, jerky, and splashy ride in the park. They were totally exhausted as they checked in at the giant ferris wheel.

Andy chose to stay back and visit with his mom. A couple guys were ambitious enough to head back for the umpteenth time to the Millennium Force, the highest roller coaster in the park. Brad and Cindy decided to wander off to the aquarium; partly because they wanted to see the sharks in the mammoth indoor display, and partly because the interior maze of the aquarium had a few dark nooks and crannies where it would be fairly easy to steal a kiss or two.

After the six o'clock check-in, they watched a comedy show at one of the park theaters, and then wandered the shops on the walkway between Jungle Safari and Frontier Village. Brad bought Cindy a pair of horse-head earrings from a tinsmith and Cindy bought Brad a horseshoe key chain from a pewter shop. As the sun began to set, they came upon a woodworking shop that made plaques and house signs. The teens bought four heart-shaped wood plaques. On one, the carver burned the word "Pogie," on another "Burgie." And on both the remaining plaques, he engraved "Brad & Cindy." With their purchases in hand and fireworks overhead, they walked, arms around each other, back to the waiting bus and the long, romantic ride home.

28

The fall semester of Brad's senior year was nothing but a blur. He was amazed at how much he could accomplish by jam-packing his schedule. His feet hit the floor at four-thirty every morning. He would be at McMichael's by five-thirty, have the stalls picked by seven-thirty, shower and change at the barn, and be in his second-hour class by nine. Brad was thankful the barn had a full bath in the elaborate observation room, and he was blessed to have been able to switch his study hall to first hour. Cindy reminded him often that it was a good thing he was a guy. There never would be time for a blow dryer or instant rollers!

When school dismissed at three o'clock, Brad would stay on campus. He could clear away a lot of homework in the quiet of the school library, while the subject matter was still fresh in his mind. This was where he completed all his assignments for life sciences and advanced composition, the two classes that often needed library research anyway. His two elective classes, electrical science and computer-assisted architectural drafting, never had homework, other than one big team project. He often took his algebra to McMichaels' with him because Andy Prescott was also taking Algebra III. Even though their assignments were always different, the formulas were not so they could help each other.

At four o'clock, Brad would scoot on home and his mom would have an early dinner waiting for him. By five o'clock, he would be at Wheatens' working Burgie, incorporating into their sessions things he was learning through observations made at McMichaels'. At six, he'd be back on the road and at seven, he would be shuffling show horses around and cleaning stalls. He was usually done with the basic cleaning job by nine, but often would put in an extra hour working with the weanlings, repairing equipment, or using a tractor and pull-behind, dragging the arena to keep it smooth. His basic pay didn't cover much other than his gas expense so he appreciated these extra hours whenever he could get them. Even though his summer barn repair job with Mr. Wheaten would cover Burgie's care until after Christmas, Brad still needed to tuck away funds for the expensive show season ahead of him.

On those evenings when the McMichaels did not have an extra odd job for him, Brad was able to spend a speck of time with Cindy. With her living in South Lyon, she was practically on his way home. One evening, Cindy gave him a copy of a mail-order catalog called *The Book Stable*. It contained over 200 books and videos all related to horses: horse behavior, veterinary care, horse breeds, riding styles, and training methods. Brad immediately decided that some of his hard-earned wages must be invested in these valuable materials. Choosing with diligence, he ordered two books or videos each month throughout the winter. By the following summer, he owned a substantial reference library. Much of what he took into the competition ring came directly from these valuable resources.

During his months at McMichaels', Brad was able to visit extensively with Bob Preston, the traveling blacksmith. Bob's shoeing van traveled a five-state area, catering only to the largest and most professional show stables. He was a friendly talker and enjoyed sharing what he knew about the care of a horse's feet and legs. Brad quickly learned the science and methodology of English pleasure shoeing; the ever-so-slightly toe-weighted steel shoes, the leather cushion pads, and the heel and toe clips. Brad asked whether Mr. Preston serviced any farms further north and was happy to learn that one of his clients was a prominent Arabian horse farm near Saginaw. Brad made a mental note to do what he could to make Mr. Preston's visits to McMichaels' run smoothly, having horses ready and running errands when necessary. He knew that, come spring, he would need to have banked enough good deeds to feel confident asking Mr. Preston to stop in for just one horse at Wheatens' on his way up to Saginaw. Plain trail shoes, like she had shown with last summer, just would not give Burgie the lift she would need to compete against those elegant performers on the breed circuit next summer.

By the time Christmas rolled near, Brad was helping with a lot of the routine clipping—muzzles, eyes, bridle paths, ears, and fetlocks. If practice makes perfect, then Brad was working toward perfection, because he was doing a *lot* of clipping! He also learned to braid a Morgan's thick and luxurious tail and bind it carefully in a tail bag to protect the beautiful hair from breakage during the dry and brittle winter. Back at Wheatens', he painstakingly braided Burgie's tail, rolled and tucked it in a soft gray hunting sock, and secured it with kite-string stitches woven with a huge needle "borrowed" from McMichaels'. People coming through the auction barn made disparaging comments about the silly grey sock with a bright red heel swish-swishing on "that horse's butt." Burgie, however, couldn't understand and Brad didn't care, so the sock stayed.

Brad's schedule allowed him to attend only one State Morgan Club meeting during the entire winter. It was the annual January potluck held at the South Lyon High School.

"Just bring potato chips," Cindy had said. "That will get you off the hook cheap and easy." Brad was glad he attended. During the meeting, the adults set up committees to handle the upcoming summer shows. He was able to jot down all the dates and locations. As he sat with Cindy, taking notes, Joe McMichael walked by with a cup of coffee and a handful of homemade brownies; Cindy's brownies to be exact.

"Well, well, what have we here," said Mr. McMichael jovially. "We must be treating you pretty good. Have you decided to take an active interest in Morgan horses?"

Brad glanced quickly at Cindy, and then kindly mumbled his reply to Mr. McMichael. "Yeah, well, maybe, thought I'd check it out."

"Good idea," beamed Mr. McMichael. "And I see you found yourself a perfect little hostess." The older gentleman beamed at Cindy.

Cindy squirmed in her seat, wishing he would take his brownies—or her brownies—and get lost.

"Well, take good notes, young man," Mr. McMichael concluded. "Who knows? Maybe someday you'll own a Morgan and we McMichaels can train it for you." Joe slapped Brad on the back in a fatherly manner and wandered back to his seat.

"Cri-ma-nee!" whispered Cindy, a look of disbelief etched on her face. "Don't McMichaels know you've got Burgie?" she exclaimed quietly, not able to hide her shock.

"Shh, no!" whispered Brad in response. Cindy looked around the cafeteria. Attentive adults were quietly debating all the little details of the summer show itineraries. She slid her folding chair back, pinched Brad's shirt sleeve between her fingers, and dragged him out into the corridor.

"Where in heaven's name do they think Burgundy Delight has been all this time? Do they think she disappeared into thin air?" she demanded in amazement.

"I dunno," exclaimed Brad in exasperation. "Mrs. Wheaten never told them who bought her, just some dumb kid. For all they know, Burgie's gathering flies in her eyes and burrs in her butt behind some old cow barn!"

"*Just* some dumb kid," Cindy repeated Brad's words, shaking her head in disbelief. Then she concluded, "They are going to be livid when they find out you've been purposely stealing all their training information for use on a real live horse. Almost *their* real live horse!" she added emphatically.

"Well, Cindy," Brad said with exaggerated sarcasm. "Do you think they would have hired me if I had said, 'Hello, Mr. McMichael. My name is Brad Bateman, and by some miracle I just happen to own one of the nicest mares ever to come out of your stable. May I work in your barn so I can learn how to beat you at your own game?'

Cindy just stared at him in wild bewilderment, and then began pacing the corridor, tapping her forehead as she walked back and forth in front of Brad.

"Think, think, think," she pondered. "What's the worst that could happen?" She continued to pace and ponder.

"They could watch me show and lose and laugh at me," suggested Brad.

"They could watch you show and win and fire you—and mutilate your body while they're at it!" exaggerated Cindy.

"That's not possible," corrected Brad, "because I'm giving my notice at the end of February. Mr. Wheaten wants me back in time for the spring sale season. And I figure by then, I'll have learned most all I can at McMichaels'."

"You're right," agreed Cindy. "After that, it will have to be all your own effort."

Brad explained his plan. "By returning to work at Wheatens', I'll be giving up all this driving twice a day. That will give me more time with Burgie and a little extra money." Then he winked at her and added, "I suspect I'll even have a little more time and money to spend with you."

Cindy failed to take notice of his flirting. She was deep in thought. "This is going to be some summer," she mused. "You, me, Andy, and Paula all in the same classes."

"Who's Paula?" That was a new name to Brad.

Cindy walked over to the closed door and peered through the narrow vertical window. "There," she said, pulling Brad to the door and pointing through the glass. "Over there; next to the woman in the red sweater. She has blond hair. Do you see her?"

Brad scanned the room until his eyes lit upon the blond teen next to the red sweater. He wondered whether he recognized her from the Cedar Point trip.

"I don't recognize her," he said.

"She's new. Moved here two months ago. I think she lives in Oxford."

"So, is she supposed to be really good or something?" queried Brad, almost nonchalantly.

"Good is an understatement," chided Cindy. "Last year she was California State Youth of the Year. Then her folks trailered her and her horse through five more states. She ended up representing three states at the World Championships."

"Hmm," Brad contemplated the potential competition.

Cindy continued, "She has a pretty nice horse. I know because he's at our barn. I've watched her and Linda working him."

"Nice horse, huh," Brad repeated.

Cindy elaborated. "His name is Challenger. He's a chestnut with a flaxen mane and tail. Looks like a storybook horse. And he's got good hock action," she added, referring to the quick piston-like lift of the back legs.

"So, is she nice?" Brad asked, referring to Paula, as he turned away from the cafeteria door.

"You know, that's the funny thing," said Cindy. "I've known her for two months and I can't answer that. One day she'll visit like she wants to be my best buddy. The next day she'll walk right past like I'm not there."

Brad was tired of all this talk. The corridor was empty and stone silent except for them. He backed against a row of lockers and pulled Cindy to him. Wrapping his arms around her, he gave her a long, sweet kiss. She returned his kiss with equal enthusiasm and warmth. Then she said, "We can get three days detention for kissing in the school hall."

Brad quickly replied, "I can't. This isn't my school!"

29

"I've got sixty-five, sixty-five, one-sixty-five," bellowed Chuck Wheaten. The auction loudspeaker rang out loud and crystal clear. It was March, and Brad's employment at the McMichaels' was now behind him, and his electrical science class was already paying off. He figured he didn't need an electrician's license to re-wire the loudspeaker. Most of the building was not up to building code standards anyway. The county fire marshall could have a heyday in any one of Wheatens' buildings.

Roads and fields were muddy, but Brad and Burgie got their rides in just the same. Brad kept her on firm ground whenever possible. Compared to last year, their exercise workouts were shorter in time, usually no more than 20 minutes under saddle, but they were more intense.

Bob Preston had, in fact, stopped in on his way to Saginaw. Burgie was now sporting a set of English pleasure show shoes that cost Brad nearly two hundred dollars. Bob had promised not to mention it to McMichaels. After all, it wasn't his business to be spreading gossip between barns. Even a good blacksmith would lose his clients quickly if he were to behave so unprofessionally. Besides, he recognized Burgie immediately and thought the whole thing was a real hoot.

"You know, Brad," he had said. "I'm the designated smithy for the All-Morgan this year. With you, Burgie, the McMichaels and all, I think I'm going to really enjoy the show!"

Pogie, Cindy's old dependable, would be left behind this year. Ramsey's Riverside Rock-N-Roll had served his time in the spotlight as a senior division park horse. This year, Mr. Ramsey was trimming him back to the junior division and Cindy would show him English pleasure. Although he had not elaborated his motives with his daughter, Bill Ramsey already knew that Paula Adams and her west coast champion, Rockford's Challenger, were going to prove to be tough competition. Pogie just couldn't rise to the challenge, and Cindy's dad knew it. He had to give his own daughter a fighting chance.

To make matters worse—or competition better, depending on how one wanted to look at it—he had already heard that Andy Prescott out of McMichaels' barn would be competing on his dad's former park champion, McMichaels' Jay-B-Boy. Bill Ramsey shook his head. How could one state produce so many absolutely glorious Morgan horses? Unbeknownst to him, there was still another Michigan Morgan who would prove to be a formidable contender in the junior rider English pleasure division—a deep burgundy bay mare presently stowed away in a shoddy little auction barn just a few miles to the north.

Throughout Brad and Burgie's intense spring training, Dorie Wheaten was ever present with advice and encouragement. Brad was surprised that most everything Dorie suggested was very similar to what he watched and learned at McMichaels'. She might not have been dressed in neat jodhpurs and paddock boots, but from within her blue jeans and flannel shirts, she barked clear and concise commands to horse and rider.

All of this was against Chuck's better judgment. He criticized the efforts of his wife and young employee, often through sarcastic teasing, or off-the-cuff comments, any time he saw them working Burgie or discussing her progress. As the summer show season drew nearer, he complained more and more about neither of them pulling their own load around the barn, although they clearly were—and he definitely was drinking more. Brad could always smell beer on Chuck's breath and, sometimes, hard liquor. Brad wondered how Mrs. Wheaten could tolerate it and why she did, yet Dorie never said a sour word about her husband. She just did what she needed to pacify him during his angry bouts, never chastising him in public, and continued to run her auction office and concession stand with quiet efficiency and good customer service.

30

Brad was scared stiff to take Burgie to the first spring show. He had invested so much time, energy, money, and heart into his project over the long winter months. Now, it was time to learn whether it would all pay off.

Cindy had made a wise suggestion. Instead of starting the season at a class A Morgan show, why not enter Burgie in one of the late spring 4-H shows, similar to the ones they had enjoyed last summer. She could not bring Rocky, because her dad said he was only to be shown on the breed circuit under the strict supervision of Linda Cramer, but she could bring her dependable Pogie along and enjoy the day with Brad.

Brad thought this was a great idea. He did not want his first show to be under the scrutinizing eyes of Joe or Evan McMichael, or even Cindy's dad for the matter. Instead, they chose a May 4 show at the Genesee County Fairgrounds, north of Flint. It was nearly two counties away. Surely, no one from the McMichael or Ramsey stables would be there.

Cindy had to get up really early to have Pogie loaded and on the road, picking Burgie and Brad up along the way. It was an extremely chilly day and a bit damp. The temperature never reached 50 degrees during the entire day. A lot of horses were skittish, having obviously not been worked enough over the winter. Some still had remnants of their winter coat while others were well turned out, surely owned by riders who took their hobby to heart.

"Are you going to go easy on me?" Brad asked Cindy in the make-up ring.

"What do you mean by that?" asked Cindy.

"I mean, are you purposely going to let me take a ribbon ahead of yours?" asked Brad in earnest. He didn't want Cindy to do that and was worried that she might.

Cindy laughed with aggressive good humor. "Heck, no! Pogie beat you last summer and he'll beat you this summer!'

"Good," Brad responded matter-of-factly.

"Now, what do you mean by that?" Cindy asked again.

"Well, I just want you to ride to beat me so I have something to measure myself by."

Cindy edged Pogie just a little closer to Burgie and looked Brad straight in the eyes. She said with emphasis on every word, "Brad Bateman, I will *never* purposely throw a class. I'm here to win!"

"Good," Brad said again.

The announcer called for English pleasure horses to enter at a trot. Fifteen minutes later Brad came out of the ring with his first blue ribbon. The girl with the big chestnut with the wide white blaze was back on the open circuit this year and she garnered second place. Pogie took third.

Back at the trailer, Cindy congratulated Brad, who was absolutely ecstatic, with a huge kiss.

"Well, either your horse shows extremely well in cold, damp climates, or you're ready for the big time," Cindy exclaimed.

"Did she look good, Cindy? Could you see her go?" he asked emphatically.

"She looked *really* good, Brad. If you don't beat McMichaels, you will at least impress them." By now they had the horses' bridles off and halters on. They were throwing light body blankets over the saddled animals because a misty rain was developing.

"My goal is to win at the All-Morgan, Cindy, but not to impress Joe and Evan McMichael. I couldn't care less about the McMichaels." Cindy knew this was not entirely true.

He put Cindy's jacket around her shoulders and reached back into the cab of her truck for his own. Putting his arm around her, they headed for the concession stand and hopefully some steamy hot chocolate.

"I wanted to impress myself with winning and impress you with my love for horses," he said as he squeezed her tight. Cindy stretched up as they walked and kissed him on the cheek.

"Just wanting to be at a horse show in this crummy weather impresses me," she said, and to herself she added, *Oh Lord, where did I find this man? I am such a lucky girl!*

31

Four Michigan class A Morgan shows prepared riders for the Michigan All-Morgan in July. At each of the shows, Cindy, Andy, Brad, and Paula juggled the top four places. If they had been on an equestrian team, they would have been unstoppable in their victory sweep. Instead they weren't on a team; they were individual contenders, each going for the blue. Andy, Brad, and Cindy were enjoying the summer of their lives, a trio whose shared memories would truly last forever. Paula, on the other hand, had difficulty mixing friendship and competition. She was often sultry if the blue eluded her, and lofty if it did not. Cindy made constant efforts to include Paula as part of their little group only because Paula's family was a Ramsey Stable client and, like Cindy, Paula was one of Linda Cramer's students.

The first show, sponsored by the state Morgan youth club was held in Mason. Because the youth club sponsored it, youth club volunteers did most of the work. It was a well-respected show among Morgan enthusiasts throughout the state, and all the big barns had horses in the ring.

Joe McMichael was at the concession counter purchasing his umpteenth cup of coffee.

"Hey, Dad," Evan came around the corner, catching his father off guard and causing him to spill hot coffee from the Styrofoam cup. "Did you see the Bateman kid? He's dressed to show."

"Really?" responded Joe without much interest. "Did he get himself a horse?"

"Dunno, I didn't ask. He was with Andy."

Joe took a sip of the piping brew. "Speaking of Andy, does he have Jay-B-Boy ready?"

An hour later, Evan and Joe McMichael were leaning against the railing when the Junior Rider English Pleasure entries trotted boldly into the ring. One, two, three, four, five . . .

"Hey," Joe elbowed Evan, "there's the Bateman . . . " but before he could finish his sentence, Evan was wide-eyed and staring.

"Dad, that's Dee Dee," he exclaimed. Joe studied the flashy bay mare pumping her knees and hocks beneath Brad Bateman.

"Well, what's going on here?" muttered Joe as he watched Brad and Burgie give a not-half-bad performance.

"I'll tell you what's going on," screamed Evan McMichael over the clapping and whistling of the admiring crowd. "She stole our horse! That's what's going on. That Wheaten dame gave you fifteen hundred dollars for a ten thousand dollar horse and her stable boy is sitting on it right now!"

"Hold on," cautioned the older McMichael. "I've known Dorie Wheaten most all my life and she doesn't have a dishonest bone in her body."

Evan was not to be calmed. "Yeah, well, I don't know how you come to know this Wheaten woman most your life, when I'd never heard of her until the day I delivered Dee Dee to her godforsaken ramshackle barn a year and a half ago, but I tell you what. Somehow, she got my Dee Dee into the hands of one of her muckrakers for pennies on the dollar. And somehow, somewhere, they found someone to finish her training off pretty darn well. Speak of the devil," Evan exclaimed. Bill Ramsey was just coming along the show-ring rail, coaching and encouraging his daughter.

"Cool it, Evan," cautioned the older McMichael.

"Hey, Ramsey," Evan called as he sauntered close to Cindy's father.

"Hush up, McMichael. My daughter's in the ring," Bill Ramsey responded without taking his eyes off Cindy, who was charging valiantly down the rail on Rock-N-Roll.

"Yeah, and so's the Bateman boy," continued Evan. "Ain't he dating your daughter?"

Ramsey's eyes never left his daughter's near flawless performance. "So what?"

"Did you train that horse he's riding?" Evan pressed the issue.

"Nope, but Linda told me he had a mare you guys ran through that auction barn up in Linden a couple years back." He tossed a quick glance toward Burgie. "Is that her?"

Evan repeated his question.

"I said, did you train that horse?" By now the riders were all positioned in the line up. Bill Ramsey turned his attention to Evan.

"Didn't that boy work at *your* place most the winter? Looks to me like you at least contributed to her training," Bill said with a wry grin.

Evan was still livid with anger. "You won't be so smug if that little stall-mucker beats your daughter," he quipped.

Bill Ramsey now looked at Evan square on.

"Number one," he said, "he's not going to beat my daughter, whether or not they're oogle-eyed for each other. She's a tough cookie. It's all about winning and she understands that. And, number two, what's got you so hot under the collar? It's just a kid and a horse."

At this point, Joe McMichael intervened on his son's behalf.

"Sorry, Bill. It's just that the mare was foaled at our place and Evan took a special liking to her early on. He was more than just a little upset when her owner's finances went belly up and we had to sell her to collect on the bad debt. We didn't have any potential buyers in the barn at the time, so I said to run her through the auction." He set his hand on Evan's shoulder, "Evan here has yet to forgive me."

As they talked, the kids left the ring: Paula with the blue, Cindy with red, Andy with yellow, and Brad with white. Two more ribbons came out behind them and four riders were left ribbonless in the line up.

By the time Andy Prescott stopped dallying with his friends and got Jay-B-Boy back to the stall area, the two McMichaels were waiting for him. They knew he had chummed all winter with Brad and the Ramsey girl, and they cornered him as soon as he dismounted.

"Hey, Andy, who finished off Bateman's horse for him?" asked Joe.

Andy contemplated the two trainers. He liked these men and considered them his mentors. He owed everything he knew about horses to them.

"I guess he did it mostly on his own," Andy replied honestly.

Joe pressed the issue. "Did you and Cindy Ramsey put any work into that mare?"

"No," Andy answered, becoming defensive with his trainers. "We offered, but he didn't want our help."

"Andy Prescott," growled Evan, "I'll be a pig's ear if you think I'm going to believe he did that nice of a job, with no prior experience. He had to have had help from someone."

Andy handed Jay-B-Boy over to a groom and was in a hurry to get out of his saddle suit. "I guess his boss helped him some."

"What boss?" demanded Evan.

"You know, that auction barn lady." Andy didn't like being caught between his friend and his riding instructor.

"That's impossible!" retorted Evan, transferring his gaze from Andy to his father. Joe just lifted his eyebrow and cocked his head.

"No, it's not," he said quietly, and slowly downed the last swallow of his now very cold coffee.

32

Two weeks later, in early June, the group gathered in for the second competition, the Lions Club Charity Show in Goodells. At one point, between classes, Evan approached Brad with the intent of starting a ruckus, but Joe intervened and the show commenced smoothly.

In late June at the Swartz Creek Kiwanis Show, Joe thought he saw Dorie Wheaten walking away from the concession stand. Was it Dorie? He just wasn't sure. It had been near thirty years since he had last seen the woman. Had it really been that long? Joe sat quietly near ringside on a canvas chair as the classes came and went. He wasn't really needed back at the stalls. Evan had a good handle on running the stable and its various employees: assistant trainers, grooms, maintenance people, and truck and trailer drivers. Now, Joe just sat and watched. Near thirty years of horses had come through his barns, hundreds of top-quality Morgan horses winning thousands of ribbons, and over a hundred state and national championships.

Joe sat up attentively and peered across the ring. The Junior Rider English Pleasure class was in the warm-up ring. He could see Andy on Jay-B-Boy and Cindy on Rock-N-Roll. Was that Dee Dee and the Bateman Boy? He quietly cursed himself for leaving his binoculars back at the truck. If that was Dee Dee, then who was the woman standing at her head, adjusting the bridle? He watched the trim figure run her hand down the horse's neck, pat the rider on the knee, and retreat to the edge of the warm-up ring. The walk was unmistakably Dorie Wheaten's. Joe shook his gray head in silent admiration. Thirty years can elapse and a simple way of walking stays the same.

"Dorie, Dorie," he whispered out loud. "It never crossed my mind that sending a good horse into your barn would pull you out of it." A tear welled up in the elder McMichael's eye. He wiped it away and went in search of a cup of coffee.

☆   ☆   ☆

At the fourth and final show before the Michigan All-Morgan, Brad placed second to Andy Prescott. Cindy's Rock-N-Roll took third. Paula garnered the fourth, which, to her, was like no ribbon at all.

After all the horses were stabled, the three kids were enjoying cold pop, crummy hot dogs, and good company atop a stack of straw bales near the end of the stalls. Andy had asked Cindy whether she was going to take her class ring back from Brad in retaliation for his besting her in the ring.

Cindy stared at Brad with a grin that burst her face and popped her cheeks.

"Of course not. I don't mind going steady with a winner. Besides, I plan on turning things back around the way they should be at the All-Morgan."

Brad leaned across the bale and gave her a big kiss.

"No way, sweetheart. I've worked too hard for it, and I don't intend to give it back so quickly."

"I'll tell you what," interjected Andy. "I bet if you place ahead of Cindy at the All-Morgan, her dad will give the ring back *and* give you the boot!"

Cindy and Brad glanced briefly at each other.

"Nooo way," they said simultaneously, and the three chuckled in good-natured camaraderie.

Just then Paula Adams walked by. "Hi guys," she said with feigned friendliness and continued down the aisle.

"Oh-h-h," cooed Andy. "She speaks." Cindy waved her hand to dismiss Andy's caustic joke. "I tell you what, guys. I am determined to break the iceberg around that woman if it kills me. If she loves horses, there must be a heart in there somewhere."

As they started to collect the trash from their lunch, Evan McMichael walked past the straw bales and stopped when the group caught his eye.

"Hey, Andy, your mom and dad's been looking for you," he quickly lied in order to have a conversation opener. Then, he switched his attention to Brad. "Congratulations, Dee Dee didn't look half-bad out there."

"Thanks," Brad replied with hesitation.

Evan continued. "I don't need to tell you that Andy here and Jay-B-Boy are out of our barn and seem to do a pretty good job of dusting your breeches in the ring." Brad glanced at Andy and could clearly see the discomfort on his friend's face.

"Tell you what," offered Evan. "You want the blues like Andy here is getting? You bring that little mare over to our place and we'll polish her off like you just don't know how." Brad felt the heat rise up his neck and into his cheeks.

"I'm doing just fine, thank you," Brad responded, trying hard to keep his voice from cracking under Evan McMichael's intimidation.

Andy and Cindy just stood there, caught uncomfortably in the middle of the simmering contest of wills between the older professional and the young amateur. The tenseness held the two men's words suspended in the humid summer heat.

"Ya? Just fine you think," surmised Evan. "You may think you're doing okay on this little Michigan circuit, but only Evan McMichael's training can take your Burgundy Delight to the world championships. You'd be eaten alive in Oklahoma City," and before Brad could respond, and to his great relief, Evan McMichael turned on his heels and strode away.

The three teens stared at each other in bewilderment. Finally, Cindy ventured, "What was that?"

Andy exhaled a big sigh. "That's my trainer and, you know what? He really is good. I mean he's a good trainer and a good guy. I don't know why he's got such a bone up his butt about you and Burgie."

But Brad didn't hear either of his friends. His brain was spinning, his thoughts a blur. After a few moments, he turned quietly to Cindy and with total composure asked, "When are the world championships?"

33

Mr. and Mrs. Bateman sat anxiously in the hard plastic seats in the Ramsey Riverside Stable section at the Detroit State Fair Coliseum. Robbie Bateman and his girlfriend were wandering the trade booths that lined the outer aisle beneath the bleachers. Jewelers, tack dealers, clothiers, artists, and photographers displayed their wares at the various booths. Matt Foxworthy, Mike Donaldson, and Pat Spielman were out in the stabling area, adding to the commotion around Burgundy Delight's stall.

"Did you see that '73 GTO in the parking lot?" Matt was exclaiming.

"Let me fix that," Pat was saying as she tugged on Brad's tie.

"Man, like I have never seen so much horseflesh," Mike was saying as highly polished ring-ready horses were paraded in and out of the stabling areas.

"And so many hot chicks!" added Matt, while ogling at a particular brunette all dolled up for a western pleasure class.

"Shut up," snapped Pat good-naturedly. "I'm here, aren't I?"

"Yeah," bellowed Mike, "but if we tried to kiss you, you'd run away, and we'd never be able to catch you!"

That was true, thought Pat. She was enjoying a very good summer of running, was well prepared for this year's Bobby Crim, and fully expected to run the twenty-six mile Columbus marathon in Ohio in October.

The past four days had been horrendous. Temperatures soared between ninety-six and a-hundred-and-two degrees for the entire All-Morgan, cooling only to the low eighties at night. Two children had passed out from heat exhaustion, one while she was on a horse's back. Fortunately, someone was standing near enough to break her fall as she slid to the ground.

Many riders had pulled their entries and forfeited their class fees. Some did so because they felt such high impact physical exertion was dangerous to horse and rider in the high temperatures. Others did so simply because the thought of pulling on a three-piece saddle suit or suede western chaps in hundred degree weather did not sound fun, and for them, showing was a simple pleasure. But the horse handlers who took their fun seriously had persevered the last four days and had earned for themselves the glory of championship night at the Michigan All-Morgan Horse Show.

"All right, guys, get outta here," chided Brad. "I need some down time before my class."

"All right, all right, we're outta here," said Mike, "but we'll be watching for you." Mike and Matt slapped Brad on the back and face in good-natured ruff-n-tumble and headed for the coliseum.

Pat said, "Tell Cindy, I said good luck, too."

"I will," Brad lied. He couldn't pass the greeting along because he and Cindy had agreed not to see each other all Saturday afternoon. They had attended a youth group meeting early that morning and had parted with a kiss. Together, they promised that each would ride the best they could that evening, and neither would harbor resentment over the judge's placing. They had also agreed to simply not spend any time together during the day. They needed to keep their minds on their own show priorities and keep the stress between them as low as possible.

Bill Ramsey was glad to see his daughter where she belonged on this most important day. Not only did she spend the entire afternoon doting over Rocky, but she also helped Linda and the grooms prepare their other horses for competition. In all, thirteen horses and seven riders represented Ramsey's stable. Bill Ramsey had actually been pleased with his daughter's performances for the entire show. She had bested Paula Adams in the English pleasure for riders sixteen and seventeen yesterday, and he hoped she'd hold that rank when they went against each other in tonight's championship. She had also edged out, by a hair, Paula's point total on the four parts of the State Youth of the Year Contest. Paula, of course, was livid and had not been seen all day. Her father had threatened to pull all of his horses from Ramsey's stable and move them to a competing farm. Bill just retorted with a firm man-to-man reproach.

"If you would tell your daughter to quit sulking around the whole blame summer and, instead, concentrate on riding like she's capable of riding, then you might be holding those blues instead of me. Don't blame my daughter when it's your girl that needs the attitude adjustment. It's all about winning, Mr. Adams," Bill Ramsey reminded his client. "And I raised me a tough cookie. She knows how to handle the competition. When it comes to your daughter, Mr. Adams, all we can work with is what you give us. You sure did give us enough potential, but she needs to do some work in the attitude department."

Mr. Adams already knew he would be taking his daughter to compete in Ohio, and other states if necessary, in order to qualify her for the Youth of the Year Competition at the World Championships.

The afternoon dragged by too slowly for Brad; his anxiety over the evening's performance constantly undermined his self-confidence. Although Dorie had come down for his classes on the previous days, she could not afford to get away from home on auction night.

☆ ☆ ☆

It was eight P.M. at Wheatens' auction barn. All the incoming horses had been number tagged, bidders had been given their bidding numbers, the coffee was poured, candy bars sold, spectators seated, and the first horse was now in the chute. Chuck Wheaten dropped his gavel to the counter and began his chant.

"Here's a nice little filly folks. Who'll give me . . ."

Dorie sat behind the cashier's window, her pre-sale paperwork completed. She glanced at her watch. Eight P.M. Down in Detroit, Brad would be saddled and ready to go. Maybe he was already in the warm-up ring. Maybe he was actually in the coliseum this very moment.

"I've got three-fifty, three-fifty, who'll give me three-seventy-five." Chuck's gruff singsong voice wafted in from the other room. Dorie left the cashier's window to check on Jackson. The old white gelding had been moved over from the loafing shed because a confrontation with an old wire fence earlier in the week had inflicted a nasty gash on his left front leg.

As she nursed the wound, her thoughts returned to Brad and Burgie. Oh, how she had wanted to be in Detroit tonight! She had been with Brad, coaching him daily, had been there for his ride yesterday, but there was no way she could relinquish her responsibility to the auction barn on a Saturday night. After all, this barn had been their sole income for the past twenty years, ever since Chuck gave up driving cross-country semi-trucks in order to be home in the evenings with her. She gave one more thought to Brad and his burgundy bay mare, then forced them out of her mind. People wanted their coffee cups refilled, and customers would soon be streaming to her window to pay for their newly purchased horses. Brad would do as Brad would do and she would hear about it in the morning; but, oh how she wished. . . .

Outside the coliseum, people were milling about in the warm night air. A few trailers were pulling out; their horses having not qualified for the championships. One by one, Andy, Brad, Cindy, and Paula joined the other riders in the warm-up ring. There were teens of various ages competing in this championship class. All those who garnered a ribbon in the twelve through seventeen age divisions were eligible to enter the championship classes, although not all chose to. The four teens kept themselves separated and even attempted to avoid eye contact. Even among friends, the tension was unbearable. The announcer called the start of the class and the gate opened. Cindy immediately moved Rocky toward the gate, but with a sudden bump of legs and a clink of stirrup irons, Paula brushed past her and into the ring, boldly catching the judge's eye.

The next fifteen minutes was a flurry of magical beauty for the audience but near cutthroat competition for the riders. Each and every horse was pushed to its peak as the incredibly talented and aggressive teens vied for the top state honor.

When the announcer called them into the line up, Brad counted thirteen contenders. After a few tense moments, the judge instructed seven riders to return to the rail at the trot. All four teens were included in the work-off. The tension mounted for both riders and audience. Mr. and Mrs. Bateman understood very little of what was going on in the ring; what the judge was looking for among what appeared to them to be thirteen perfect horses and thirteen perfect riders.

Matt and Mike decided it was much like a custom car show where almost everyone works his tail off and produces a flawless vehicle, but a judge still has to pick the best of the best—an impossible task.

Finally, the judge handed her place cards to the ring steward who in turn relayed the winning numbers to the announcer's stand via walkie-talkie. The winners were called in reverse order, starting with eighth place.

"Ladies and gentlemen, we have the results of the Junior Rider English Pleasure Championship at the Michigan All-Morgan Horse Show. In eighth place, Sheridan's Suzie Q, ridden by Nicole Riley of Wake Forest, Illinois. In seventh place, SummerBreeze's Storm, ridden by Roger Schumacher of Royal Oak, Michigan. In sixth place, McMichael's Jay-B-Boy, ridden by Andrew Prescott of Northville, Michigan. In fifth place, Burgundy Delight, ridden by Bradley Bateman of Linden, Michigan. In fourth place, Crescent Moon, ridden by Rebecca Simpson of Sarnia, Ontario, Canada. In third place, Ramsey's Riverside Rock-N-Roll ridden by Cindy Ramsey of South Lyon, Michigan."

The announcer paused as riders came forward to accept their ribbons and exit the arena. "Ladies and gentlemen, your Junior Rider English Pleasure Reserve State Champion is Rockford's Challenger, ridden by Paula Adams of Oxford, Michigan; and your Junior Rider English Pleasure State Champion, ladies and gentleman is Starlet April Dawn, ridden by Bruce Davenport of West Valley, Virginia.

Exhaustion overwhelmed the teens and disappointment that the state championship went to an out-of-state rider was a tough pill to swallow. Paula remained in the coliseum to take her reserve championship victory pass, a long tri-colored ribbon draped around Challenger's neck and streaming across his shoulder. The other three teens gathered in the steamy starlight outside. As usual, Andy was the first to ease the tension.

"Bet I can be the first one down to the wash rack," he said. Without another moment wasted, they trotted off toward their respective stalls. In no time, three naked sweaty horses, totally ignorant of the ribbons they had just won, were standing in bliss under a shower of cool water gushing from three hoses.

Mr. and Mrs. Bateman, Mr. and Mrs. Prescott, Mr. and Mrs. Ramsey, Robbie, Matt, Mike, and Pat arrived to find their elite champion riders—still completely dressed in three-piece riding suits and boots—in an all-out battle of the hoses, screaming and squealing under the drenching onslaught of icy cold water.

☆ ☆ ☆

"Are you spending the night?" Cindy asked Brad as they slow-danced at the exhibitors' party.

"No, I don't think so," he replied. "One more night on a stall cot will do me in."

"I told you yesterday Dad said you could sleep in the fifth wheel," Cindy reminded him, referring to just one of the elaborate trailers the Ramseys had parked at the show.

"No thanks, I think I'll head out tonight, get Burgie bedded down at home, and me, too."

Cindy turned her lip down in a feigned pout, but Brad had already made up his mind. He said, "I told my folks to leave the light on when they get home and to expect me around two."

Cindy said, "I want to be with you when you tell Dorie you placed in the championship."

But Brad responded, "No, I thought I'd leave the ribbon tied to Burgie's stall. That way, she'll find it first thing in the morning."

34

The drive home seemed particularly long. Brad did not pull away from the state fairgrounds until almost one o'clock. The exhibitors' party had ended and bedraggled exhibitors and their families, trainers, instructors, and assistants had all wandered off to their respective beds in hotels, motor homes, campers, trailers, and stalls. A good number of rigs were pulling out with Brad. Some would be driving for just an hour. Others were heading back to states as far away as Florida and Virginia.

The expressway lines blink-blinked past Brad, the green highway signs glared in his headlights. It was a relief to finally see road signs on the overpasses that were familiar to him, closer to home.

Off in the distance, the sky held a rosy glow; lights from a small town, thought Brad, though they seemed out of place. He saw his exit and his truck pulled the trailer up the ramp. As he maneuvered the familiar country roads, the glow grew larger, more distinct. Brad began to wonder if it could be a fire. As he pondered the possible location, his heart skipped a beat. He began to imagine it really was a fire at some familiar place; a home whose family he knew or a business he frequented.

Brad's pulse began to race as his imagination got the better of him. The glow was now clearly a fire, heating up the already muggy summer night. As the pickup continued down the familiar road toward home, turning the bend a mile away from Wheatens', it became painfully apparent to Brad. The auction barn was a blazing inferno!

Brad wheeled the truck and trailer to a stop on the shoulder of the road. In his shock, he couldn't think. Even in the depth of night a number of cars filled with curious spectators were passing him, heading closer to the catastrophe. Brad could see lights flashing from a half-dozen emergency vehicles, and he was afraid to proceed, afraid of what he might find.

With trepidation, he slowly pulled back onto the roadway and idled closer to the devastating scene. Now, he could see the fire-fighters at work, hopelessly attempting to quench the raging flames. There was no question that the main barn was a total loss.

Brad drove slowly past the scene, feeling helpless and alone. His eyes scanned the small crowd of people, silhouetted by the fire in the black of the night. Some were standing dumbfounded, others scurried about, but he could not pick out Chuck or Dorie in the smoky haze. Beyond the main barn, its drive, a corral, and a loafing shed used for the summer riding stable, was Wheatens' farmhouse. Safe from the fire and removed from the crowd, Brad pulled Burgie's trailer up the drive and around the dark side of the residence. He found the Wheatens sitting in silence on their porch steps, quietly watching their primary means of income going up in smoke. They turned to acknowledge his presence.

"Leave Burgie where she is," Dorie said wearily. "We'll pull her out when everyone leaves."

Brad knew that the value of the building was greater than any animals that may have been in it. Still, he was afraid to ask. He sat quietly next to Chuck.

Chuck was the first to speak.

"We lost five horses that had been left after the sale. Willy's chickens were in there, too."

Brad's throat was tight. He didn't want to ask the ultimate question.

"Jackson?"

Dorie Wheaten began to sob out loud and Brad knew their de-voted Jackson had died a horrifying death. His stomach churned at the thought.

Dorie tried to pull her thoughts together. "Your mom called earlier, as soon as she got home." She tried to manage a smile. "Congratulations."

"Yeah," Brad responded with no emotion. "We did good." The ribbon that lay on his truck seat now seemed so incredibly unimportant.

"Go call your mom," Dorie instructed. "She'll be sleeping light. Tell her you don't want to pull Burgie out of the trailer yet. When the flames die down a bit, we'll walk her out to the big pasture with the riding stable horses. Go on now."

35

It was a Sunday in late August and Brad was helping the blacksmith trim hooves on thirty or so riding stable horses. A hundred and fifty feet away, the scorched earth, a few charred boards, and a lonely stretch of new foundation blocks were the sole reminder of the auction barn.

Brad pondered as he rasped away on the soles of the horses' feet. Every Saturday night for over twenty years, people gathered on the wooden bleachers. It was now just a place in space. Bleachers had been there. People had been there. Horses had scurried in and out every Saturday. Now it was just thin air. Brad stared and wondered whether he saw the ghosts of all those horses and all those people. He heard the noise. "Sixty-five, sixty-five, I've got one sixty-five . . ."

Chuck had since reapplied for his diesel license and was doing long hauling. Sometimes, he was gone for days at a time. Brad wondered how he could get the license, being such a heavy drinker, but he guessed that wouldn't show up on a driving test.

So much had happened since the All-Morgan. Cindy had registered for fall classes at Washtenaw Community College. She had every intention of one day inheriting her father's stable business, and he insisted a two-year business degree would serve her well.

Pat had earned an athletic scholarship to Michigan State University, but wouldn't be starting classes until late September. Andy would be leaving the state soon, as he had been accepted into a pre-law program on the east coast. Brad, with the help of his high school counselor, had secured a job with Morton Building Company, a national leader in free-span buildings: churches, gymnasiums, fire halls, and some of the nation's most elaborate horse facilities.

   Tomorrow, he would leave for a week-long orientation at their main office in Morton, Illinois. Cindy had promised to work Burgie while he was gone. After that, he would spend the fall swinging a hammer and shovel, and helping with post construction clean up throughout southeast Michigan. From January to May, he would continue his engineering and construction studies while interning at Morton's corporate headquarters.

   Throughout September, without lessening her dedication to, and efforts with Rocky, Cindy also worked Burgie on any day Brad couldn't get home in time. She had not discussed this with her father, because she was sure it would not set well with him. Even if Burgie was not competing at the World Championships in Oklahoma City, which was just six weeks away, still, the mare was a horse outside the Ramsey stable. Bill Ramsey just thought it didn't make common sense to help potential competitors, but in Cindy's heart, Burgie was inside *her* stable. Secretly, she was still wishing Brad could be with her in Oklahoma in October.

   The ringing of the telephone startled Dorie and jarred her from her work at the kitchen table. Gone was the dusty little office, with the bare wood floor and lone window that had been her personal space for two decades. She scoured the *Flint Journal* in search of employment ideas. Once September came and went, the riding stable would be closed for the winter and money would be really tight. Susan Bateman had encouraged her to enroll in a real estate course to secure a sales license.

   "You can specialize in rural properties," she had suggested, but Dorie would need money before Christmas, and a fledgling real estate agent usually suffers at least a few incomeless months while they learn the nuances of the trade. No, she couldn't imagine a life without horses in it every day. Even the comings and goings of auction horses had been better than no horses at all.

   Dorie Wheaten was lost in hopeless daydreaming of owning a riding school, full well knowing she had neither the finances nor the reputation to get one off the ground, when the ring-ringing of the phone jarred her back to reality.

   "Hello, Wheatens' Auction, er, Riding Stable," Dorie corrected herself. "May I help you?"

   "Dorie?" a tenuous voice hesitated at the other end of the line. "Joe McMichael here."

Dorie's heart stopped. Then she quickly composed herself and replied, "Yes, Joe. Long time no see. How are you?"

"I'm fine, Dorie, just fine, and you?"

"Fine, fine too, thank you," Dorie lied. She didn't know what to say next so silence fell over the line.

"I hear Chuck's renewed his trucking license." Joe decided getting to the point was the most comfortable thing to do. "I could use an extra man in October. Wondered if he might want to contract himself out on special assignment."

Dorie's brain went blank. Chuck would never drive for Joe McMichael, not on his life. The voice at the other end of the line continued.

"Dorie? Dorie? Is Chuck there?"

Once again, Dorie pulled her thoughts together.

"Joe? Thank you, Joe, for the offer, but we don't need your handout. Chuck's doing just fine. Being back on the road seems to be good for him." She hesitated, then added, "You know it's what he always loved." Her voice trailed away.

"It's not a handout, Dorie," Joe defended his offer. "I'm short on drivers for the World Championships. I know Chuck knows trucking, and I know he knows horses. I was just hoping with the fire and all, that he could make himself available." Dorie pondered Joe's offer.

"Well, Chuck won't be home for two or three days, and I can't speak for him," she finally said. "How about if I ask him to give you a call."

"That's fair enough," Joe concluded. Then with a little hesitation, he added. "It was good talking with you, Dorie."

"You, too, Joe," she conceded as she quietly returned the phone to its receiver.

☆　☆　☆

"No . . . No.. Joe, I'm booked up." Chuck Wheaten's voice sounded old and haggard. At the other end of the line, Joe McMichael wondered at how the years must have weathered Chuck. He wondered to himself: *"Did my voice sound so old to Dorie last week? Hers had sounded just the same as it had when we were young."* Now Joe was beginning to feel old, just conversing with Chuck; it seemed to drain his emotional energy.

"I'm not interested in hauling horses anymore," Chuck added. "Canned goods and dry goods are a lot less hassle."

"Well, you know that, and so do I," confided Joe. Then he added slowly, "You always were good hauling horses. You know, thirty years is a long time for two old men to be holdin' a grudge. Maybe it's high time we partner up again."

There was only silence at the other end of the line.

"I can sweeten the pot, Chuck, if you want," Joe said with apparent caution. "If you would be willing to drive, we'd easily have the extra space to haul that little mare along. You know the one you've been keeping for your barn boy."

Still there was silence. Chuck was trying to think, to sort out the issue. No, he did not want to work for Joe McMichael. Yes, Dorie would be forever grateful if he could get Brad's horse to the World Championships. No, he did not want his wife near Joe McMichael.

Finally, he broke the silence.

"All right," he agreed in a low, slow gruff. "I'll haul for you just this one time, but Dorie will be busy here closing down the riding stable for the winter. She'll not be able to ride along."

Joe contemplated Chuck's response, wondering why he mentioned that.

"I bet she'd enjoy Oklahoma City in the fall, but I can understand her needing to be back home," he said. He had almost mentioned that he thought he had seen her at a show last June, then thought better of it.

Chuck sealed the deal by saying, "And Joe, the only reason I'm doing this is so the kid and the mare can go along."

"Sure thing, Chuck, send him over to see me," Joe assured him. "And Chuck, would you let us break the news to him? I'm sure Evan would enjoy that."

"Whatever," Chuck grumbled with a genuine lack of interest. He dropped the phone heavily onto its cradle and went looking for a beer.

Joe McMichael sat at his desk, contemplating the deal. Evan was still livid about Dee Dee being out on the circuit. Now he had found a way to end this rift with his son.

36

Brad stood nervously in the office at the McMichaels' Training Center. He had not been there since he left their employ seven months ago. What could they want with him now? Chuck just said it was important and he shouldn't waste any time getting over there. Could it be a job offer? Surely not!

Brad heard the sound of boots, dirt being kicked from the soles. Joe and Evan McMichael entered the office together.

"Welcome back to McMichael's," said Evan wryly, stretching his arm for a less than boisterous handshake. Brad hesitated, then returned Evan's greeting with skepticism. Joe shot a disparaging glance toward his son.

"Have a seat, Brad," Joe pointed toward a leather chair as he walked behind his desk and sat down. He pointed for Evan to take a seat on the short sofa. "We'll get right to the point," Joe continued, "after all, we are all men here, aren't we?"

Brad took the seat with caution, as if it might bite him on contact. He perceived tension in the room and began to think he was sorry he had come. The older McMichael pulled a manila file folder from his desk drawer and quietly set it before him. "Evan, here, tells me he thinks you want to take your mare to Oklahoma City. Is that right?" he asked forthrightly.

"Well, yes, I would, as a matter of fact." Brad's lack of trust in Evan McMichael and his continued skepticism kept him cautious. But, he continued. "I think Burgie deserves the opportunity."

"Dee Dee," corrected Evan.

Joe shot his son a second disparaging glance. "Do you think you can win?" asked Joe, looking steadfastly at Brad.

Brad's stomach was squirming on the inside but, on the outside, he held his nerve and returned the stare.

"I think I learned a lot at the All-Morgan. I'm a good observer." Brad looked from Joe to Evan, picking his words carefully. It was Evan who responded first.

"You may be a good observer, but you're not a showman. You'll be . . . "

"Evan!" The older McMichael had had enough. He scowled at his grown son and looked back at the teen. "Well, young man, I think you do have a chance to win at the World. You've already proven yourself here in Michigan, as far as I'm concerned."

Brad shifted uneasily in his chair while Evan wondered angrily at his father's compliments. The older McMichael continued.

"And, like you, I think Burgie has earned the right to show at the World. Has Chuck Wheaten told you he applied for a driving job with us?" Joe noted that Brad appeared to be genuinely surprised.

"That's right." Joe continued. "And, he wants us to take your mare along. But, Evan here says to me, 'Why would we want to do that, Dad, if we think that Bateman boy might beat us at our own game?'"

Evan's bewildered look indicated that he had no idea what his dad was saying. *Where in the dickins was he coming up with this ridiculous story?* But the older McMichael continued. "So, I said to my boy, we'll take Dee Dee, or Burgie rather, to Oklahoma City as a favor to Chuck, being as he's a friend from way back when." He watched Brad for any signs of suspicion as he continued. "However, to offset the risk of losing to you, we're going to make you an offer."

Brad listened carefully, not knowing where this was all leading.

"Now, understand, lad, you don't have to accept our offer," Joe cautioned, "but, it seems to me, that this is the only way you can afford to get your mare to Oklahoma. And, if you choose to accept our offer, it will be a confidential offer, not to be shared with anyone outside this room."

The men were toying with Brad and he was growing angry, losing patience.

"What's your offer, Mr. McMichael?" he blurted out with a firm and mature voice that surprised even himself.

Now, Joe shifted in his seat and Evan sat on the edge of his.

"Here's the deal," Joe stated, leaning forward in his chair and folding his hands on top of the manila folder. "We haul your mare to Oklahoma City. If she wins the World Championship Junior Rider English Pleasure Division, we get her first foal as payment for our hauling her." Brad's ears perked up. This was beginning to sound like a fair deal. "If she loses," Joe continued slowly, not taking his eyes off Brad. "If she takes anything other than grand champion," his gaze pierced a hole through Brad, "we get your mare."

Brad's head went dizzy and Evan just about slipped off the couch. Brad gripped the arms of his chair while Joe McMichael sat patiently at his desk.

"What's the matter, Bateman," Joe said quietly. "You look pale. Aren't you ready to play in the major league?" Brad fought to gather his composure and his confidence. This was all happening too fast. But Joe continued to press, making it difficult for the younger boy to think clearly.

"Listen, kid," Joe said, emphasizing the word 'kid.' "You've been flirting with us pro's all season, and as best as I can tell, you're flirting with the daughter of a pro as well. We're curious to know just what you're made of," and with a sly smile he added, "and I suspect that young Ramsey girl is, too."

Brad didn't respond, so Joe continued, "Do you understand, Bateman? This is your day of reckoning. Either you're in—or you're out."

Brad just stared at Joe McMichael. *You first-rate jerk!* he thought. The silence was unbearable. The tension in the room could only have been cut with a chain saw.

Finally, Joe McMichael stood and slowly pushed the manila folder toward Brad. With steady resolution he repeated, accenting every word.

"Bateman, are you in, or are you out?"

Brad stood slowly and with purpose. His eyes shifted from Joe to the manila folder. He reached forward and took it in his hand. Working ever so hard to hide his shakes from these two men he once respected but now despised, Brad opened the folder. It was a formal contract, neatly typed, cementing Joe McMichael's malicious offer.

A fleeting vision of Cindy Ramsey, the dream of his future with her, and the ecstasy of Oklahoma City flashed before the young man's eyes. With firm and resolute confidence, he said, "I'm in."

37

The next six weeks flew past. Brad developed a love/hate relationship with his new job at Morton Building Corporation. It was, after all, the gateway to his dream career, and his wages were desperately needed to afford his and Burgie's upcoming trip to Oklahoma. In addition to stall fees and entry fees, there were hotel rooms to pay for and eight days of restaurant food. Plus, he was buying a brand new Lane Fox saddle and weymouth bridle. In addition, the construction work kept him from time he could devote to preparing his horse for the world championships.

"For heaven's sake," Cindy reassured him. "You can only work her once a day or she'd burn out. Besides, I can sneak over here after school every single day if that's what we need to do." Cindy was absolutely elated that Brad would be with her. This was the very last time, they would be able to compete in the junior division. It was the pinnacle of her youthful career. The memory would go to her grave with her, and she desperately wanted Brad to be part of that. He had not told her the gruesome details of his deal with McMichaels.

Cindy had not yet told her father that Brad and Burgie would be competing. She was sure he would expect and demand her total dedication to Ramsey's Riverside Stable—and, for good reason. The future credibility of his stable's reputation depended on the outcome of the world championships; and, therefore, so did Cindy's future livelihood. She, however, confidently justified her work with Burgie because, clearly in her mind, her dedication to Brad figured strongly into her future, too.

Unbeknownst to either of the teens, Dorie Wheaten also worked with Burgie every single day.

☆ ☆ ☆

Every year, throughout every fall, caravans of horse trailers migrate to Oklahoma City. Motor homes, semis, stock trucks, fifth wheels, and four- and two-horse trailers wind along the nation's highways from the forty-eight contiguous states and from the many provinces of Canada. Horses are even flown in from Hawaii, Alaska, and numerous European countries. Oklahoma City is the home to the world championships of many wonderful breeds, not just the majestic Morgan Horse. It is the horse show capital of North America.

This week, Oklahoma City was dedicated to the Morgan horse. The caravan from Ramsey's Riverside Stables had set out on Saturday, as had most of the Michigan contingency. It was a long two-day drive to Oklahoma City, and most farms wanted their horses settled in by late Sunday. They would then have Monday and Tuesday to recover from the long haul before the show started on Wednesday.

The McMichaels, however, were delayed by a day. Evan had come down with a dour case of the twenty-four-hour flu, and he was expected to drive one of the rigs. Joe had felt it imperative that all four of their vehicles stick together. Mechanical problems on the highway are compounded when horses need care.

They finally pulled out of Northville early Sunday afternoon. Chuck had nine horses in the big rig, three abreast in three angled rows. Seven horses represented McMichaels' Training Center; the eighth was Burgie; the ninth was Paula Adams' Challenger. Bill Ramsey's caravan was completely full, so for a hefty fee, the McMichaels had offered to take the bright chestnut along with them. A second vehicle, driven by a stable hand named Benny, hauled tack and equipment, plus miscellaneous provisions including water buckets, show clothes, and food. The third was a cube van driven by Evan McMichael. It was packed full of hay and grain for the horses. Joe McMichael brought up the rear in a truck hauling a fifth wheel-enclosed trailer behind. Inside was his cherished antique carriage to be shown in the historical Americana class. All of the farm's clients and their families, including Andy Prescott, would be arriving later by plane.

Michigan's usual brilliant October color change had turned ugly, with sleet pulling the radiant leaves from the trees and rendering the highway slick. The constant whomp, whomp of the windshield wipers wore thin the nerves of all four drivers. By nightfall, they had traveled south down I-75 and west on I-70, only getting as far as Terre Haute, Indiana. The sleet had turned to rain, and was now clearing altogether, but Joe decided to call it a night. He knew Evan was still feeling poorly and felt they could make up for lost time tomorrow.

Brad shared a hotel room with Chuck Wheaten. From behind the closed bathroom door, he could hear Chuck putting through a long distance call.

"I love you, Dorie," he heard the gruff man murmur from the bedside. "I don't like being away from you; can't wait to get back to you . . . " Brad purposely stayed in the bathroom until he heard the receiver return to the handset. When he came out, Chuck was gone. Brad turned on the television and casually surfed the channels. A little while later, Chuck returned with a twelve-pack. The next morning, Brad counted seven empty cans.

On Monday, it was at least an eight-hour drive from Terra Haute to Oklahoma City in a normal car. The conglomeration of vehicles and number of passengers, both human and horse, inside the McMichael caravan, made it even longer. To make matters worse, Brad had a devil of a time rousting Chuck out of bed that morning.

It was after dinner before Oklahoma City finally seemed within reach. Brad had bumped along in the semi cab most the day, small-talking with Chuck. The World Series was winding down to its final game, so listening to that absorbed a fair part of the day. At dinner, Brad decided to switch vehicles and ride along with Benny. Benny used to clean stalls with Brad, and they enjoyed each other's company. Chuck had become surly as the day wore on and his company wasn't very pleasant.

It had been drizzling lightly for most of the day and now, heading toward dusk, the rain was picking up. Benny's wipers were slopping on high speed, flop-flopping obnoxiously. He turned on his headlights as he trailed Chuck's semitrailer's taillights.

"Man, he doesn't hold the road very well," Benny commented to Brad.

"Oh, I don't know," Brad replied nonchalantly. "I rode with him all day yesterday and most of today. He seemed to be doing just fine."

"Yeah? Well, look at him now. He's all over the road." Benny motioned ahead with his hand. Just as he said so, the huge semi swerved over the centerline, then back in place. Immediately, it swerved over the centerline again, but this time it overcorrected and went off the right side of the road. Within a matter of seconds, it careened off the soft shoulder, jackknifed its cab, and slid the trailer down a steep ditch. The entire trailer was deeply embedded in mud and dirt at a dangerously uncomfortable angle.

Brad panicked! Burgie was in that trailer along with eight other precious animals, including Challenger and Jay-B-Boy! Benny threw on his emergency flashers and wheeled off the road. He grabbed a mammoth flashlight from under the seat as he raced toward the semi cab. By the time Evan and Joe pulled their rigs over and scrambled down the ditch, Benny was shining a beam of light through the broken window. Chuck Wheaten lay unconscious, blood trickling from his head. Empty beer cans were strewn throughout the overturned cab.

Benny ran back to his truck to call 9ll from his cell phone. Evan grabbed his flashlight and scrambled up the wheel of the behemoth cab. Carefully scaling the slippery side of the trailer, he reached for the side door. It opened easily enough but, because the van was tipped at a 45-degree angle, the weight of it made it difficult to lift.

Evan cast a beam of light across the scrambling, screaming horses.

"What do you see?" shouted Brad.

Evan studied the situation without comment. Finally, he replied, "Actually, they all look to be in pretty good shape, considering."

The rain had dropped to a fine mist that was almost refreshing, and Evan left the door open so the night air could circulate around the animals. As he slid back across the trailer side and scrambled over the tire, he added, "They sort of look like they're in crazy veterinary restraints. If they just keep their heads about them and don't thrash about too much, we may be okay."

Brad wanted to rush to Burgie, to assure himself she was uninjured, but it was impossible. *Why,* thought Brad, *did I leave Chuck alone in that cab when I knew he'd been drinking the night before?* He turned his attention back to Joe, who had been attempting to revive the unconscious and bloodied driver.

In what seemed like an eternity, paramedics were on the scene and Chuck, still unconscious, was taken by ambulance into Oklahoma City. It was nearly an hour, an unbearable hour, before an industrial-sized tow vehicle arrived to rescue the truck. Everyone agreed it was probably safer to pull the vehicle up out of the ditch with the horses still in it, than to attempt to unload the animals at an angle where it would be impossible for them to get their footing.

Another hour passed before the cab and trailer were upright on the shoulder of the highway. Other than the broken side window and a lot of scrapes and dents, the rig had weathered its slide into the ditch quite well. However, without Chuck, there was not a man in the group who could maneuver the truck's sixteen gears and get it into the city. The tow truck driver put a call out over his CB radio, and within minutes a minivan pulled over. In the night, Brad could make out the silhouette of the driver, with his wife and two kids. He heard the younger child ask, "Are all the horsies dead?" The woman hushed the youngster as the man handed her the keys to the family van. She put the vehicle in reverse and positioned it at the rear of the caravan.

Under the stars, appearing in the clearing night sky, the stranger approached Joe McMichael, the most senior of the group. He stuck out a friendly hand and said, "Fred Simms here. I usually haul new cars, but I think I can get this more primitive form of horsepower over to the coliseum for you'all."

"How far is it?" queried Mr. McMichael.

"Oh, fifteen, twenty minutes maybe. I'll take it easy in case you got some injured ones in there."

Brad cringed at the thought.

"Well, we've got a problem with some torn wires and there's not enough light here to do a vet check. Even if it was necessary, we couldn't do surgery on a dark highway. Figure it's best to baby them into the city." Then he added, "We sure do appreciate your being here for us."

"No problem," replied the Good Samaritan. "Oklahoma City takes good care of its horse people. Let's git goin'."

With caution lights flashing on all five vehicles, the tired caravan chugged the last few miles into Oklahoma City.

By the time the McMichaels' caravan limped into the well-lit coliseum parking lot, word had spread among those who had arrived ahead of them. Bill Ramsey, Joe's hottest competitor and oldest horse-show buddy, was the first to meet them.

"How's the old man?" he asked immediately. "Heard he was drinking."

"Damn fool might be dead," mumbled Joe, careful not to let his crew overhear. "I'm sorry, Bill. Challenger's in that truck." Bill saw the concern on Joe's face.

"Yeah, buddy. Well, so are your horses. Let's get them unloaded and see what we've got."

One by one, the beautiful show horses were backed down the ramp. Each was visibly shaken but otherwise unharmed. The last to come was Challenger, who had traveled in the front right of the trailer. Evan encouraged and coaxed, but Challenger did not want to move. The wiring for the inside lights was obviously broken so Evan had to work with his flashlight plus what parking lot light was coming through the van's side door. Even with limited vision, he could see that Challenger's eyes were wide and glazed over. Joe and Bill were escorting a veterinary doctor toward the vehicle.

"Get in here, Dad," Evan called toward the approaching men. "Challenger doesn't want to move and he looks like he's going into shock."

As the three men neared, Evan gasped, "Oh my God," The steel rod from the feed rack had impaled the horse's shoulder!

☆　☆　☆

Brad worked closely with Benny and two other grooms to make sure the other eight horses were well bedded down. They went over each horse meticulously, searching for open wounds or swellings that may have been previously missed.

Confident that they had done all they could, Benny got directions to the hospital, and he and Brad headed out.

It was a different scene there. Everything was clean and bright. Brad had the sudden desire to collapse on one of the steel beds lining the halls. Friendly staff directed them past the emergency room and into the critical care unit. They found Chuck still unconscious, hooked up to an elaborate life support system. Brad took it upon himself to call Dorie and he drudgingly searched out a pay phone.

38

Tuesday was meant to be a day to let down and relax before the start of the world championships on Wednesday. Instead, it turned into a rushed and stressful day for the entire McMichael crew. Horses were shampooed and groomed, then lunged with meticulous attention given to signs of possible post-accident trauma. Challenger had been transported to the Colorado State University veterinary hospital and would remain there for the next month. Paula Adams had arrived that morning with her parents and immediately went to see her horse. Dorie Wheaten had also arrived Tuesday morning and had taken up vigil at her husband's bedside. Chuck Wheaten, who remained on life support, had slipped into a coma during the night.

On Tuesday evening, Joe and Evan McMichael, Bill and Rita Ramsey, and Brad and Cindy gathered at the hospital in support of Dorie Wheaten. Her face was puffy and her eyes swollen from hours of nonstop crying and no sleep. They encouraged her to go to dinner with them, but she chose to stay near her husband.

"You go on without me," she urged. "I want to be here."

They all felt hesitant about leaving her alone but she said, "Now, all of you listen. Chuck did this to himself. No one made him drink those beers. I love him, bless his heart, but he belongs here right now and you all belong at a horse show."

The group shuffled uncomfortably as Dorie continued. "This here's the world championships and you're all professionals. Now pull yourselves together and win us some ribbons. I need at least one happy memory out of all this. Now go on with you! All of you!"

Brad leaned over and gave Dorie a tender kiss on her cheek and a big hug. "I'll be back tomorrow night," he promised. The six people vacated the crowded little hospital room, leaving Dorie to doze upright to the tink-tink, beep-beep of Chuck's bedside monitors.

39

Brad stood still and let the aura of the World Championships surround him. It was late Tuesday night and a good dinner warmed his belly. He had worked Burgie during the day and she had performed extremely well. Now, she was settled into her stall. Heaps of clean straw, a stuffed hay bag tied to the wall, and a fresh bucket of water cozied her in for the night. Snatches of conversation drifted through the barns from those early arrivals whose stabling areas were already completely arranged. Most horses had stalls with drapes to shield their evening sleep from the overhead lights. The tack stalls with their fancy curtains doubled as dressing rooms for the competitors. Most farms had paid for extra stalls and hauled in sofas, wet bars, and VCRs to impress their clients and potential clients. Here and there a dog was tied, serving as the stable mascot.

In other areas, barn crews were working into the night to get their stalls gussied up and their horses bedded down. Out on the drive, trailer after trailer continued to pull into the lot, delivering state champion horses, glorious horse after glorious horse.

Brad wandered away from the McMichaels' stabling area. Joe and Evan had been talking quietly with their staff and Brad was an outsider. When owners and trainers talked competitive strategy, they just as soon not have others around. Tonight, the McMichaels were talking about Burgie.

Evan twiddled an empty Styrofoam cup between his fingers and pondered.

"Do you think that Bateman boy has any chance at all of winning the English Pleasure Championship with our mare?" His father waved a silent finger in the air as a sign of caution to his son.

"I suppose, Evan, we should not be calling her *our mare* yet, but I would have never brought the kid if I thought he could win. The way I figure it, that boy doesn't have a cat's chance of walking away with a ribbon Saturday night. There's too much pressure on him. He knows he's out of his league now and, pardon the pun, but there's too much riding on his winning. There's no way he's capable of taking that mare into the ring and pulling a world championship performance out of her. He's got too much at stake. She'll feel his fear and miss a beat or two, or three, and we'll watch them take the gate. Next year, we'll bring her back to win."

Evan pondered his father's summation, and then added, "Sure sounds like you've got him figured. My angle was just a little different. I figure, even if Dee Dee gives the best she's got under Brad, it's still just the best she's got under Brad. You know, I can't help but admire the kid, but a showman he's not. I like the way he can solid up a horse, and, we can thank him for the miles he's put on Dee Dee, but I don't think he can spell the word 'spunk.' And, if he doesn't have spunk, he doesn't have the championship."

The McMichael crew shut down for the night. In a barn two buildings away, Burgie munched her hay and, out in the drive, Brad watched the endless caravan of trailers pull into a row and shut down their lights. He was glad his stall assignment was far from anyone he knew.

☆   ☆   ☆

In the Ramsey camp, all was quiet except for a dim waver of flashlight under a tack stall curtain. Cindy and Paula shuffled the last of their dog-eared pages into their notebooks and snapped their pens closed.

"If I see one more flashcard, I'll barf," moaned Paula.

"Ditto," chimed Cindy. "You have to give us credit, though. If I don't know an answer, you do."

"And vice versa," quipped Paula. "Too bad we can't do this youth thing in twosomes. We'd have it in the bag."

"You betcha," agreed Cindy. "You know, last year the speech made me sick; I mean really sick. I threw up as soon as I was done."

Paula looked surprised.

"You're kidding! That's the part I'm least worried about. It's those multiple-choice, fill-in-the-blank, true-false, how-many-ways-can-we-give-you-a-trick-question crap that rattles me."

Cindy continued her own train of thought. "I took speech in school this year, just to make this easier, but now that I'm here, I'm not so sure it did any good."

"Don't worry, Cindy, you'll do fine." Paula stood and collected her belongings. "And Cindy, I really want to thank you for letting me borrow Rocky for the pattern ride. It's hard enough not to think about Challenger laid up the way he is, but to go home without competing at all would be the end of the world. I just want you to know how much it means to me."

"No sweat, Paula. It was my dad's idea as much as mine. Let's hit the hay." To herself, Cindy said, *It was ALL Dad's idea. He must be trying to keep his clients happy, and I'm not at all happy about it!*

"No, let's hit the hotel," laughed Paula

And with a tired chuckle, the girls ambled away from the barns.

☆   ☆   ☆

Wednesday morning found hundreds of people scurrying around even before the sun peeked over the Oklahoma City horizon. Horses had awakened in their portable homes and were demanding attention. Strange and uncertain neighs echoed from far corners of the mammoth metal barns and were answered from equally strange and uncertain neighs in some other corner. Unappreciative horses stomped and swerved and splashed water on their grooms in the wash racks. Others, scheduled for the early morning halter classes, were already dry and standing in their cross-ties. Grooms on short step stools combed manes, unbraided tails, oiled faces, sanded hooves, and double-checked the fittings on the flashy show halters that would be used to parade these dashing animals through the in-hand classes.

The saddle and buggy classes would start after lunch and continue late into the evening. In and amongst all of this, the youth would gather at the east end of the auxiliary arena to complete the first leg of the National Youth-of-the-Year competition—the Judging Contest. Four geldings and four mares had been offered as volunteers. The youth would judge each set separately.

Twenty-seven teens were gathered in the arena when the horses were trotted in. Both Cindy and Paula were hoping for a smaller group, but even at twenty-seven that only represented

half the states. Both girls went to work sizing up the animals.
They scratched notes quickly across their pads as the handlers
turned the horses from right to left and trotted them away from
the young judges. The geldings were corralled out, the mares paraded in, and the process began again. When the last horse left
the ring, Cindy was surprised to note that her watch indicated
more than three-quarters of an hour had flown by. She settled herself into the stands to compile her notes and was devastated to
discover they were a total mess. In their absence, the horses became muddled in Cindy's brain and she wondered whether she
had jotted the correct notes by the correct animal. Oh, why did
she suddenly feel so incompetent? She reminded herself that she
had performed well on this effort back in Michigan, so took a deep
breath and started writing. When the test organizers called time,
Cindy shook the writer's cramps from her fingers and handed
over her effort to one of the women. She looked around, but Paula
was nowhere in sight. Had she been able to leave early because
she completed her task so quickly and correctly? Or had she become frustrated, turned in a half effort, and gone for a Coke?
Cindy wouldn't know until the results were posted before dinner.

Early in the afternoon, Andy, Brad, Cindy, and Paula shared
chilidogs with horse-crazy teens from all across the country. The
conversations were timid as the kids strained to remember
whom they had met at other shows—regionals throughout the
summer months or even last year's nationals. Andy, Paula, and
Cindy made last-minute mental pictures of the pattern they
would be riding that evening. Brad was glad that he had chosen
not to compete for Youth-of-the-Year. It gave him more time to sit
back and enjoy the big picture without worrying about nitpicky
details unrelated to Burgie's performance. As the girls continued
their "strategizing," Brad's ears fell friend to a conversation
among a group of kids who would be competing in the command
class that afternoon. Memories of his and Burgie's past competi-
tions on the open-show circuit gave Brad a bittersweet sense of
being left out. Burgie had become darn good in those command
classes. That, however, was when quiet and competent obedience
was the goal he had sought. Now, by his own choice, she had been
turned toward this English pleasure championship. Her chance
for the thrill of victory and glory rested upon her ability to offer
the most dynamic and animated performance of her life.

Brad's thoughts jerked back to the possibility of the devastating agony of defeat and total loss. He had rolled his dice and they were suspended in air. He had long since realized he had risked too much, but it was too late now. He forced the thought from his mind, excused himself from the group, and wandered off to see which class was showing in the ring.

☆   ☆   ☆

By four o'clock, twenty-seven chattering contestants crowded the bulletin board outside the show office. Just like in school, half the group thought they had performed better than they had, and the other half thought they had performed worse. A seemingly disinterested woman coaxed her way through the crowd and posted the results of the morning's judging competition. *How could she be so nonchalant?* thought Cindy. *My life is hanging on this!*

"We might as well wait until the herd disperses," quipped Paula. "The score won't change if we rush the board." Paula was right. Cindy took a deep breath and observed the gathering. Squeals and groans filled the area in equal proportions as the teens crowded the board and searched for their entry number. Cindy feigned calm and wondered whether Paula was doing the same as they brought up the end of the line and scanned the sheet. Cindy's head spun as she located #128. Second out of twenty-seven! She checked a second time just to be sure. Second out of twenty-seven! She held her breath while Paula's finger moved up and down the sheet.

"I can't find my number. Where's #230?" Paula's finger continued up and down the sheet until Cindy, in frustration, slapped it out of the way. Her chest froze. Paula's #230 was in the number three spot! Out of twenty-seven entries, how could they be so close? Cindy suddenly sensed a rush of anger mixed with guilt as she realized that she really did not want Paula to do so well. She shook herself silently and said, "Wow, Paula, I guess we really are doing this as a twosome."

"Right on, girl." Paula slapped a highfive toward Cindy, who did not have time to return the gesture, and Paula slipped away into the afternoon.

Sitting at the picnic table at dinner, Cindy wrestled with thoughts of the remaining three phases of the youth competition. She didn't want Paula to be so close to her. Not at the table now, not in the competition, and not in her life. She had spent the entire summer being kind to Paula and got nothing but snootiness in return. Now that Challenger was laid up, Paula suddenly needed a friend.

Linda Cramer swung her leg over the seat of the picnic table and dropped in between the two girls.

"So, are you two going to keep this youth thing neck-to-neck to the bitter end?" She was smiling and in good cheer, so Cindy took the cue and offered a friendly response.

"You don't think I'd want a friend that doesn't know a Morgan when she sees one, do you?"

Paula threw a surprised smile. "So, okay, we know 'em when we see 'em. Let's get in our duds and find out whether we can ride 'em!"

Linda laughed out loud. She really loved these two girls. She slapped their backs simultaneously, pulled away from the table, and chided, "Yeah, let's get you in your duds and see if you can ride."

☆   ☆   ☆

Unlike other classes, where all the horses compete in the ring together, the youth pattern is judged one horse at a time. Each rider enters the ring alone, performs her or his pattern, and exits the ring. The most they would have to do is adjust the stirrup leathers for Paula's longer leg. They even chose a red and white brow band and girth for Rocky because they would match both Cindy's navy and Paula's black saddle suit.

Rocky seemed a little edgy, but not more so than either of them had handled at home. Linda had spent a good thirty minutes working him down in the warm-up ring while the girls were dressing. The pizzazz Rocky would need for his English pleasure class Saturday night was not near so important now. Tonight, they needed for him to give them a smooth and steady performance so that the pattern would unfold as gracefully and consistently as possible. For just a moment, Cindy wished her dad had agreed to bring Pogie along for just this class. Pogie was so dependable. On the other hand, she reasoned, working Rocky tonight would help him become comfortable with the ring prior to his upcoming Saturday night performance. And, having Paula ride him also would do twice as much good. They had already decided that Cindy would take him in the ring first because he was hers. Then, they'd let him relax through the performance of three or four other horses before Paula returned him to the ring.

When they arrived at the in gate, they were surprised to find only seventeen horses prepared to show. Assuming that Rocky was the only one going in twice, that meant nine contestants had already thrown in the towel. Cindy could understand such behavior at a hometown five-dollar-a-class open show, maybe. But, why come all the way to the nationals and then not go in the ring? She wondered how she would respond if she had judged well enough at the state and regionals to warrant the nationals, just to come here and score at the bottom of the stack on the very first of the four events. The irrelevant thought quickly dissipated as the organist's music drifted from the barn, a signal that the announcer was preparing to call them in.

Bill Ramsey pressed his cigar into the blacktop and ambled into the arena. Trudging up the cement stairs, he found a seat away from the crowd and brushed away the dust. He watched one rider after another perform the identical pattern and made mental notes. He'd known many of these kids, at least by sight, most of their lives. It seemed like just yesterday they were in the kiddie corral playing Legos, while their parents competed. They all looked so mature now. How many cumulative hours of effort were represented here tonight? How many parents had pushed their young riders as hard as he had pushed his Cindy? Which cherished child would hold the trophy Saturday night? For which parent would the dream come true? How many of the remaining young riders would go home to the open arms of understanding parents? How many would have to face the disappointments their parents couldn't hide? Ramsey's chest tightened because he knew why he was sitting here now. Ramsey's Riverside Stables' entire advertising campaign for the coming year rested on Rocky winning the Junior Rider English Pleasure Championship Saturday night. Tonight, it was his job to size up two riders.

☆ ☆ ☆

Brad sat quietly high up in the bleachers. He couldn't bear to be near the in gate where Cindy and Paula would be chatting. Quiet concentration before the class remained his preferred mental state, and it was easier to do that away from the girls. He watched Cindy's apparently flawless performance and made a mental note to give Rocky a carrot for treating her so well. Andy Prescott glided through his performance on McMichaels' Jay-B-Boy the way a McMichael rider should. He left the ring with the same look of confidence with which he had entered. The organist started repeating melodies. Brad had already decided she had no more than nine songs in her entire repertoire, or so it seemed. Paula entered the ring to the smooth strains of "Lara's Theme," from *Dr. Zhivago*. It was a beautiful song and a beautiful performance. Although Brad had seen Paula work Rocky back home, he had not remembered her looking so good. The horse was tall and big, and his barrel consumed the length of her longer legs well. She completed her pattern and awaited the judge's nod for dismissal before exiting the gate.

Brad wondered how one could ever be a judge. It was one thing to work a horse until you felt you had brought out the very best it had to offer, but it was quite another thing to compare very bests among riders or horses. It was a task he was sure he would never undertake. For now, he had to wait out the remaining riders before they all returned to the ring to learn their fates. He remained in his seat.

Brad's butt had long gone dead on the hard plastic arena seat before the last of the eighteen patterns had been completed. The sound of the announcer's voice calling the riders to return to the arena as a group snapped him from an uncomfortable snooze. He rubbed an aching neck and strained to pick Rocky from the group. There was the black bay with one rider on his back and another at his side.

"Sixth place goes to #73—blah, blah." The name blurred away past Brad's attention. It was a number he didn't recognize belonging to some kid from Texas. The announcer continued, "In fifth place #187—blah, blah." Again, Brad ignored the remainder. "Fourth place is awarded to #128—Cindy Ramsey of Ramsey Riverside Stables riding Ramsey's Riverside Rock 'N Roll."

Brad clapped enthusiastically, thankful that Cindy had taken Rocky into the ribbons. He wasn't surprised but now wondered whether the black bay could do it twice. He watched as Cindy collected her white ribbon on foot, leaving Paula to tend Rocky.

Cindy exited the ring and stood to the side, stroking the silky ribbon, her eyes remaining on her dad's favorite horse.

"The third place award goes to #42—blah, blah from blah, blah, blah." Brad stood to work his way down the bleachers to where Cindy was standing, as a rider from Connecticut collected the bright yellow and rode from the ring. But he stopped short as he heard the familiar "#230" fall from the announcer's mouth. Paula had beat Cindy in the pattern! Brad's eyes fell quickly to where Cindy was standing, quickly enough to watch her body quake momentarily as Paula commanded Rocky forward toward the ring steward. He quickened his pace, suddenly realizing he should have been at her side all along.

Paula diverted her own gaze away from Cindy as she passed her at the out gate. None of them was aware of the announcer awarding the blue ribbon to Andy Prescott.

Mr. Ramsey remained fixed in his plastic bleacher seat long after the class was dismissed.

40

Neither Brad nor Cindy had performances on Thursday, so they planned to spend a good share of the day at the hospital. Now, they sat at a hard cafeteria table nursing a cup of coffee with Dorie Wheaten. They had been there for an hour small talking about all sorts of things. There was a lull in the conversation and it was Cindy who brought up the subject, asking her question tentatively.

"Mrs. Wheaten, would you tell us how you know Mr. McMichael?"

Dorie toyed with the spoon in her coffee mug and, with a melancholy sigh, said, "Oh, you don't want to hear worn-out stories about things that happened before you two were even born."

The kids couldn't help but note the sadness, the tiredness in her voice and it was Brad who said, "Yes, we do. I know you're better than twice my age but, next to Cindy, you're my closest friend."

The two teens watched Dorie's face drift off in time as she began . . .

☆ ☆ ☆

It had been thirty years since Dorie Wheaten graduated from Culver Military High School in Indiana. Leaving home to attend Culver's boarding school was an expensive endeavor, but the opportunity to be with horses every day was worth it. Her school grades had been good, but her riding had been excellent. As a member of the Culver Black Horse Brigade, she rode in the Presidential Inaugural Parade during her senior year.

Dorie could not have known where life would lead her. Tuition and board at Culver had drained the meager college fund her parents had set aside, so college wasn't a strong possibility. At eighteen, the world seemed huge and opportunities endless. The one thing Dorie knew for sure was that her future would be filled with horses.

Immediately after graduation, she secured a job as a groom, less than her ability but at Sun Up Farm, a well-known Saddlebred show barn near Lansing, Michigan. Even though the position wasn't exactly what Dorie had hoped for, it seemed a good foot in the door. Amos Bigelow, the farm manager, was a nationally known trainer of five-gaited horses, and he promised to take Dorie on the winter Sunshine Circuit throughout the southern states if she worked out well.

Dorie's employment with Amos consisted of morning and evening feedings, veterinary assistance, and complete responsibility for show horse grooming and equipment care. She worked seven days a week with every third Monday off. In return, she earned $80 a week plus an apartment in the barn.

The nicest thing about Sun Up Farm, though, wasn't Mr. Bigelow, or the trainers, or even the horses. The best part was that her high school sweetheart, Joe McMichael, had also landed a job with Amos. Joe would serve as assistant trainer to Dave Busick, Amos's head trainer.

Dorie's shortsightedness would eventually be her downfall. Joe and Dorie had a spat about the positions before finally agreeing to accept them. Dorie was every bit as good with horses as Joe, and Joe knew and admitted it. She often pulled ribbons ahead of him back at Culver and on the open circuit. But thirty years ago, most farm managers thought it didn't look good to have female trainers on the payroll, and Amos Bigelow had that streak of chauvinistic discrimination in his bones.

Horse trainers were expected to be aggressive and dynamic in the show ring, and most stable managers during that era felt that women just didn't fit the image. It would be hard for Dorie to work her way up to assistant trainer at Sun Up Farm, and she knew it would probably be impossible to ever earn the title of head trainer as long as Amos Bigelow was there.

Still, Amos held true to his word and took Joe and Dorie along with the rest of the barn crew when they headed south for the Sunshine Circuit that winter. They hauled a full-sized semi-truck through five southern states from November through February. They were back in Michigan in March, exhausted and road-worn but in possession of more championship ribbons than they could count.

The following year, Dave Busick left his position at Sun Up. Joe was offered the position of head trainer and he jumped at the opportunity. Dorie, however, was not promoted to Joe's old job as assistant trainer. A new man was brought in and Dorie remained the groom.

The situation was unbearable and truly unfair. When the new man didn't feel like working his string of horses, he would pay Dorie to cover for him. Joe didn't mind because it gave him and Dorie opportunities to work horses together, as they had when they were back at Culver. Dorie knew, if she ratted on the new assistant trainer, Amos would most likely not believe her. She insisted that Joe expose the truth to Mr. Bigelow, thus giving her at least a fighting chance at the assistant trainership. Joe refused, however, claiming that ruffling feathers could possibly cost them both their jobs. Dorie was devastated that Joe would not support her.

During high school, Joe and Dorie had planned to open a training stable of their own. Marriage had never been discussed, but maybe it had been assumed. Joe was crazy about Dorie. She was bright and bubbly and fantastic with horses. He knew all too well that she was every bit as good, if not better, at training the high-powered horses than he.

After two years on the circuit, however, life seemed less rosy. Dorie wanted desperately to train and ride Sun Up Farm's top show horses in competition and earn a name for herself, but Amos wouldn't hear a word of it.

Joe claimed that his heart went out to Dorie. He would wrap his arms around her slender body and rock her slowly, kissing her tears while claiming that he just had no control over the situation. They discussed the possibility of Dorie applying for trainer positions at other show barns but such places were so far and few between that they'd never see each other. Even if she were to find a manager who would trust the success of his horses to a woman who had not yet earned a public reputation as a trainer, she'd find herself in the show ring constantly competing against the man she loved. In fact, probably the only time they'd have a chance to be together at all would be when they were competing against each other. Joe would beg her not to leave. He would say he couldn't live without her. Dorie would agree that leaving didn't seem like the right path toward the marriage they both envisioned, so Dorie stayed on at Sun Up, feeling more resentful as the months flew by.

"You'll show right alongside me when we have our own place," Joe promised, encouraging Dorie to hang on for a while longer. He'd laugh and add, "And you'll probably beat me every time and steal my ribbons."

However, all the while he talked, a while longer became a while longer and a while longer. Joe knew they weren't earning enough to save for a place of their own, and Dorie knew it too. After a time, Dorie finally realized that Joe was in his heyday, earning a fantastic reputation as a trainer and Dorie finally realized, after too long, that her own career was not a priority with the man who claimed to love her.

A year later, in her pain and loneliness, Dorie married Mr. Bigelow's semi-trailer driver—Chuck Wheaten. She hadn't stopped loving Joe, but she was harboring three years of growing resentment toward him and there were no signs of anything better ahead. Too much emptiness had grown between them, and Chuck was there with open arms.

Chuck had become a good friend of Joe and Dorie's while employed by Mr. Bigelow. The trio had enjoyed a lot of horse shows together during the past three years, but Chuck wasn't a horseman, he was a trucker. He was no competition for Dorie and, when it came to desires and goals, he was happy enough to share hers. He resigned his position at Sun Up to drive cross-country rigs for an industrial manufacturing company. Amos couldn't compete with the wages offered by the larger company, and Chuck reasoned that driving for someone else would earn marriage and farm money quicker. It would also, he reasoned to himself, speed the process of taking Dorie as far away from Joe McMichael as possible.

Early in their marriage, Chuck and Dorie leased ten acres with a small house and barn. A lesson program seemed an ideal way for her to fill her time and make a small name for herself. She advertised for riding students in the local paper and while Chuck was on the road, she gave as many as fifteen lessons a week on the one horse they could afford.

In no time at all, she was booked full and ready to purchase a second horse. However, the problem was that the riding program only went smoothly when Chuck was out of town. After being on the road for two weeks at a clip, he insisted on having all of Dorie's time for himself during his brief visits home. There was nothing wrong with this, of course, Dorie wanted to spend that time with her husband, too. Chuck had little control over his schedule and never knew ahead of time when he'd be home so it was impossible to plan her lesson schedule in advance. It was both embarrassing and unprofessional to cancel students with little or no notice every time Chuck's diesel cab pulled into the drive. It was a terrible way to run a business, and customers often quit because of her inconsistency. Discussions about the scheduling always led to fights. Finally, Dorie just gave up the idea. Once again, with a second man, Dorie found herself having to compromise, with her dream drifting farther and farther away. She even began to wonder whether she was still competent. What had become of the rising star of Culver Military High School? Where had she made her first poor decision?

Whatever resentment Dorie had she managed to repress to keep the marriage smooth. When Chuck's back went bad, he had to stop driving trucks. Dorie wasn't happy about her husband's chronically painful back, but she was glad to have him off the crazy trucking schedule. In the interim, they had not yet secured enough finances to fund their first nice farm, so when the auction barn came up for sale, they purchased it with what little disability money Chuck had from his old job. It wasn't Dorie's dream stable, but it gave her the chance to be around horses again and gave Chuck something to do with his time.

Cindy had refilled Mrs. Wheaten's coffee mug twice and, now, Dorie sipped the last of her brew. She looked at the kids who had, obviously, been totally engrossed in her story.

"You know, Brad and Cindy, like everybody else, my life has been dictated by the tyranny of small decisions, and I'm the one who made those decisions. Every person deserves to be loved—really loved . . . adored . . . respected. If I married Chuck for the wrong reasons, that wasn't Chuck's fault. I know lots of people think I'm a fool to stay married to an alcoholic; that he isn't good enough for me. But I know the opposite is true. I was never good enough for him. Dorie picked up the coffee-splattered napkin and wiped away new tears.

41

Why did they have to schedule the National Youth-of-the-Year written examination for eight in the morning! Cindy grumbled as she pulled herself out from under the sheets. The hard spritz of the shower water flooded her face and woke her fully. She stayed in longer than usual and then took her time towel-drying her hair.

There was a loud rap on her door.

"Cindy. Hey, are you up?" It was Paula bugging her to go over the flash cards one last time. Cindy, however, just did not want to study with Paula.

"Naw, Paula, I'm all studied out," she called from the bathroom. "Why don't you go find Brad and ask him to run through them with you?" Cindy plopped her towel on the hotel vanity. She didn't even bother to answer the door. With little hesitation, Paula headed off to find Brad.

Back at the show grounds, she found him lunging Burgie on the open green beyond the warm-up rings but decided not to interrupt. In silent contemplation, she hoped Brad and Burgie edged Cindy out in the Saturday night Junior Rider English Pleasure finale. She had never thought about it earlier. Her sole thought had been for her and Challenger to come out on top. That was just a painful memory, and she was resenting Cindy's increasingly cold shoulder. Brad noticed Paula and softly commanded, "Whoa, Burgie."

"Good morning," he called. Paula just waved in response and went in search of a breakfast Coke.

An hour later, Paula was grueling over the written examination. It was divided into five sections: horse evolution and behavior; anatomy and physiology; tack, equipment, and training protocol; breed association rules and regulations; and breeding practices, including new artificial insemination techniques. She glanced across the room at the group of middle schoolers completing the junior youth test booklets. Their booklets were visibly thinner, even from a distance. Paula thumbed through her numbered pages—twenty! She glanced to her other side and noted that Cindy was already well into her booklet. With a sigh of resignation, Paula put her pencil to work.

☆   ☆   ☆

The bright afternoon sun warmed Cindy's back as she sat on a saddle blanket behind the barns. She could hear the cluck-cluck of horse handlers lunging their animals farther out on the green and, for just a moment, imagined a horse escaping his line and trampling her lithe body there on the blanket. Silly thought! Horses never purposely trample things. She'd watched enough of them make some pretty wild spins and turns just to dodge a kitten or some such thing in their paths.

She was so glad the written exam was behind her. Quite frankly, she felt pretty confident in her performance, but she knew that, just like in school, confidence sometimes proves false and the grade ends up much lower than expected. Just the same, it didn't matter because it was over. What she got would be what she got.

The image of Paula's face crept into Cindy's brain. Had Paula been struggling with the test this morning or had Cindy just read into Paula's expression what she had wanted to see? "Oh, this is terrible," she murmured out loud. She was just beginning to like Paula and now she was hating her for all the wrong reasons. She reminded herself of a lesson Linda Cramer had taught her years before.

"Take your heart out and leave it on the gate as you enter the ring," Linda had tutored, "but don't forget to pick it back up on the way out." Cindy repeated the phrase over and over in her mind. *Don't forget to pick it back up on the way out. Don't forget . . .*

Cindy began to think about tonight's public speaking competition. Whoever won the Youth-of-the-Year would be campaigned around the nation to speak on behalf of the Morgan breed. Oh, drat! Why did she not have Paula's composure in public! *Nonsense!* she chided herself. *I did just fine in Michigan!* Four o'clock came and went but Cindy did not bother to check the bulletin board at the show office. The whole Oklahoma scene was lasting way too long. And, like Paula said yesterday, rushing to the board wouldn't change the score.

At dinner, Cindy purposely picked a spot at the picnic table between two older stable hands. She was in no mood for conversation. The oral competition was looming closer and closer. Cindy found her head light and her stomach sick at the thought. She decided to pass by the rest of her plate and was just getting ready to swing her legs from the bench when Paula plopped down beside her, feet out, back to the table.

"Are you avoiding me because it's more fun to be smug by yourself?" Paula purred as she stole one of Cindy's potato chips.

"I don't know what you're talking about. I've been off practicing my speech." Cindy folded her paper plate around the last of her food and collected her cup, but Paula continued.

"Did you notice how few kids were there with us this morning?"

"No, I hadn't thought to count," Cindy replied.

"Six." Paula took Cindy's cup and sipped the red punch.

"Where'd you get that number? I'm sure there were more than a dozen," Cindy corrected.

"Guess again," Paula said assuredly. "They were all juniors. I counted. The only seniors were us six who placed in the ribbons last night."

Cindy contemplated Paula's observation. Who would want to roll out of bed for a twenty-page exam when they knew they were really out of the running? She should have been feeling like one of the elite just to have been there, but this all or nothing, number one or number nobody kept her from reveling in her accomplishment.

"Well, Braino, see you tonight." Paula stood to leave. "Are you still planning to wear your green skirt?"

"I dunno," was all Cindy replied. Paula shrugged her shoulders and went in search of some food.

Braino? What did Paula mean by that? Cindy dropped her plate into a plastic-lined steel drum and wandered over to the show office. No one was near. As she approached the posted notice, it was clear to see that Paula was right. Just six numbers were on the senior sheet and #128 graced the top of the list. Elated, Cindy jogged back toward the barns where Linda Cramer was to meet them. Linda would drive them back to the hotel in order for both girls to look their best for this evening's public presentations. She hadn't even bothered to look for Paula's number. It rested quietly in the number three spot.

Burgie stood quietly in her cross-ties. Brad had just finished working her in the warm-up arena and she worked wonderfully. Two days on the show grounds were enough to settle Burgie, and she was perfectly comfortable offering Brad a dependable ride. Brad found himself feeling conspicuous working Burgie in front of these show people; people who had been competing all of their lives. He much preferred the open roads behind Wheatens' Auction Barn. There, Burgie would open up because she wanted to, not because she was being urged by the cluck of the rider or the snap of the crop.

Now, Brad brushed his mare meticulously. He quietly contemplated the fact that she might not go home with him and his chest muscles began to tighten around his heart. Then, he shook the fuzz from his brain. *No,* he thought. *Tomorrow night we'll ride. We'll ride hard and we'll ride sure.* Even Cindy Ramsey and her high-faluting Rocky would not keep them from the national championship! He had not come this far just to roll over and play dead. He'd show them all what the "barn boy" could do!

Brad had long ago convinced himself it was not his job to worry about how Cindy might react to his winning. She was tough. She understood it was all about winning. Because he had finally confided to her his "winner-takes-all" deal with the McMichaels, she now knew his stakes were high. Too high! As he spoke those internal words, his stomach turned in sad remorse. Again, shaking the feeling, he tossed the brush in the box, released Burgie from her ties and returned her to her stall. He wanted to clean up before sitting in on the public presentations.

Punch and cookies were being served as guests entered the conference room. It was located on the second level at the west end of the main arena. Ventilation was terrible and perspiration was beading on foreheads even as the people just sat in their folding chairs. Brad checked the wall chart before taking the last seat available—right next to Joe McMichael. Paula was scheduled to speak first, Cindy fifth. Brad tried to put himself in the contestants' places. He would rather speak first and get it over with. He guessed that Cindy would as well.

A refined woman in a moss-green suit walked to the podium and leaned into the microphone.

"Would you please take your seats so the final portion of our Youth-of-the-Year competition can begin." Brad thought the announcement was rather redundant since all the seats had been taken. It was the same woman who had been posting the results outside the show office. The six senior contestants took their assigned seats at the side of the stage. She removed a hanky from her pocket and patted her brow. She leaned into the mike once again.

"As you know, tonight's oral competition is the last of four performances required as part of the World Championship Youth-of-the-Year competition. The American Morgan Horse Association is proud of each and every one of these fine young people. They have persevered in preparation for this week in ways beyond what most of us adults would endure. As a result, we may want to remind ourselves that most of these young adults now know more about horses, and about the American Morgan Horse in particular, than many of us. They have represented our breed across the nation over the past summer to thousands of beginning horse riders. Most of the new members who will be joining the American Morgan Horse Association, and its state affiliations over the coming year will be joining as a direct result of the efforts of these young ambassadors. No matter how they score on their tests this week, they too, like their fine horses, are the pride and product of America.

"As you know, a topic was assigned to these young adults eight weeks ago and they have spent those weeks researching and planning their speeches. This evening, our speakers will enlighten us on 'How the Morgan Horse Can Play a Major Role in the American Recreational Industry in the New Millennium.' The judges have been advised to rate the speeches as follows: Sixty percent on factual information, twenty percent on creativity, and twenty percent on presentation. So, with no further ado, let me introduce our first speaker of the evening, Miss Paula Adams of Oxford, Michigan."

Cindy watched Paula approach the podium. A quiet, mauve suit graced her svelt stature over an ecru blouse. Just enough conservative lace adorned the collar: not too frilly, not too drab. Her lapel sported a gold brooch—a horse, of course. Drat! Even her shoes matched perfectly! She must have had them dyed. Paula's question earlier at the picnic table came back to Cindy now: "Are you still planning on wearing your green skirt tonight?" Cindy wanted to barf.

Paula's speech was spectacular. Did Cindy expect anything less? This was really Paula's forte. Surely, she should become a politician or a marketing representative for some huge corporation. It was in her blood. How could she speak while stepping away from the podium so casually? How could she use her hands as such graceful extensions of her explanations? Why does she *not* have to cling to the podium to keep from passing out? Why doesn't she drop her cue cards? Cindy wondered if Paula's three-by-fives were even damp with sweat. Oh, let this night be over!

Back at the hospital, Dorie quietly consulted with the doctors. They had advised her to remove Chuck's life-support system and let him slip peacefully away. Dorie, though, asked whether they could wait a couple more days. It wasn't that she thought a miracle would bring Chuck out of his coma; rather, she wanted to wait until the kids had returned to Michigan. She planned to stay on in Oklahoma City for a few days, maybe take in a museum or a couple movies. She needed time to ponder her future and would catch a plane home alone later in the week.

42

Saturday came at last. The fourth and final day of the World Championships was a real stretch for those who had survived the earlier eliminations. Cindy had not even left her hotel room. She admitted her cowardice to Brad and begged him to check the morning bulletin. Not only would he find the scores from last night's public speaking but also the total tally, and thus, the grand winner of the Youth-of-the-Year competition. He now stood outside Cindy's door, hesitant to knock. Paula had, of course, placed first in last night's oral, and no one could deny that she deserved it. Brad had to run his finger all the way down to fifth place before he stopped at Cindy's name. The only speaker to place behind her was a young man from Wyoming who had literally forgotten his cards at his hotel and, in panic, forgot the major portion of his speech.

"Hello?" Cindy responded to the quiet rap on the door.

"It's me. Brad. Let me in before someone sees me and rats to your dad."

Cindy slipped the chain off the door and twisted back the dead bolt. She pulled on the door and Brad slipped in.

"Have you had breakfast yet?" he asked, knowing that she hadn't. Everyone was totally sick of stadium food and he had spotted a Denny's across the street from Cindy's hotel. Compared to stadium food, Denny's looked pretty good to him.

"I'm not really hungry," Cindy responded. "I think I've lost at least ten pounds in the last four days. The food's too crummy to eat. My stomach is always sick. I've mostly chewed on ice for breakfast, lunch, and dinner."

"Yeah, well, I've noticed, and I'm taking you out to breakfast. Pull on some pants and I'll take you to Denny's."

Cindy suddenly remembered that she was only half dressed! She had slept in one of her dad's super-long dress shirts and, even though her undies weren't showing, it was pretty obvious that she was not wearing shorts.

"Gosh!" Cindy yelped as she grabbed yesterday's jeans off the chair and ran to the bathroom. Brad dropped smiling into an easy chair to wait.

A few minutes later, Cindy reappeared, much improved. Her hair was combed and pulled back into a scrunch comb. She had applied just some basic makeup and performed a quick scrub and spit with her toothbrush. She plopped down on the edge of the bed and asked the big question. Brad reached across and slid the back of his hand down Cindy's arm slowly, coming to rest in the palm of her hand. Cindy entwined her fingers around his and a premature tear trickled down her cheek.

"It's that bad, huh?" she quietly queried. She didn't let Brad answer. "I mean, I know she placed first. We all know she placed first. But I figured the numbers last night. If I placed second, I beat her overall. If I placed third, I tied. If I placed fourth . . . " Brad's eyes met hers, and she knew.

Cindy slid to the floor and landed between Brad's open legs. She laid her head on the side of his jean thigh and began to quietly sob. Brad continued to grip her fingers in his one hand and ran his other hand through her hair. When it came to rest at the scrunch comb, he removed it and let her hair fall around her shoulders. He scooted forward until his hips slid down from the chair and nestled on the floor in front of her. He pulled Cindy to him. Rocking slowly, he lifted her face and kissed every part of it.

"I love you, Cindy," he whispered. "I love you with all my heart. I love the tough part of you. I love the noisy part of you. I love you all over. And I love this part of you, too. We're going to learn from this. And someday in the not too distant future, we're going to own the nation's best show barn. I promise you this."

Cindy sobbed even harder. "Oh, Brad, how can you say these wonderful things when I'm hurting so bad?" she wailed. "My life ended last night and you're talking about our future?"

Cindy stopped short. The pain in her sinuses gave way to a sudden realization. She had failed miserably and Brad was telling her he loved her. Not her dad. Brad.

Cindy reached forward and took the bulk of Brad's sweatshirt in her fingers. She wiped her eyes, thankful that she had foregone mascara a few moments ago. She looked into his eyes and they were smiling. In the safety of his friendship, and looking for a funny diversion, she buried her face in the material and blew her sinuses clear.

"Cri-ma-nee!" Brad bellowed. He pushed her away emphatically and pulled the sweat off over his head.

"You give me one of your sweats or I won't take you to breakfast," he threatened.

As Cindy searched her drawer for a sweat large enough for Brad, she asked the all-important question. "So, where do we go from here?"

"Well," Brad surmised, "we still need to deal with tonight. Paula's out of the picture. Boy, that sounds terrible. No one would wish this on Challenger. But, the fact is, it's one less horse to deal with. You and I, sweetheart, have to go neck-to-neck. You will never forgive yourself if you don't put everything you've got into Rocky's ride."

"But Brad!" moaned Cindy. "My winning will cost you your horse! How could I live with that for the rest of my life?"

"Do it, Cindy. I've already thought this through. You've got to do it. It was wrong of me to put us in this predicament in the first place. If I lose my horse, it will be no one's fault but my own. Remember what Dorie said yesterday about the tyranny of small decisions? Well, call mine the tyranny of dumb decisions! Besides, if I think you're laying back for me, it will only weaken my resolve, and we could both end up losing out. How could we live with *that* for the rest of our lives? Bring out your best, Cindy, and I promise you, Burgie and I will be our best. We'll give you a run for your money like you've never seen. But, honey, you've *got* to promise me . . . "

"What, Brad?" Cindy stood stone still, gripping the sweatshirt in her hands. "I'll promise you anything."

"Promise me, Cindy. Promise me we'll love each other tomorrow no matter what."

Cindy stared deep into Brad's eyes. She didn't blink. She didn't falter. She looked all the way to his soul. For her entire life she had looked forward to riding and winning the Junior Rider English Pleasure Division at the World Championships; the pinnacle of her riding career. Everything she had ever done had led to this day. She took a deep breath.

"I promise," she said.

Brad took the clean sweatshirt from her hands and slipped it over his head. It wasn't until they were halfway across the street that he looked down to see the front motif—tiny pink puff kittens scampering over a bouquet of glitter hearts. He ripped it off, turned it inside out, and pulled it back over the head. Much better!

43

The Ramsey Riverside stabling area was a quiet scene. A lone horse stood in the wash rack quietly accepting his bath. Bill Ramsey, leaning forward in a folding chair, cigar and coffee in hand, was in quiet conversation with Linda Cramer.

"You can't do this, Bill," she was whispering. "It's a sin!"

"Oh, it's not a sin," he responded, waving his cigar past his face in a dismissive gesture. "I watched the two of them Friday night and Paula is clearly more comfortable with Rocky. She definitely has better command of him."

"But Cindy is your daughter and she's worked Rocky all summer!" Linda snapped back, trying to maintain a whisper.

"Linda, do you want a job next year? This is all about winning. Cindy's tough. She can handle it," Bill Ramsey continued. "Besides, she's the one who tossed her youth award out the window by tutoring the competition!" Linda was aghast.

"But you're the one who loaned the horse to Adams so his daughter could do the pattern class! Cindy studied with Paula because she thought you wanted her to!"

"Oh, hogwash," retorted Ramsey. "I wanted to keep Adams just happy enough not to sue me for massacring his horse out there on the highway! I never expected his kid to look so good on Rocky! Do you know what it would mean to have the National Youth of the Year also capture the junior rider English pleasure title?" he continued. "The press coverage would the phenomenal! We'd be on the cover of half the horse magazines in the nation. We wouldn't be able to handle the training contracts that would come our way. I expected it to happen this way all along; I just expected it would be my kid, not his. Think of it, Linda!"

"I am," she said emphatically. "I think we'd get just as much press having both the National Youth of the Year *and* the world champion English pleasure youth rider coming out of the same barn. It would show that we're not just working with one wonder girl." Linda attempted to show Ramsey her logic. "Wouldn't it be better to be able to say, *We've taken more than one girl all the way to the top. We can take yours, too?*"

Ramsey slowly shook his finger back and forth. "No, I think the double punch is an opportunity we shouldn't pass up. Besides," he added, "we have the Prescott boy to contend with. He's stiff competition for our girls."

Linda had been pacing in front of Ramsey. Now, she stopped short and turned toward him. "Bill, she's your own daughter! You can't need to win that badly! That's not called tough; that's called vicious! You're compromising your own child's respect for you!"

"Oh, hogwash, Linda!" Ramsey snapped in defense. "Cindy can show horses for the rest of her life! Don't tell me I can't handle my own daughter!"

"Bill! She's not a horse that doesn't know what's going on out there in the ring! She's not a world-class stallion you can push around to show how powerful *you* are! She's a human being; she's your daughter; and, in case you haven't noticed lately, she's a woman! She's not going to be around for you much longer. This fool move may win you a class but it's going to cost you your family! And, Bill Ramsey, I don't have to tell you that you're not the only man in her life; she's got another waiting in the wings! You can't be *that* blind." Suddenly, Linda stopped as she realized what was really going on.

"I don't believe it!" she bellowed. "You're punishing your daughter because *you're* not number one anymore! How dare you! I may not remember being a teenager any more than you do but, by golly, I know what it means to think like a woman. And, I can tell you right now, Billy Ramsey, this one's gonna backfire on you!"

Ramsey rose from his chair and snubbed his cigar out on the pavement.

"You've got this all figured wrong, Linda. I raised me a tough cookie. She's not some wimpy woman. She thinks like a professional competitor. This is all about winning for our farm and she'll handle it." He pulled a fresh cigar from his pocket and walked away.

44

As soon as breakfast was finished, Brad and Cindy headed back to the show grounds. They both had a lot to do today. As president of the Michigan youth club, Cindy had meetings scheduled with club presidents from around the nation. They would already be addressing how to improve next year's show and setting up lines of communication for the coming twelve months of youth activities. Brad had a horse to prepare. Obviously, McMichaels would leave him on his own today. Their money was riding on Andy Prescott and McMichaels' Jay-B-Boy. He set to work lightly sanding Burgie's hooves.

Cindy bounded between the stalls in the Ramsey Riverside grooming area. Bill Ramsey pondered what she could possibly be so chipper about. Surely, she must know that last night she missed the mark by a mere three points. Linda cast a cautious glance at both of them. Using an empty coffee cup as an excuse, she slipped away to the concession stand. She felt sick to her stomach with what was about to happen. She swore to herself that she must love that girl more than her own dad did. *How could he do this to her? How could he justify such a despicable decision to his own daughter?*

"Cindy? C'mon over here for a second."

"Sure, Dad, what's up?" She feigned nonchalance, knowing what was coming. In fact, she was surprised that he was being so calm and cool. He had commented earlier about her studying with Paula, but she reasoned it was he who loaned Paula the horse. It wasn't studying with Paula that cost her the title. Paula had outscored her on riding and speaking. Those were Paula's talents, and she earned those points fair and square. Cindy also knew, that the title went on total points, and Paula would probably have scored lower on the written test, if not the judging contest, had she not had Cindy's help.

Bill Ramsey pulled up a nearby chair and motioned for Cindy to do the same. He didn't waste time saying what needed to be said. "Cindy, we've made the decision to have Paula ride Rocky tonight."

"What?" gasped Cindy, jumping to her feet. "Dad! Did I hear you right?"

In a quiet, patronizing way, her father explained the logic of putting Paula in the ring, but Cindy heard none of it. Her mind was a blur. Nothing registered. Somewhere in the distance, her father's voice slipped in and out.

"It was Linda's idea," he was saying. "She thought it best for marketing." . . . "She said you were a tough cookie; a good businesswoman." . . . "Linda said you could handle it." . . . "You would know it was all about winning; that you were part of our team."

Cindy stared away from her father, her throat tight, no words coming out. *Linda! How could she? Linda is part of me! How could she?* Cindy turned away, but her father caught her by the arm.

"Where are you going?" His grip held her firmly in place.

"Let me go! Let me go! I'm going home! I'm calling Mom! I'm going home!"

Bill Ramsey loosened his hold and watched his little girl race from the barn. *It's best,* he thought. Actually, he could not have hoped for a better response. She'd be safely on a flight home, leaving him to deal with the pressure of tonight's performance. He would have plenty of time to make amends when he returned home.

45

Cindy sat in the dirt hugging the receiver of the pay phone near the concession stand. People milling about stared at her. Eyes swollen, hair disheveled, face splotchy, she felt like screaming at them all. *Yeah, and I puked up my breakfast, too! So what?!* Her mother's line was busy. *Please, Mom, hang up. Please, Mom, hang up now.* She rose on her knees and punched in the number again. Still busy. A tap on her shoulder spun her around. *Linda!*

"HOW COULD YOU? HOW COULD YOU? HOW COULD YOU?" Small gatherings of people blatantly turned to stare at the screaming girl.

Linda was shocked. "How could I? What did he. . . . ? Cindy, talk to me."

☆ ☆ ☆

By four o'clock Brad had Burgie ready for her class. They had limbered up in the warm-up ring before enjoying a messy bath together. Back in the cross-ties, he toweled her down good, brushed her out, and checked every possible place there could be stubble the clippers might have missed. He had spent a half hour just brushing her mane and tail. The hooves were meticulous and pre-polished. Brad complimented himself. He may not be the most dynamic rider in the world, but he sure had learned how to turn out a good-looking horse. With nothing more to do, the space between him and his horse grew quiet. As Brad quietly ran a brush through Burgie's mane, an eerie thought came to him. Someday, when he and Cindy had their own training stable, they would most likely compete against Burgie's babies; foals with the McMichael prefix before their names. His sordid visions were interrupted by a steady, quiet voice.

"Brad, we need to talk." He turned and found Cindy standing at his side.

46

Seven o'clock came all too soon for Bill Ramsey. It came not quickly enough for Evan McMichael. The fall sun was beginning to set on Oklahoma City, but the biggest part of the night was just beginning at the fairgrounds. The junior color guard had performed their parade to start the championship night. The national anthem had been sung, and the first class of the evening, the Junior Rider English Pleasure Championship was waiting its call to the ring.

Paula collected her composure atop Ramsey's Riverside Rock-n-Roll. Bill had given her fair warning, and she knew what he said to be true: if she were nervous, Rocky would fidget. Her concentration had to be unwaveringly on her horse. Her mind could never leave his body; they had to move as one. She glanced quickly about to see if Cindy was lurking in the shadows. No one had told her Cindy had gone home. They should have. It would have settled her and left her to mind her horse. Rocky danced about a bit and Linda Cramer reached up and took his reins.

"Thatta boy, Rocky. Relax, Paula. Just ride him like you did Thursday night and you'll do fine." Paula drew her confidence from Linda. If Linda were on her side, she'd do okay. She could only imagine that Cindy did not voluntarily give up her mount for this performance. But now, Linda's relaxed attitude assured her that Cindy must have been comfortable with this decision. She would do as Linda said. She'd take Rocky into the ring and ride him just as well as she had on Thursday. Their performance had been flawless—and it would be again tonight. The aura of the evening filled Paula Adams and she became sure, quite sure, this would be her glory night.

Andy Prescott trotted up to the group on McMichael's Jay-B-Boy. Joe and Evan McMichael were not leaving Burgie's defeat up to Ramsey's Riverside Rocky. Their ace in the hole was Jay-B-Boy and, without going into details about their secret contract with the Bateman boy, they didn't mince words letting Andy know how much was at stake. The pressure, however, didn't bother Andy one iota. First of all, it wasn't really pressure because, personally, he had nothing to lose. Four years from now he'd be out of college and off in some professional practice. Horses and horse showing would pretty much be something in his past. So, tonight was just a really big game, and he loved it. Andy pulled his horse to a halt near Rocky and tipped his hat to Cindy.

"Paula!" he said in surprise.

"Hi, Andy. Wanna go riding?" Paula flashed a sly, flirtatious smile that sparkled in the evening dusk.

"Where's Cindy?" asked Andy in puzzlement.

"I guess she got sick," Paula lied. "You're not afraid to ride against me, are you?" Andy loved the game.

"No way, woman. You may have beat me on Thursday but that was just because we were riding alone. Jay-B here thrives on herd mentality. Whatever your Rocky does, Jay-B will just feed off it. We'll leave you in the dust."

Paula threw her head back in friendly laughter. The banter was fun.

"Hey, Andy. If I beat you, will you buy me a Coke at the exhibitor's party?"

Andy winked. "I'll buy you a Coke even if you don't beat me."

"Deal," quipped Paula. "Hey, have you see Brad? He should be here by now."

Andy glanced around the gathering. There were twelve horses prepared to enter at the announcer's call, but no Brad and no Burgie.

"Maybe he's turned chicken," Andy mused. "It wouldn't be the first time someone cut a class."

"That doesn't sound like Brad," responded Paula. "Even if he's going down, he'd go down fighting."

The organist began a warm-up tune in the arena. It seemed she was playing the same tune for the millionth time. Trainers gave their horses a final slap on the rump and moved away so the riders could pick their spots in the line-up. Bill Ramsey gave Paula a wink and a wave of his cigar from where he leaned against the solid wooden half-wall that formed the entryway to the main arena.

"Eat 'em up, little lady," he said under his breath.

Evan McMichael was giving last minute instructions to Andy, but Bill Ramsey noticed Joe McMichael surveying the crowd.

"Hey, Joe. Where's your stable boy?" Ramsey quipped.

"Don't know," muttered McMichael, only half aware that Ramsey had asked the question he had just asked himself. "But if he's not here soon, he'll miss the in gate."

Bill Ramsey grinned in amusement.

"Hey, Joe. Maybe he's waiting around the corner listening for the two-minute call. Remember how when we were kids, we used to wait 'til the last second so we could storm the ring like we thought we owned the place?"

The organ music stopped. People slowly moved closer to the edge of the performance arena. The snap of the microphone echoed in the cavernous building. The announcer drew the mike to his lips and began his chant.

"And now ladies and gentlemen, after three hard days of competition, and some one hundred and fifty classes under our belt, our Saturday evening finale is about to begin. Young riders are gathered outside our doors atop some of the most high-powered horses the Morgan world has to offer. They have challenged these horses, and themselves, throughout the summer, and the fruits of their labor lie in the honors they bring here with them tonight. All of them are blue-ribbon riders from the many state and regional shows held during this exuberant show season. If we may ask our organist to welcome these dynamic young riders to Oklahoma City and, gate man, please open the gates!"

The organist went into full gear. Axle Foley's theme song from the movie, *Beverly Hills Cop,* flooded the arena and reverberated off the walls. The crowd stood on its feet as the gate man swung open the gates.

One after another, the dozen contestants trotted boldly into the arena, veered right, and proceeded around the ring. Paula held Rocky back. She had already decided to be the fifth horse into the ring. She didn't want to be last because the judge would then have her eyes on too many other horses. She did, however, want to hold Rocky back long enough for him to become excited about the commotion of the class. He came through the gate with head high, nose tucked, and forelegs churning the dirt. Paula's gaze was well over her horse's ears and down the long wall of the arena ahead. She was in total control. Three more horses entered before she completely circled the arena and arrived back near the in gate. Jay-B-Boy burst through the gate just as she approached, and she moved Rocky smoothly to the left to give Andy and Jay-B-Boy ample room. Riding stride-for-stride alongside Andy, she threw him a kiss. Andy winked back and, without missing a beat, moved his horse boldly forward and away from Ramsey's Riverside Rock-N-Roll. It was time to go to work, and under all his composure, Andy secretly knew Paula Adams would be a hard act to beat.

Bill Ramsey remained near the in gate, casually wondering what had happened to the Bateman boy. Joe wondered, too, with a little more than casual concern. If Brad chose not to compete, in some last minute hope to save Dee Dee as his own, he had another guess coming. McMichael's Training Stable had funded her trip west, whether or not she competed. If they were to take the mare by default, well, so be it.

The announcer's voice came over the mike. "Last call for class number 218—Junior Rider English Pleasure Championship; last call for class number 218." He quickly double-checked the roster in front of him. Yes, there was one horse missing. "We are looking for entry number 86."

From the far end of the entry tunnel came a shrill whinny and the pounding of hooves. The gate man turned in surprise as a bright bay horse charged the arena. With every slam of the hooves came the deep snort of a dragon. BOOM! BOOM! BOOM! BOOM! A thousand pounds of massive moving muscle dominated the entryway as a glorious Burgundy Delight made her grand entrance at the American Morgan Horse World Championships. That little bay mare from Wheatens' Auction Barn, with all the road miles under her belly, was ready to strut her stuff!

Bill Ramsey's cigar fell from his mouth as his eyes popped out of his head. Atop that glorious mare, *Cindy Ramsey charged through the gate to claim her moment in time!*

Burgie was spectacular! Bold, forceful, and solid. Her cadence was perfectly balanced, rhythmic, and flowing. The deep, solid bass of the music surged through Cindy and into her mount. She knew her mission and had no question about her ability to complete it. Burgie sensed her strength and lifted her legs like there was no one else in the ring. Joe McMichael stared in disbelief.

Evan McMichael stared in disbelief. But when Paula Adams turned her head to stare, Rocky caught the shift in balance and skittered toward the center of the ring. It took Paula just three strides to right herself and return her mount to a smooth performance at the ring's edge, but she knew all too well the toll those three strides would take.

Brad Bateman walked slowly up to the ring, still in his pink sweatshirt turned inside out. He came to a stop next to Joe McMichael.

"Damn you, boy!" snapped McMichael.

"I checked our contract, sir." Brad reported quietly without diverting his attention from the competition. "There's nothing there that says I had to ride my horse."

"Damn you!" snapped McMichael again. And with that, he stormed off to call coaching cues over the rail to Andy Prescott.

Fifteen minutes later, it was all over. Thirteen sweat-frothed horses were in the lineup; reins soaked with lather. Thirteen exhausted riders sat perfectly still awaiting the judges' decision. The announcer snapped the mike once again and began his chant.

"Ladies and gentlemen, we have the results of class number 218—Junior Rider English Pleasure Championship." The silence of the coliseum was broken only by the snorts and stomping of the horses. The announcer started his count from eighth place. Out of thirteen horses, any ribbon that came out of this ring would be a lifetime treasure. However, as Paula Adams exited the arena, she kept her gaze away from Bill Ramsey. She tossed her pink fifth-place ribbon into the steel drum trash barrel next to the rail. As she slid from Rocky's saddle and walked the sweat-soaked horse back to the barn, she heard the announcer bestow the second place, reserve championship ribbon to #122—Andy Prescott, riding McMichaels' Jay-B-Boy. By the time, the announcer presented his final honor, Paula had shoved a sweaty Rocky back into his stall and was bent over, flooding her hair, her head, her brain with the freezing rush of water from a nearby hose.

☆   ☆   ☆

Back in the arena, Cindy Ramsey was taking her victory ride on Burgundy Delight; the tri-colored ribbon draped completely around the horse's neck, the mammoth red rosette blanket resting graciously over the bay mare's shoulders as she glided past the crowd's standing ovation. She brought Burgie to a panting walk before passing through the exit. In her emotional exhaustion, she spotted her father standing behind the gate. Cindy brought Burgie to a full halt and gazed at her father. He opened his mouth to speak, but she cut him off.

"You should be proud of me, Dad. I'm a tough cookie. I knew you'd understand. It's all about winning." She gave Burgie a quiet nudge and the beautiful bay mare ambled into the cool night breeze. Bill Ramsey watched in silent contemplation as his daughter slid off the horse and into Brad Bateman's waiting arms. He was still standing there when a large arm encircled his shoulders from behind. He turned to face Joe McMichael eyeball to eyeball.

"What do you think?" Joe ventured.

"I think us two old boys just got beat by a couple of kids," grumbled Bill.

"Damn kids," muttered Joe in reply.

"Damn good kids," corrected Bill.

"I've never heard you cuss," mused Joe.

"Didn't have a reason to, up to now," replied Bill.

"Let's go find us a beer," suggested Joe.

"Don't drink," replied Bill.

"You do now," corrected Joe.

Bill dropped his cigar and smashed it into the pavement, making a mental note to talk to Dorie Wheaten. Linda Cramer had long been begging for help back at the farm, and Bill knew who was truly responsible for Burgie's brilliant performance. He was determined to secure an employment commitment from Dorie before Joe McMichael could solicit the trainer. Little did he know, nor would he ever know, that, not only would Dorie Wheaten *never* work for Joe McMichael, but she would devote the rest of her working life to defeating him in the class-A ring.

Bill wrapped his arm over Joe's shoulder in a double lock and the two old friends sauntered off into the October Oklahoma night.

Appendix A

A hunt saddle (Figure 1) has knee rolls to support the rider when sailing over fences. Burgie was not destined for the hunter/jumper circuit, thus the hunt saddle was inappropriate.

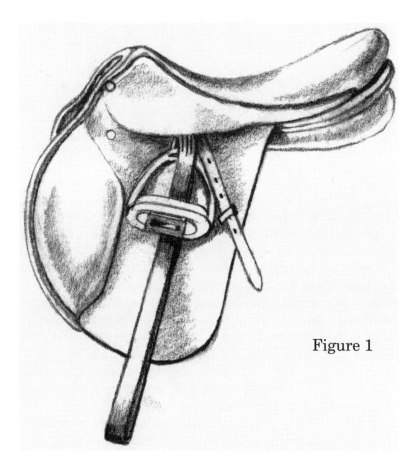

Figure 1

On the Lane Fox saddle (Figure 2), also called the flat or cutback saddle, the pommel (top front) is cut back about four inches. This

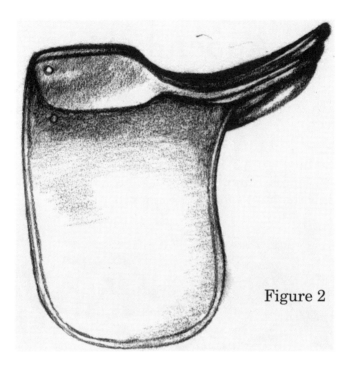

Figure 2

makes it possible for high-headed horses—primarily Morgans, Arabians, Saddlebreds, and Tennessee Walkers—to more easily lift their arched necks. The Lane Fox saddle is also designed, by being more flat at the cantle (top back), to cause the rider to sit about four inches further back on the horse. This would be a disadvantage to a jumper (or racer) who uses its hips as a major power source. For an English pleasure horse, however, this design puts less of the rider's weight on the horse's shoulders, making it easier for the horse to high step.

Where one might call the hunt saddle the "balanced" seat because it puts the rider's weight at the horse's center of balance, one might also call the flat saddle the "balanced" seat because it requires more balance on the part of the rider.

The flat saddle is fitted with wide side panels to protect the rider's handsome riding suit from the sweat of the animal.

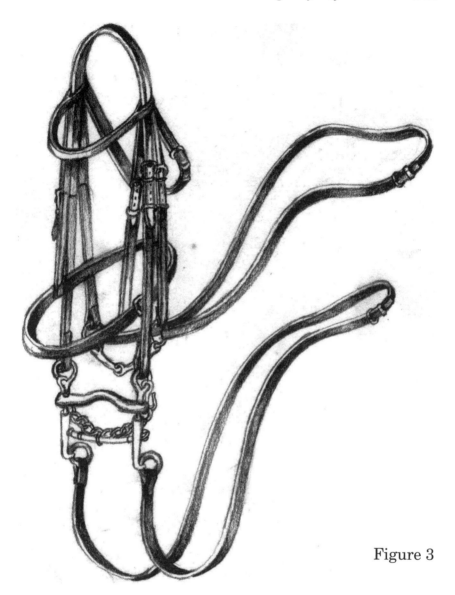

Figure 3

The weymouth (double) bridle (Figure 3) has two bits instead
of one; a thin snaffle, called a bridoon, to maneuver the horse and
raise its head, plus a curb, somewhat similar to a western bit, to
encourage the horse to tuck its nose. Because the spine of the animal is connected from the poll at the base of the brain all the way
to the tip of the tailbone, tucking the horse's head causes the

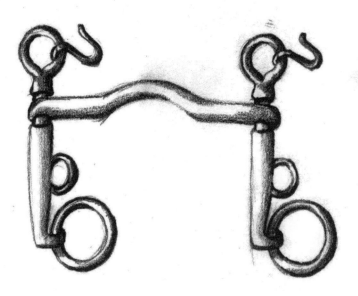

spine to raise and fill under the saddle, and encourages the horse to pull the rear legs up under itself for a more balanced ride. Two sets of reins extend from the bits. A rider must have very steady hands if he expects to use the weymouth bridle in such a way to get the desired response from the horse.

Appendix B

The open show circuit is an interesting one. Crossbred horses compete, like the ones that come through auction barns like Wheatens'—good deals found by solid horse people who know what they are looking for. But purebred horses compete as well. In and amongst the crossbred, sometimes called grade, horses one can always find a nice mix of Quarter Horses and Paints, Morgans and Arabs, and the spotty-rumped Appaloosas. Tennessee Walkers are showing up more often now and every show is always graced with a few golden Palominos. In addition, there are always a few horses that come down from the class A circuit to compete against the open show horses. Class A shows are sponsored by individual breed associations, so a Morgan is judged against other Morgans, Quarter against Quarter, and so on. Trainers and riders who compete on the class A circuit generally believe they have a better animal, but who's to say. Putting the horse out on the open circuit first gives the horse a chance to do his "stupid" stuff, like shying away from loudspeakers or being nervous in a noisy crowd, where class A judges wouldn't see— sort of getting the bugs out of the system. Also, if a training barn is bringing up new riders, they can get over being ring-shy out on the open circuit. Those class A trainers want their riders to dazzle the ring when they go big time.

Sometimes, a class A rider will drop down to the open circuit because she has a chip on her shoulder. She's not winning against the big training barns so she'll look for a place where she thinks she can steal a ribbon. The fact is, most of the open circuit riders are every bit as good as the riders from the big barns—and sometimes better.

More often, class A families enter the open shows for two better reasons. First, because they love to show and want to be on their horse, in the ring, somewhere, every weekend of the entire summer no matter who is sponsoring the show, and second, because the open circuit has a reputation for being pretty darn friendly. There usually are no trainers on the open circuit, though sometimes riding instructors. More often, supervision and mentoring comes from volunteer 4-H leaders and a group of parents who enjoy working with the horses as much as the kids do. On the class A circuit, parents are reasonably considered clients who will, for the most part, hand a child and a checkbook to a trainer and go sit in the stands, leaving all the preparation and coaching to the trainers and instructors. On the 4-H circuit that same parent will be up at four A.M. right along with his or her child, shampooing and braiding the horse and hauling it to the show in their own trailer.

About the Author

Colleen Pace has owned horses for 34 years, and has offered riding lessons to new, and non-horse-owning beginners for 26 years. When her son, Andy, was young, he competed on the Michigan Morgan Horse circuit with his little red mare, Summer-Breeze's Storm, while Colleen volunteered as a youth leader for the state club. As a "senior" trail rider, she continues her ties with old friends in the Michigan Justin Morgan Horse Association.

Over 450 youth and adult riders have been introduced to riding under Colleen's supervision at Riverbank Farm in Davison, Michigan. Over 3,000 Girl Scouts have earned their Horse Lovers Badge at Riverbank Farm. Every July, her riding students enjoy a field trip to "Championship Night" at the Michigan All-Morgan.

With an honors degree in business from the University of Michigan–Flint, Colleen founded the American Association of Riding Schools®, the nation's first comprehensive riding program designed especially for non-horse owners. She continues to oversee the program at Riverbank Farm, including private instruction, scout and school programs, birthday parties, and pony experiences for children too young for lessons.

Are You a Horse Handler *and* a Writer?

The sport and hobby of horses is huge and diverse. The American Association of Riding Schools Press publishes teen fiction that is true to today's U.S. horse industry. You can give new horse enthusiasts a better understanding of our exciting world of horses by writing about your special breed or riding style. For submission guidelines, write The American Association of Riding Schools Press, 8375 E. Coldwater Rd., Davison MI 48423-8966 or e-mail us at *colleenpace@onemain.com*

The Pepperoni Pony Club

" Pepper "

Finally!

An affordable horse club for kids who may not even own a horse! That's right! You can live in a subdivision with a too-small yard or at the top of a high-rise apartment! You can join all by yourself, or gather a group of friends to meet and enjoy club materials together. For membership information, write:

The Pepperoni Pony Club
American Association of Riding Schools,
8375 E Coldwater Road
Davison, MI 48423-8966
Or visit our website at www.ucanride.com

"Pepper," and "The Pepperoni Pony Club" are trademarks of The American Association of Riding Schools, Inc.

Are You a Riding Instructor?

Do you prefer working with new, and
non-horse-owning beginners?
Do you own, or do you want to own your own business?
The American Association of Riding Schools® has
developed the nation's most affordable and enjoyable
introduction to the sport and hobby of horses.
We offer marketing, programming, and business
management support for those stable owners
who truly want to serve the entry-level rider.
Call or write today to learn how your lesson program
can become a member of
The American Association of Riding Schools®:

The American Association of Riding Schools, Inc.
8375 E. Coldwater Road
Davison, MI 48423-8966
810-653-1440
colleenpace@onemain.com
www.ucanride.com